PRAISE FOR *CHOOSE YOUR OWN MISERY: THE OFFICE ADVENTURE*

"I worked for many years in an office exactly like the one in *Choose Your Own Misery: The Office Adventure*. So at first this book made me laugh peals of delighted laughter at its loving reproduction of office life. Ha ha!, I laughed. Oh, how I laughed at this droll little book. Then, slowly but irreversibly, it filled me up with dread."

—Jesse Andrews, author of the *New York Times* bestselling *Me and Earl and the Dying Girl*

"[F]or former *Choose Your Own Adventure* fans and devotees of dark, dark humor."

—*Publishers Weekly*

"Hell, the only reason for going to work is to goof-off reading Jilly Gagnon's and Mike MacDonald's book, *Choose Your Own Misery: The Office Adventure*!"

—E. Jean Carroll, former writer for *SNL*

"*Choose Your Own Misery: The Office Adventure* [is] the most addictive, clever, and honestly hilarious decision tree you've ever read."

—Zack Bornstein, segment director at *Jimmy Kimmel Live*

"Sorry, I've been spending every waking hour lost in your maddening madcap narrative labyrinth. I'll try to send a blurb for the book by the deadline!"

—Jamie Brew, Associate Editor at *Clickhole*

"It's time for you to choose your own miserable adventure, just like you do every day of your miserable life, but now in hilarious book form!"

—Nate Dern, Head Writer for *Funny or Die*

CHOOSE YOUR OWN MISERY

THE OFFICE ADVENTURE

BY MIKE MACDONALD & JILLY GAGNON

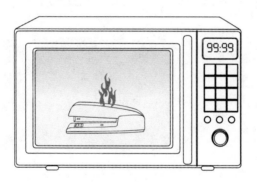

DIVERSIONBOOKS

Diversion Books
A Division of Diversion Publishing Corp.
443 Park Avenue South, Suite 1008
New York, New York 10016
www.DiversionBooks.com

This is a work of fiction. Names, characters, places and incidents either are the
product of the author's imagination or are used fictitiously. Any resemblance to
actual persons, living or dead, events or locales is entirely coincidental.

For more information, email info@diversionbooks.com

First Diversion Books edition January 2016.
Print ISBN: 978-1-62681-924-5
eBook ISBN: 978-1-62681-923-8

To Paul Houseman.
The frog in a blender joke still isn't funny.
It never was.

WARNING!!!!

Do not read this book straight through from beginning to end! These pages contain too many different forms of misery for any one person to experience end to end. And it will feel like all your choices are meaningless if you do it that way, since they'll lead, inexorably, to existential absurdity, and while that's basically true of both life and this book, that's a pretty grim way to read.

The shit that happens to you in this tome of endless, unavoidable misery is still your choice, on some fundamentally meaningless level. You are responsible because you choose, and frankly, you're too old to keep blaming how things turned out on your parents. After you make your choice, live with your shit. The rest of us have to.

Think carefully before you make a move...or don't. Frankly, it won't make much of a difference. None of what we do makes much of a difference. We're all just programmed to die.

BEEP BEEP BEEP BEEP!

The shriek of your alarm clock bores straight through the front of your skull into the softest, most sensitive part of your brain.

How in god's name did you get here? What has happened to you?

Doing your best not to move the throbbing wreck of your head, you examine your surroundings.

You try to open your eyes, but are immediately stabbed by icepicks of light, and close them again, groaning.

You're going to have to Helen Keller your way around your bed.

You seem to be alone. But that means there's no one to blame for the piss spot pooling around your crotch. Fuck.

BEEP BEEP BEEP BEEP!

Portions of last night are coming back in flashes. All of them are of you, alone, plus vodka, with reruns of *Perfect Strangers* playing on the television.

You start searching for the alarm, eyes still closed, knocking over a glass of something liquid in the process.

It has to be around here somewhere.

You squeeze your eyes shut as sweat beads roll down your forehead. You can taste vodka on your breath.

Stop thinking about vodka. Think of anything else in this world but vodka.

You immediately think of every single vodka drink you had last night.

BEEP BEEP BEEP BEEP!

You actually want to die. Getting up for work is *not* an option at the moment.

If you want to call in sick, go to page 2.
If you want to hit the snooze button on your alarm clock, go to page 3.

IN FACT, GOING INTO WORK AT ALL TODAY ISN'T AN OPTION.

You fumble on your nightstand for your phone. No one should be in the office for almost two hours. You know it's a cop out, and it'll probably make your manager ask questions tomorrow, but right now, the idea of actually speaking to a real person is impossible to wrap your shattered head around. By tomorrow you'll have a good enough answer for her.

You tap in the office number.

"Hello?"

Shit, no one was supposed to *answer*.

"Uh, who's this?"

"What do you want?"

The fog over your brain clears momentarily. You recognize this creaking, wavery voice. It's Betsy, the ancient receptionist. Who apparently sleeps under her desk.

"Uh, sorry, I didn't expect anyone would be in at this hour. I was just calling because I've been up all night sick and I really don't think—"

"You don't have any sick days left," she says sharply.

"Well, I guess…just use one of my vacation days, then, please."

"You know you've already used nine out of your ten vacation days."

"I understand that, but I'm too ill to—"

"And it's only March."

If you want to use your last vacation day, go to page 4.
If you want to backtrack and go into the office, go to page 6.

YOU HIT THE SNOOZE BUTTON AND ROLL OVER.

Seconds later the alarm blares again.

Trying to crack through the crust on your eyelashes, you squint at the clock. 7:36 AM. If you don't get up now there's no way you're going to fit in a shower.

You could just skip the shower altogether and rely on the cloaking device of perfume. If you did that you could get another…thirty minutes of sleep?

Leaning up on your elbow is making you nauseous. Grasping at the clock feebly, you reset the alarm for 8:00 and roll over.

You open your eyes, feeling marginally better. Good thing you squeezed in that extra…three hours of sleep? SHIT. How did it get to be 10:30?

Slipping out of your still-damp underwear and stepping into the pair of pants near your bed, you pick up the alarm, shaking it, as though that will somehow flip the numbers back.

Apparently you never hit the "on" button when you had your brilliant idea about resetting the alarm. Pants still tangling around your legs, you shuffle as quickly as you can over to your closet. Unfortunately, your depth perception is still off, and you pound your knee into the doorjamb.

Screaming in pain, you bend over to clutch your knee, hitting your forehead against the edge of the open door. Eyes tearing up, you grab at the nearest shirt and shrug into it.

You just have to hope that no one at work has noticed your absence, yet.

If you sign your laptop into the work server and start 'working from home,'
go to page 7.
If you call a cab you can't really afford and race into the office,
go to page 8.

You think about it. If you go in, you'll still have that vacation day. Lord knows you're going to need it at some point, possibly even worse than you need it right now.

But at this point, even if you do go in, Betsy will probably tell your boss that you tried to call out. And then you'll have to have a talk about "your attitude lately."

Screw it. If you need another day off, you'll just take it unpaid.

"I guess I've just been having a really unlucky year, Betsy," you say. You try to make your voice sound more mucousy. "I just wouldn't feel right coming in until I get an all-clear from my doctor."

"A doctor? I thought you just had the Irish flu," she wheezes. "What's wrong with you?"

Shit, you hadn't thought of that. What's serious enough that you'd need to see a doctor, but not so bad that you'll have to start digging into unpaid time tomorrow just to keep up the ruse? Your brain feels like it's packed with cotton-wool. Rubbing-alcohol soaked cotton-wool. Think. THINK.

"Um...it's...I think it's...bronchitis?" You cough weakly for emphasis.

You hear a sort of muffled, strained shriek coming out of the phone, sort of like the sound you'd expect manatees to make when mating. Maybe she misheard you? Or saw a mouse? You thought you'd picked something just-this-side of innocuous.

"Betsy? Are you there?"

"How could you bring that into our office? You've probably contaminated the whole place already! Oh lord, Oh lord, and you brought me coffee yesterday, oh Jesus Christ..."

"Betsy, settle down," you say, "It's just bronchitis. Anyway, I'm pretty sure I'm not contagious..."

"Just bronchitis? Just. *Bronchitis*? Have you ever dissected a bronchital lung? HAVE YOU?

"Well, no, but..."

"And if you're not contagious, why would you need a doctor? Oh lord..."

"It's probably just a cold. Or allergies! It might even be allergies. I just wanted to rule bronchitis out. I'm almost sure it's not bronchitis. In fact, I'm feeling better, I think I can just come in, and we can pretend…"

"NO YOU WON'T! You will *not* come back into this office, and spread your, your, *contagion*," she makes the word sound like it's been coated in shit, "around me. I am extremely susceptible. A doctor needs to clear you. I want to see the test, I…"

"Betsy, Betsy, calm down," you say, sighing. "I'll try to get in to see the doctor, okay?"

"You'd better do better than try. I'm serious, if you come in here and spread…"

"I will. I'll see the doctor. Okay?"

If you call your doctor for an appointment, go to page 9.
If you trust that senility will erase this conversation from Betsy's memory,
go to page 11.

"Yeah, I really do need to save that for…" you can't think of any reason you'd actually need the day. Except a hangover worse than this one, which you can't even bear to imagine. "…later. I'll be in soon."

You look over at the clock and realize that because of your attempt to play hooky from work, you're now running seriously late.

There's no time for a shower; you're just going to have to use that Axe hanging out at the back of the bathroom medicine cabinet—how did you even inherit that in the first place?—and hope your sweat doesn't smell too much like vodka.

You grab some cleanish-looking clothes from the floor and put them on.

You grab the can of "Anarchy For Him"-scented Axe and start spraying the entire 6-foot radius around you…but nothing happens. Even you can smell the clammy, processed-alcohol scent already creeping out of your pores.

Now you're even later. Frantic, you dig through the cupboard under the bathroom sink for something—anything—to cover the smell of your shame.

You come up with a mostly-empty bottle of your ex-roommate's perfume and a can of Glade air freshener.

The air freshener somehow seems like the better choice. That roommate was a hippie.

Spraying a massive cloud, you twirl through it and run out the door to catch a cab.

Go to page 12 to continue.

YOU PLACE YOUR LAPTOP ON THE KITCHEN COUNTER. YOU'RE JUST going to have to hope that if you log in to your office server remotely now, no one will have noticed that you've been offline the entire morning.

You open up your laptop and navigate to your company's remote access login site as you begin to mop up a spilled vodka and orange juice.

It asks you for your office VPN password.

Shit.

You know the IT people made you set this up, but as far as you can remember, you've never once worked from home.

You did write it down at the time. And then you tucked it into your desk drawer at work, where it will do you absolutely zero fucking good.

Frantic, you try entering every password that you've previously used.

Nothing.

Gritting your teeth, you type in the last idea you can think of: p-a-s-s-w-o-r-d

A window pops up. Maybe you've made it in?

"We're sorry you're having difficulty accessing our network today. In order to help you resolve this as quickly as possible, your issue has been flagged as urgent and forwarded directly to our IT department, who will be contacting you shortly."

You let out a scream of frustration.

You look over at the microwave clock. It's already 11 AM. Even if you were to go into work now, you'd have to take half a vacation day. Half your *last* vacation day. Which would trigger a meeting with your boss, guaranteed.

If you want to call your doctor's office and try to wrangle a note for work, go to page 14.
If you want to call IT and plead with someone to fix this, go to page 16.

YOU HAIL A CAB, WHICH, THANKFULLY, COMES ALMOST IMMEDIATELY. You point the cabbie towards the office and lean back, relieved.

It's only when you get there and pull out your wallet that you remember—sort of—the late-night pizza order. Oh my god, why did you give that kid a $20 tip? Who cares if he likes photography, you needed that money.

You have no cash, and this cab doesn't take cards. There's an ATM at the end of the block, but just as you're about to step out of the cab, you see your boss exiting a town car about ten yards in front of you, leaning into the window to continue his conversation with someone inside; if you go to the ATM he'll see you, and probably expect to talk to you. You look down at your stained, wrinkled pants as you check your breath against your palm. It smells like metabolized vodka and unbrushed pizza-mouth.

And it's nearly 11 o'clock already.

Oh yeah. That conversation probably shouldn't happen.

If you want to risk it and head to the ATM, go to page 19.
If you want to run in the opposite direction, pulling a cab-and-ditch, go to page 18.
If you want to just sit in the cab a minute and hope your boss goes away, go to page 20.

Fortunately, the word "bronchitis" gets you an appointment almost immediately. Apparently everyone but you thinks it's a "real" disease. You head into the doctor's office for the test.

"So what can we do for you today?" your doctor says, studiously avoiding eye contact.

"Well, what have you got for hangovers?" You chuckle weakly, but your doctor is looking at you with the mixture of pity and disgust that you've come to expect from him. Why haven't you switched doctors yet?

"I'm kidding, just kidding," you say. "I'm actually here for a bronchitis test."

The doctor has you open wide.

"I don't see any signs of bronchitis. Or redness, or irritation, for that matter. Frankly, if I didn't know better, I'd assume you have no reason to be here whatsoever." He sneers at you. "Either way, I think you're in the clear."

"Would you mind just doing a swab? And maybe writing me a note? It's a long story, but my work needs to know I don't have bronchitis…for sure."

The doctor rolls his eyes exaggeratedly, but he swabs your throat.

"Anything else you've been having problems with?" he says, already halfway to the door.

"Just running into stuff. The usual," you quip.

"What do you mean?" He sits back down, looking at you with concern. It may be the first time you've ever seen the look on his face.

"Oh, nothing. I've just had this weird lump on my back for the last few weeks, but I'm pretty sure it's just me being a klutz. I probably banged myself on a doorknob or something."

"Still, that shouldn't take more than a few days to heal. We could be looking at a sub-dermal hematoma, or even something worse. Can I take a look?"

"Sure, of course, but it's really nothing," you say, raising your shirt and spinning so the doctor can see.

10

"Hmmm. That's not good," he mutters.

"Not good how?"

"Well I'm not sure. But I'd like to take a small sample and send it to the lab for some tests."

Of course. That's what you get for telling your doctor the truth.

If you head home to fret over WebMD for the rest of the day, go to page 21.

If you head into the office to distract yourself and salvage your sick day, go to page 22.

"I'm gonna go make that doctor's appointment, okay, Betsy?"

She grunts what you assume is assent, and you hang up.

Now you're starting to feel nervous. Not about your fake bronchitis; about missing even more work. There is a chance, after all, that you'll eventually want to *plan* to take time off, rather than drink it away. And if you skip a shower, you can still be into work pretty much on time. Sighing, you reach for the cleanest-looking shirt in the pile at the bottom of your bed and get yourself as pulled together as five minutes allows.

Fortunately, Betsy isn't at the front desk when you skulk in. It's Gina, who sneers at you maliciously. But that's to be expected; ever since Gina told you her boyfriend had called her a "six, maybe a seven on a good day," and you didn't disagree fast enough, she's hated you.

You settle in at your desk, and after the fourth cup of coffee you're feeling anxious enough that you actually work on your presentation for a solid ten minutes.

Just as you're starting to feel like this day might not be the most terrible one of the week, you hear a nasal, high-pitched screech, followed by a thump. You turn to find Betsy—who's fallen flat on her ass at the shock of seeing you—clutching onto a massive "Get Well Soon" card as she attempts to scoot away from your desk.

So much for senility.

Go to page 63 to continue.

You call a cab.

You anxiously pace the sidewalk in front of your house. Jesus, this cab is never coming, maybe you should call the dispatcher again? Finally, though, it arrives. And it smells terrible, like shit cooked up in BO that's then been eaten and shat out again.

You feel your stomach churn.

The cab driver speeds away from your house, racing to the red light at the end of the block, then abruptly hits the brakes. The tires screech in protest.

"Motherfucking idiot drivers can't make it through a single cock-sucking light," he mutters under his breath. Somehow it makes the cab smell worse.

You can feel your stomach fly into your mouth.

The entire ride is agonizing, filled with hard stops and jumping starts. Finally you arrive outside your office.

As you reach for your wallet, the car jolts forward again. Oh Jesus, here it comes.

"Blaaaaaaaaaaaaaaaagggggghhhhh."

You've just puked all over your shoes.

"Blaaaaaaaaaaaaaaaaaaagggggggggggggghhhhhhhh."

You can't stop puking all over your shoes. Dear god, you need to catch your breath. Has anyone ever died from hangover-puking too much?

"Blaaaaaaaaaaaaaaaaaaaaaaagggggggggggggggghhhhhhhhhh."

You think you feel a blood vessel in your eye burst. A long string of saliva dribbles down from your mouth and hits your knees.

"Get the fuck out, you shit stain!" the driver screams.

You reach for your wallet, hoping to find a massive wad of cash.

"GET THE FUCK OUT!!"

You run out of the cab, trying to ignore the squelching sound your shoes are making—it could turn your stomach again. You can wash the shoes when you get upstairs. It'll be fine. Just get in the elevator, and…

Just before the doors close a delicate hand shoots between

them. Your crush, Alex, walks into the elevator.

It's clear, from the affronted look on her face, that she's smelled your shoes.

If you want to blame the puke on a homeless person, go to page 24.

If you want to pretend nothing has happened, go to page 25.

14

AT THIS POINT, EVEN IF YOU DO GO IN, THAT VACATION DAY IS SHOT. Your last vacation day.

But if you had a doctor's note, they'd have to accept it as sick time. It might be unpaid, but that would be better than losing your last sliver of hope.

You call the main line.

"Hello?" an ancient voice croaks.

Great. It's Betsy, the puckered old receptionist.

"Hey, Betsy. I'm glad I reached you," you say, trying to sound as sick as possible. "I just wanted to let you know I'm home sick."

"Again?"

"Yes. I guess I've just been having a really unlucky year," you say. You try to make your voice sound more mucousy. "I wouldn't feel right coming in until I get an all-clear from my doctor."

"A doctor? I thought you had another bout of the Irish flu," she wheezes. "What's wrong with you?"

Shit, you hadn't thought of that. What's serious enough that you'd need to see a doctor, but not so bad that you'll have to start digging into definitely-unpaid time tomorrow just to keep up the ruse? Your brain feels like it's packed with cotton-wool. Rubbing-alcohol soaked cotton-wool. Think. THINK.

"Um…it's…I think it's…bronchitis?" You cough weakly for emphasis.

You hear a sort of muffled, strained shriek coming out of the phone, sort of like how you'd expect Tinkerbell to fart. Maybe she misheard you? You thought you'd picked something just-this-side of innocuous.

"Betsy? Are you there?"

"You've probably contaminated the whole place already! Oh lord, and you brought me coffee yesterday…"

"Betsy, settle down," you say, "It's just bronchitis."

"Just bronchitis? Just. Bronchitis? Have you ever seen an entire cluster of alveoli explode at once? IN REAL TIME?"

Is that even possible to see?

"It's probably just a cold. Or allergies! It might even be

15

allergies. I just wanted to rule bronchitis out. I'm almost sure it's not bronchitis. In fact, I'm feeling better, I think I can just come in, and we can pretend…"

"Has the doctor cleared you?"

"Well not yet, but…"

"If you show your face in here without proof that you're free of…contagion," she makes the word sound like something she just stepped in on the sidewalk, "I'll be forced to report it to HR. I'll have to—"

"Don't worry, I'll make sure the doctor clears me, okay?"

She hangs up on you without another word.

Go to page 9 to continue.

16

YOU'VE GONE TOO FAR TO TURN BACK NOW. THERE'S ONLY ONE WAY out of this that you can see: you'll have to call the IT department.

"Yeth?" The voice on the other end sounds preemptively annoyed.

"Hey, I was just calling because I was having trouble logging in remotely. It said a report had been sent to—"

"Mmhmmm. Yeth, I thee you." You never thought that much contempt could be worked into an adenoidal lisp.

"The thing is I'd been working from home all morning, and then suddenly the system booted me, and, um, now my password doesn't seem to be working," you say, quickly.

"Yeah, that'th not what happened."

"How do you...what do you mean?"

"I *thee* you. Ath in I can thee your computer? Your firtht login attempt wath five minuteth ago. Nithe try though." He snorts derisively.

"Yes, well, previously I'd been working on...on some documents I had saved to the computer's drive, and..."

"Whatever. I honethtly don't care. I'll rethet your pathword if you want, but my report ith gonna thay you didn't log in all morning. You know, like how it *actually happened?*" He snort-chuckles to himself for about a minute. "Thooooo...maybe work on your excyuth before you thow up to the offith again."

"NO," you shriek. "No, there's no reason for that. What if... what if I bought you...a rare collectible comic? Would your report be more...accurate then?"

"Are you theriouth right now? You know not all IT guyth are fat slobth who live with their parentth, right?"

You've seen the people who work in IT at your company. No matter who you're talking to, at least half that description definitely applies. It doesn't seem wise to mention that, though.

"No, I mean, yes, of course I do. That was silly of me. What I meant to say was...was that maybe we could help each other out. Since my boss would be a little...confused by your report, otherwise."

"You don't have anything I want," he says flatly.

"There must be something," you plead.

"Well…" he pauses for several seconds. You can hear the slight wheeze of his breathing. "I gueth there'th *one* thing you could do for me."

"Anything," you say eagerly.

"It seemth to me that you have a 'thpethal' connecthin with an ekthtremely attractive woman we work with. I'm thur you've notithed her, too. She'th the angel of the HR department."

You have no idea who this guy is talking about. Unless he means…

"Wait, Debby?" No, you must have forgotten someone. Debby snorts when she laughs, wears velour skirts a size too small, and constantly drones on about presidential history. It can't be…

"Yeth, Deborah. I've been hoping to…connect with her, but I…haven't found the right moment. But thee theems to be very friendly with you."

It's true, you are one of the few people who doesn't just walk away from Debby mid-sentence.

"So you're saying…if I get you a date with Debby…"

"Your report will be 'accurate.'" He snort-chuckles again. With a laugh like that, maybe they *should* get together.

But there's no way this is going to work. You're not even sure which IT guy is on the line.

"Would you be able to, erm, 'correct' my vacation time so that it reflects those two other days I was actually working from home, uh, Brian?"

"Jethuth, Brian hathn't worked here for a year. It'th Anthony." He sighs exaggeratedly. "But yeth, I think I could manage that… if thee puth out on our date."

If you agree to help prostitute Debby to this mystery IT man,
go to page 26.
If you decide you can't do this, you'll just take your chances with your boss,
go to page 28.

You open the door, looking into your wallet as though you're finding the right bill, all the while watching the cabbie out of the corner of your eye. As soon as he picks up his cell phone and starts yelling at it in some kind of Middle Eastern-y language, you jump out and run in the opposite direction of your boss's town car, turning down the alley that will spit you out near the rear entrance to your office building.

Stopping to catch your breath—Jesus, you are in terrible shape—you head in the loading dock door. Eventually you manage to find a service elevator to your floor.

Luckily, not only has no one seemed to notice your absence, but you manage to make it to your desk before your boss makes it in.

After a half-hour or so, your heart rate has finally settled down. You head to the break room for a cup of coffee.

Passing through reception, you see two police officers, deep in conversation with Gina, one of the receptionists, who has hated you ever since you agreed with her about her nose being "kinda big."

She looks at you, squinting with malevolence, and points.

Now the officers are looking at you, too.

Gulp.

If you confess about the cab in the hopes that it will lessen your punishment,
go to page 29.
If you try to play it cool, go to page 30.

"FUCKIN', $23.50."

"Oh, you know what, I'm realizing I don't have any cash," you say, peering into your wallet as though you didn't already know that.

"Oh, GREAT. So now *I'm* supposed to eat that fare? No fucking way you ignorant shart. Let me tell you something, dickcheese—"

"No, no, of course not. There's an ATM just at the corner. I'll run over there and grab you your cash."

"I'm keeping the meter on. Twat."

You grit your teeth.

"Fine, you should. I'll only be a minute."

You rush out the door. If your boss just keeps his head in the window a few seconds longer, you'll be past him, and…

"Fancy seeing you here!" you feel a touch on your arm. "Where's the, uh-uh-uh fire?" Your boss chuckles indulgently as you turn, painfully fake grin plastered on, to speak to him.

"I just had to grab some cash at the ATM." You head that way. He follows you over. Great.

"Really? How quaint. You know, I'm thinking of starting to live a cash-free lifestyle."

"Is that right?"

"It is. I honestly think it's a remnant of the past. In the next five years…"

You nod, feigning interest, as your boss drones on. At least he's not commenting on your uncombed hair. Or the smell.

Or the fact that your account is apparently overdrawn. Fuck.

You look over; the cab driver has stood up outside his door and is gesturing at you.

And, of course, the meter has been running this entire time.

If you want to offer the cabbie an I.O.U., go to page 32.
If you want to try to borrow the cash from your boss, go to page 34.

Maybe if you just wait for a minute or two, your boss will go in and you can sneak into the office unnoticed.

"Hey, cockbreath, I said the fare's $23.50." The cab driver squints at you in the rearview, obviously annoyed.

"Sure, yes. I'm just…" You pull out your wallet and start rifling through it, as though looking for money, still staring out the window. What the hell is your boss talking to that guy about?

"Are you gonna pay or what, asshole?"

"I am, I am. I just…it appears I've…um…misplaced the cash in my wallet."

"Why'd you get in a cab without cash?"

"Well…why don't you have a credit card terminal? Aren't all you guys supposed to have those now?"

"Us guys? US FUCKING GUYS? What are you trying to fucking SAY?" Up until this point you hadn't really looked at your cab driver. Now that you are, it's clear that he's some kind of Middle Eastern.

"No, not like that. I meant cab drivers."

"Oh yeah, sure you did, you chode," he says, snorting derisively. You have to admit, you're impressed by the inventiveness of this ongoing tirade of cursing; this might not even be the guy's first language. "I bet you did."

"No, honestly, I'll go to the ATM in a minute, if you would—"

"You'll go to the ATM. NOW."

The cab driver is screaming at you now. But at least your boss is finally stepping away from the town car. Oh Jesus, because he's noticed you. He's coming over to the cab.

"I'm not gonna take shit from some pathetic, smegma-smelling motherfucker like you…"

Oh dear lord, your boss is almost here. You don't think he's spotted you, though. At least not yet.

If you want to try to duck out the opposite side of the cab and run for it,
go to page 36.
If it's too late, you're just going to have to explain this to your boss,
go to page 35.

YOU HAVE TEN DIFFERENT "LUMP" TABS OPEN ON YOUR BROWSER.

"Leave the lump exposed to the air whenever possible," you read.

Even though you're not totally comfortable with your own topless rolls and folds, you remove your shirt, looking away from the mirror as you do so.

"80% of all lumps are benign, which means they're not cancerous."

So there's a 20% chance that you've got cancer? As far as statistics go, that's basically like 100%.

Given that you actually hold your cell phone to your ear (and you like to smoke. But only when you drink—well, also when you're hungover. And you never eat kale, and you think your cat looks kind of Russian...like CHERNOBYL Russian), it's probably more like 80/20 in cancer's favor.

It's time to face the facts—you have cancer that will no doubt attack your immune system and ravage your flabby body within weeks. Come to terms with it already!

If you want to call a lawyer and begin the process of drafting up a will,
go to page 38.
If you want to cut the lump out yourself with a kitchen knife,
go to page 39.

YOU NEED A DISTRACTION. ANYTHING TO KEEP YOU FROM THINKING about the lump, the test results, the very likely possibility that you'll die, alone, without ever having had a threesome.

This is the only situation you can think of where you'd actually prefer going into work.

You make sure to get your doctor's signature before leaving. After you scared her with the bronchitis call this morning—which even now, less hungover, doesn't make any sense to you; it's only bronchitis, and it's not even that contagious—Betsy's not likely to cut you any slack on this one.

When you get into the office, it seems like no one's around. Great, the one time you were actually *hoping* to have some idle chitchat with someone—anyone, even Gina, even though she's hated you ever since you admitted you liked her old haircut better—you can't find anybody.

As you walk past the conference room, you see why—half the office must be in there.

And your boss is looking straight at you through the window, eyebrows vee-ing down in anger. He gestures towards the door.

You head inside.

"So glad you could join us, uh-uh-uh," he says, his fake laugh-tic even more grating than usual. "I assume you've brought your presentation with you? Perhaps on…" he glances at you disdainfully. You can see him taking in the wrinkled pants and unwashed hair. "…A flash drive?"

"Well," you say, dropping your voice lower than usual. You look down at the floor, holding your gaze there for a few seconds. "I have to be honest with you all, I just don't feel up to giving this presentation today. I don't think I could…" You sigh heavily, rolling your eyes dramatically heavenward. "Do it justice."

"Really," your boss says, his eyes narrowing. "But surely you've had it completed for some time now, yes? Uh-uh-uh." God, that laugh reminds you of an ape that's just discovered its own genitals.

"Of course," you say, "but I'm finding it hard to focus right now. You see, I just got in from the doctor's office, and…well, I don't know how to say this, but…" You try to work up some tears. "He found a lump."

The room exhales collectively, clearly on your side, if only for the next twenty minutes or so.

"Oh, god, I'm so…I didn't…uh-uh-uh, sometimes you just don't realize what other people…" Your boss looks around frantically. "What I mean is, let me take you to lunch."

"Or I could," Debby—your weird, aggressively unfashionable, sort of annoying, but nice-enough-to-count work friend from HR—says from the back of the room, the buttons on her sateen blouse straining as she leans towards you. "If you need someone to talk to."

If you take your boss up on the lunch offer, go to page 40.
If you opt for lunch with Debby, go to page 41.

24

"I KNOW WHAT YOU MUST BE THINKING, AND LET ME JUST SAY——" you begin.

"There's no need for an explanation," Alex says, looking away, putting her hand up in front of her face. Well, mostly her nose.

"But it wasn't me—a, um, homeless man unfortunately…was ill all over my shoes this morning," you say stumblingly. "I was trying to give him some food. Organic food," you add.

"I *really* don't need an explanation."

"You know, it isn't the first time he's done this to me, but what can I do? He needs to eat, and I feel morally responsible for my fellow man…"

"Okay."

"A little…mess on my shoes is a small price to pay…"

The elevator doors open and Alex half-runs down the hall.

If you want to clean yourself up in the bathroom, go to page 42.
If you want to try to convince Alex of what's definitely not the truth, go to page 43.

By the time you reach your floor, both you and Alex are doing your best not to gag audibly.

You'll just have to wait another few weeks before you work up to asking her out. It'll be fine—this will just be a funny story you two share some day, right?

You head to the bathroom, rinse out your shoes with an expertise born of experience, and head back to your desk.

Although you detest most everything about your company and job, there's something comforting about your cubicle. It's home to your favorite break room mug, your ergonomic computer wrist supports, and your trusty laptop…which is where, exactly?

SHIT.

It takes you all of a millisecond to realize that you forgot it at home. You stare at your empty desk space mutely, face contorted in horror.

It's even more galling since you *knew* you weren't actually going to "really dig in" on that presentation you're supposed to give today. Have you ever *once* actually completed work from home? But even if it's just a prop on the conference room table, you can't do the presentation without the laptop; it'll be too obvious that you're just bullshitting the entire thing.

If memory serves (debatable, considering your current state), the laptop is sitting on your kitchen table, exactly where you left it when you walked through the door last night.

If you want to grab a loaner computer for the day, go to page 44.
If you want to run home and grab it, go to page 45.

"WELL…" YOU PAUSE. THE IDEA OF TRYING TO TRADE DEBBY FOR A couple days of time off feels strangely like pimping her. But then, Debby won't even know you got a pay-off for setting her up on a date, so from her point of view, it will totally be like free will, right?

The IT guy snorts. "Well? Thall I jutht remove that latht thick day from your PTO pool?"

Desperate people don't have the luxury of black and white morality. You have no choice.

"No, I'll get you the date. Or at least I'll try to set you two up. If it doesn't go well, it's not my fault."

"I underthtand that. But I'll need to thee proof of your good-faith effort in that cathe, at leatht if you ekthpect me to keep up my half of the bargain."

"Alright. It'th…I mean, it's a deal. I'm coming in now."

"Yeth, that way we can repair the 'thudden connectivity ithues' you've been ekthperienthing." He snickers lightly and hangs up the phone.

No one seems to notice you sliding into your desk. So far, so good.

You start typing up an e-mail to Debby, BCCing Anthony.

> Debby-
> I wanted to write you for a friend who's too shy to let you know what an amazing woman you are.
> Let me describe this friend, first: quiet, and sometimes gets overlooked, but has a lot going on beneath the surface. Great sense of humor—on the sarcastic side, and sometimes you don't see it right away, but it's there. Sometimes feels underappreciated, and a little lonely (I guess that's true of all of us, right?), but keeps fighting the good fight, anyway.
> Oh, and here's the kicker: this friend works in our office. And has fallen for you.
> Would you make my friend's day by saying yes to lunch? Who knows, maybe one day this will be your crazy "how we met" story…
> Let me know,

You let it fill in your work signature.

You start reading it over again after you press send. Huh. It almost sounds like you were describing yourself.

Were you describing yourself?

You've never really considered Debby attractive—she looks kind of like the dorky, doughy secretary in an '80s screwball comedy, especially in the ill-fitting wardrobe department—but why not? It's not like you're a 10; even if you factor in "personality points" you're probably a 6, tops. Maybe more like a 5½.

Why should Anthony get to find love while you have to continue on alone?

An email comes in from Debby. She must have liked the sound of Anthony. You sigh.

> Of course I'll say yes to "your friend." This "friend" sounds like the person I've always been dreaming of. ;P
> Tell your "friend" that I'll be waiting by the elevator bank at 1:15. See this "mystery friend" then!

Hmm. Debby seems to think you were talking about yourself. You feel a swell of pride…followed by a wave of desire. The reply wouldn't have included the BCCed person. So far, Anthony doesn't know anything. She could have said no…

If you want to try to snake the date with Debby, go to page 46.
If you want to be the bigger person, and tell Anthony it's a go, go to page 48.

You want to say yes. God, you need that final day off…

…but you can't. You just can't prostitute someone else, even if it will get you off the hook. Even if it is just Debby.

Sighing heavily, you speak up:

"I'm not comfortable with that. I suppose I'll just have to come in and explain about the connectivity issues I've been having face to face."

The IT guy snorts thickly.

"Good luck with that. The report ith going to thay ekthactly what I thaw on the therverth, FYI."

"I understand that. Thank you for your…help."

You hang up. Taking a deep breath, you pull on a pair of cleanish-looking pants. You're going to have to hope your boss believes your version of events…

Go to page 49 to continue.

THERE'S ONLY ONE WAY TO DO THIS: CONFESS EVERYTHING RIGHT away and hope it will win you leniency.

"I'm so sorry, I know it was wrong, but I've never done anything like that before, and, well…honestly, I just didn't know what to do. I panicked. But he should have had a card reader, and he was yelling—it was a little scary, honestly. So…you know, my reaction makes a lot of sense."

The cop nearest—tall, black, and with a hefty gut—squints at you.

"What exactly are you referring to?"

"When I skipped out on the cab fare a couple—" wait, no. You should have been in by 9. "I mean this morning. That's… that's why you're here, right?"

"No," the cop says, voice low and careful. "We're here about the alarm that was tripped last night. This nice lady suggested that you might know something about that," the cop says, pointing towards Gina, who's smirking spitefully.

"Oh. No, I don't know anything about that. I went home at the normal time. Around 6ish, I think," you lie. You left at 4:53.

"Alright, then I suppose we'll have to find someone else to talk to about that. As far as this cab issue goes, though, I have to tell you that it's not only illegal to not pay your fare, it's unfair to the hardworking cab drivers in this city. Hardworking drivers like my father." The cop sighs wistfully before continuing. "You see, a cab driver has to pay just to rent his cab every day, so until he makes a certain amount…"

The cop keeps droning on about how what you did was wrong. As if you didn't know that already. You're taking it, nodding as though you care at appropriate intervals.

…and then you spot him, chatting with Gina in the corner, his stuttering tic of a laugh floating across the room, "uh-uh-uh."

Your boss. Shit, he definitely can't overhear *any* of this.

If you want to wait the officer out and hope your boss doesn't hear, go to page 51
If you want to cut the officer off mid-sentence and hope there's not too much blowback, go to page 50

30

Just be cool. They don't have any proof; after all, if the guy doesn't even have a card terminal in his cab, there's no way he has a security camera, right? It probably wasn't even a legal cab! They don't know it was you. They can't. Just stay cool.

"What can I help you with, officers?" Your voice sounds like helium escaping a balloon.

The cop nearest you—short, chubby, and pasty-pale—looks down at a notepad, sighing extravagantly.

"We're hoping to find someone in the office who was around at the time of the incident. Usually in these cases, it's accidental. This young lady," the cop points towards Gina, who's scowling at you from behind the reception desk, "indicated you might have some information on what happened."

"What incident are you referring to?" you ask as casually as you can.

"Last night's security scare. The alarm was tripped around…" the officer checks the notepad, "10:45 PM. According to security camera footage, an individual in a black hoodie, approximately 6'2" tall, slim build, was in the building at that time. Do you have any idea who that individual might be?"

Actually, you might. It's coming back to you, now, that time a few weeks ago when, drunk and without a bathroom option, you came into the office late, almost tripping the alarm yourself in the process. (Thank god you convinced them to change the code to 0000, "So deceptively simple no one can possibly ever guess!") You'd almost pissed yourself when a familiar, hoodied individual emerged from the kitchenette just as you were passing by.

"Uh-uh-uh, sorry to scare you," he'd said. "You working late, too?"

"Um, yeah," you'd managed to slur. "Just heading to the bathroom before I go home."

"Great. Well then, see you tomorrow, bright and early!"

You hadn't really thought about how strange it was at the time, but now, looking back, it had to have been at least 9, maybe 10 PM when you ran into him.

Just then, your boss walks into the lobby.

"What's going on, officers—is this one causing you some trouble? Uh-uh-uh," he says, pointing your way.

"No, actually we're here about last night's alarm scare. We were wondering if anyone had any information on what happened?"

If you want to tell the officers it was your boss, go to page 53.
If you want to wait for your boss to speak up for himself, go to page 54.

Y<small>OU HEAD BACK OVER TO THE CAR AT A TROT, SO YOUR BOSS WON'T BE</small> right on your heels. And so the meter will stop that much sooner.

"So listen," you say through the passenger window. You're panting, and sweating pretty heavily. God, you're in rough shape. "It turns out my bank is having some sort of…error with my account right now…"

"Oh I should have KNOWN you were the kind of motherfucker that's always overdrawn. Ballsack!" the cabbie spits angrily.

"Listen, what would you say to an I.O.U.? I'm certain I can work out this situation with my bank fairly quickly, and you obviously know where to find me…"

"I don't give a shit about your fucking I.O.U.s."

"Well I'm at a loss," you say. "My understanding is that card readers are mandatory, so——"

"Here's what you can do for me, you fucknut," the cabbie says. "Get me an interview."

"Well, I'm not certain that will be possible, but…" You look at the cabbie. He looks crazed; is his left eye actually twitching? "I'll certainly try. Here—that's my cell phone number. Call me later this week and we can figure it out."

Still feeling guilty, you write down your actual number. The driver looks at it, snorts, and drives away, so fast he nearly clips the side of your head.

Within a few hours you've forgotten the incident—after all, you being overdrawn is basically a weekly occurrence—when the receptionist, Gina, shows up at your desk.

"Some guy named Ahmed is here for you," she snips.

"I don't know anyone…" Wait, that has to be the cabbie. Fuck. "Never mind. Did he ask for me by name?" You hadn't written it on the paper.

"No, he just asked for the 'doughy, dandruffy shithead that smells like booze tears.' I assumed he meant you." She smirks and walks away, snapping her gum. Gina has never really liked you, at least not since that time you told her that you guys were equally lucky that beer goggles existed.

You head out to the lobby, and there he is, wearing a rumpled suit several sizes too big, his hair slicked back with what looks like a pint of motor oil.

"I'm ready for this fucking interview," he says.

If you want to call security, go to page 55.
If you want to try to reason with the cabbie, go to page 56.

34

THERE'S ONLY ONE THING TO DO.

"Oh, jeez, this is what I get for shopping online," you say, turning to your boss. "Apparently someone has accessed my account and made some fraudulent purchases. You don't have…" you try to do some quick mental math, "$50 I could borrow, do you?"

"Well, that depends, uh-uh-uh," your boss says, pulling out his wallet.

So much for "going cashless"—you spot at least $200 in there.

"Depends on what, sir?"

"Sir? That's my dad! I'm 'Pal.' Uh-uh-uh." He slaps a heavy hand on your shoulder. "But seriously, if I lend you this money, I expect you to pay me back."

"Of course," you say, nodding like an eager dog. "I would never dream of not."

"Not in money, in something far more important."

"Oh. What's that, sir?" Is he going to ask you for a blowjob? Would you say yes? How long is it until payday, again?

"I'd like you to sit down with me after lunch to discuss your financial situation, and work out a plan. I want to make sure all my employees are taking care of business, after all, both at work AND at home! Uh-uh-uh."

"Oh, absolutely," you tell him, breathing out in relief. You're pretty sure you would have said yes to the blowjob, and that would never have really washed off. "When should I be there?" you add, pulling the cash from his hand and starting to walk towards the cab.

"2 PM. Sharp."

If you want to go to the meeting, go to page 57.
If you want to blow it off and think up an excuse later, go to page 58.

IT'S TOO LATE, NOW, YOUR BOSS IS JUST FEET AWAY FROM THE CAR. He looks at the cab driver, who is screaming obscenities so intensely his face is starting to turn slightly purple, then looks at you in the back seat, raising an eyebrow. He opens the door.

"What's, uh-uh-uh, going on here, fellows?"

"Oh, it's nothing," you begin, but are cut off by the cabbie.

"Why don't you ask this taint-licking fuckwit what's wrong, huh? Fucking people like this. I'm not gonna just sit here and take it from you, pink-dick. You hear me?"

"How about we all get out of the car," your boss says, his voice cautious, "and talk about this, uh-uh-uh, calmly."

"Oh I'll GET outta the fucking CAR," the cabbie says, throwing the door open and walking around to your side. He grabs your arm. "Get out, shitbag. The man in the nice suit told you to, you smegma!"

You stand up, but you're still a bit wobbly from the hangover, and stumble back against the door.

"Step back, sir," your boss says, pushing between you and the cabbie. "You're disgracing your profession, and by extension, uh-uh-uh, all the transportation and carriage-services professions. I will not have you assaulting an employee of mine. Why, if you're not careful, someone will call the police."

"You wanna call the fucking police?" The driver pushes your boss out of the way, roughly. "I'll give you cunts an excuse to call the fucking police."

Then he punches you in the face.

Your face feels like its splitting into a million tiny face particles. Fuck! You crumple to the ground.

"Oh, that is the last straw, sir. It's one thing to assault the proud heritage of which you are but the latest iteration, but assaulting my employee? Uh-uh-uh, that is a step too far, sir, and I'm a witness." He smirks triumphantly, turning towards you. "Shall I call the police for you? I think you should press charges immediately, before this gentleman entirely sullies his noble profession," your boss says, phone in hand.

If you want to call the police, page 60.
If you think you ought to explain that the cabbie has a reason to be upset,
go to page 59.

YOU SLIDE ACROSS THE BACK SEAT, LUNGING FOR THE OPPOSITE DOOR. Your boss can't have realized it's you, yet. If you just get out of here, now, you'll...somehow get out of this?

You fumble at the handle for a few seconds—oh god, it's taking you too long—and finally manage to wrest the door open...

...just as your boss opens the door opposite. You slip outside, but it's too late.

"Where are you going? There's traffic on that side, uh-uh-uh."

"This dingleberry is trying to run away without fucking paying," the cab driver says over his shoulder. "Try to tell me you're looking for your wallet, you sack-smell. I know your game. I know it," he mutters to himself.

Your boss stands up and looks at you across the roof of the car.

"Is this true? Were you trying to, uh-uh-uh, *stiff* this hard-working driver?" Your boss's eyebrows vee downwards as he stares at you.

"No, I...he doesn't have a card reader, you know," you sputter.

"Do you know how much it costs to rent a cab in this city? DO YOU?" Your boss's face is turning red. "Hundreds. They have to make back hundreds before they make a single CENT."

"Well I'm not sure if...wait, how do you even know this?"

"My father was a hansom cab driver, and his father before him. It's a hard life—the stabling fees alone can take food out of your children's mouths. Some days we went without so that the horses could have fodder! But it's a noble profession. Until people like you," he spits out the word like it tastes bad, "come along and destroy any pride good men like this have."

The cab driver has gotten out of the car and is looking at your boss, obviously confused, but nodding his agreement nonetheless.

"Here, sir, let me pay the fare," your boss says, reaching for his wallet. "You'll never get it if you wait on this deadbeat. I should know, I'm his boss, uh-uh-uh."

The cabbie takes the money and your boss looks at you again.

"But not for too much longer. Go to my office, now. You can wait there while I have HR draw up your severance papers."

You knew you shouldn't have ordered that fucking pizza.

The End.

You grab the vodka bottle that's conveniently already opened and sitting on your kitchen counter. It looks like it has a few ounces left in it still.

You pour yourself a drink as you scroll through the list of contacts on your phone.

You must know at least one lawyer, right?

Hmmm, you decide to call your dad's best friend, though he retired a few years back. He was a lawyer. Or at least an accountant. Either way, surely he'd be able to give you some advice.

The phone starts to ring.

"Hello?" a voice says on the other end.

You hang up in a panic.

What are you thinking? You have no assets to bequeath. Hell, you probably owe friends and family more money than you actually have in your savings account. Even if your dad's friend was a practicing lawyer, you probably couldn't have afforded that call.

The thought instantly depresses you.

You text your work sort-of-friend—Jesus, even your work friends aren't friends—to tell everyone you're sick, really sick. It might not fly, but what does it fucking matter, you're going to die soon. Alone.

On the plus side, there are at least a few ounces left in that vodka bottle…

Go to page 1 to continue.

YOU RUMMAGE THROUGH A MUG FILLED WITH FORKS AND KNIVES UNTIL you find something that's probably sharp enough to do the job.

Luckily, you're still a bit numb from the hangover, so carving out this growth shouldn't hurt too much.

You grab a bottle of vodka, conveniently already open on the kitchen counter, and take a splash of it.

You also douse the knife in a sloppy attempt to sterilize the blade.

You steady your right hand and start feeling around for the lump.

Easy does it…Easy does it…

Oh shit—that incision was pretty deep. There seems to be a lot of blood pouring out of you. Maybe you cut through an artery? Are there arteries on backs? That's probably an academic question, considering the current situation…

If you want to cauterize the wound yourself, go to page 61.
If you want to call an ambulance, go to page 62.

"That's so sweet of you to offer, Debby, but I think I just need some time to process what I might be facing before I try to talk about it. Maybe we could discuss the presentation over lunch instead," you add, turning to your boss, forcing a strained smile onto your face.

"No, no, you shouldn't be focusing on that at a time like this," he says, his shoulders dropping in relief. Clearly he doesn't feel like talking about maybe-cancer any more than you do. "We'll just take your mind off everything with something tasty, uh-uh-uh."

You try not to grit your teeth, and to look grateful.

You wouldn't have bothered if you'd known he was planning to take you to SaladXPress. Even the croutons here somehow look wilted. You load up on some sort of mayonnaisey macaroni-and-canned-peas dish. At least you're not paying.

Your boss leads you to one of the particleboard tables, sticky rings from other diners' sodas patterning the top.

"I just have one question," your boss asks, shoveling a forkful of shredded beets and ranch dressing into his mouth, one marbled purple strip clinging to his fat lower lip, "I thought Betsy told me you were going in to get a test for bronchitis?"

Shit.

If you want to undermine your boss's faith in Betsy's competency,
go to page 65.
If you want to try to blame this on some sort of cancer-fear,
go to page 66.

"THANKS SO MUCH, DEBBY," YOU SAY, TURNING TO HER GRATEFULLY. Sure, she's strange, but you're still far too hungover to contemplate sitting through an entire meal with your boss. "I could really use a friend right now."

Debby looks at you hungrily. Hopefully that's just about the food?

It isn't.

You've barely made it out of the office when Debby stands up on tiptoe to whisper in your ear. You can feel a roll of velour-squeezed flesh pressing your hand to your leg.

"I'd love to discuss your…*interest*…in the Delano Roosevelts further over lunch, if you know what I mean. SNRCK!" She snorts wetly near your cheek. "Do you want to be Franklin or Eleanor this time? I'm…open to different possibilities, shall we say…SNRCK!"

You smile vaguely, trying not to let your terror shine out through your eyes.

Or your arousal. For Christ's sake, why would weird sexually suggestive references to FDR turn you on at all? You're disgusting.

"I know where the janitor keeps a wheelchair," Debby purrs thickly. It sounds like an outboard motor driving through a bowl of cottage cheese.

If you want to run away, now, go to page 67.
If you want to explore Debby's innuendos further, go to page 68.

LITTLE CHUNKS OF VOMIT FALL FROM YOUR SHOES AND SPLATTER on the floor as you make your way into the bathroom. Once inside, you turn on the faucet and dump both shoes into the sink, throwing your socks away.

You can hear someone shuffling around in the stall directly behind you—you need to hurry up and get these shoes back on before they finish.

But you don't hear a flush. Huh.

Then you hear whispers from the stall.

That's kinda strange.

You turn around, straining to hear what they're whispering.

Maybe if you bend down, you'll be able to hear better, since the door won't be in the way.

You hunch over until you see a pair of shoes—no, wait, there are two pairs of shoes shuffling around in the stall...

If you want to linger outside the bathroom to see who comes out, go to page 69.
If you want to ask who's in the stall, go to page 70.

YOU SPRINT OFF AFTER ALEX TO FURTHER EXPLAIN THE SITUATION.

Maybe you could add a little more detail to your story. Call the homeless guy Clancy, say? Nobody would make *up* the name 'Clancy' for a hobo—it's way too obvious.

"Johnson, I need you in my office right away!"

Johnson? You're not Johnson. You're not even remotely close to looking like that fat slob.

Or are you?

Either way, that's Barbara Houseman yelling at you, the CEO of your company. You'd better play along with this whole "Johnson" thing.

"Johnson, take a seat. We need to chat," she snips, loudly slurping her coffee.

You walk into her office hesitantly, almost as if the floor is covered in bear traps.

This is the first time you've ever sat down with the CEO, and your shoes and socks are covered in vomit.

"I'm going to be straight with you, Johnson," she says as she sets down her mug. "Margins were paper thin last month, shares are plummeting, and we're bloated with staff."

If you want to end this charade right now and tell your CEO that you're not in fact 'Johnson,' go to page 71.
If you want to play along, go to page 72.

YOU HEAD INTO THE IT DEPARTMENT. AS ALWAYS, THE FIRST THING you notice is the smell—old soup and Breathe Right strips. You try to breathe through your mouth.

"Any chance I can get a loaner for the day?" you ask the nearest IT guy.

"It'th thlim pickingth. We've got a Thamthung, but it doethn't have Offithe on it," he replies, never taking his eyes off the fanfic site he's reading.

"I kind of need Office. I mean, doesn't every PC ever made have Office?"

"No. I altho have a MacBook Air, but a few of the keyth don't work," he adds.

"Which ones?"

"The E. And the enter keyth. And all the numberth. Oh, and the thpace bar."

"Um…alright. I guess I'll take the Samsung, then."

The IT guy—is it Brian? Andy? You should really know this by now—reaches for the Samsung.

"Be careful not to unplug it. It will inthtantly thut off if the power thupply cutth out," he says sternly.

There's really nothing to say to that, so you just walk away.

You see your boss walking down the hallway in the opposite direction.

"Looking forward to that, uh-uh-uh, big presentation," he says as he passes you.

"Get your hopes up!" you say with a forced laugh. Hopefully it was convincing enough to mask your anxiety and fear, seeing as the presentation isn't nearly finished, yet…or started.

Go to page 73 to continue.

Yup, exactly where you left it, on the kitchen countertop. You grab the laptop, slam the door behind you, and start jogging towards the nearest subway station. You can't afford cab fare again.

On the platform, you see a person pacing back and forth. That's funny, from the back, it kinda looks like you.

The person turns around and your jaw drops in disbelief. Same too-close eyes, same slightly-froggish mouth, same pooch. Jesus, it's your doppelganger! Only in a much nicer blazer.

Apparently your look-alike doesn't notice you, and continues to walk frantically up and down the platform, mumbling incoherently.

You see the lights of an approaching subway car. Good, at least you won't be TOO horrifically late.

Your doppelganger lets out a scream you can hear even over the screeching brakes of the subway, "Fuck my liiiiiiiiiiiiiiiiiiife!"

…while jumping into the path of the oncoming train.

Blood splatters everywhere. Some of it lands near your shoe. Is it on your face? Jesus, did it get on you?

HOLY. SHIT.

Go to page 74 to continue.

46

YOU SHOW UP AT THE ELEVATOR BANK AT 1:15, ALONE. DEBBY'S waiting, breathing rather rapidly, a motion that shows just how much strain the middle buttons of her sateen blouse are under.

Shit, you might have made a big mistake, here.

"Hey, Debby, I, um…"

"I thought your mysterious 'friend' might have been you. SNRCK!" Debby snort-giggles in a way that makes her tiny eyes—heavily shadowed in electric blue—disappear into the doughy folds of her cheeks.

Yup, definitely a mistake.

You head downstairs to the SaladXPress in the lobby, Debby's "favorite" restaurant (as though you needed more proof that this was a bad idea) and try to keep the conversation neutral. And not to watch when she stuffs bites of rubbery, bubblegum-pink "ham salad" into her mouth.

"Well this has been a lot of fun…Madam First Lady," she adds in a gurgling whisper. "Unless you're feeling more like Mr. President today. I'm not picky. SNRCK!"

What is she talking about? And why is it making you mildly horny?

Whatever, it doesn't matter, you just need this over.

"Ummm, haha, yeah. I should be getting back, though. Lots of work."

"Of course. The leader of the free world's work is never done," she says, winking exaggeratedly.

"Sure." You stand up and head to the elevator. She can follow if she wants.

Trying to avoid her in the ten square feet of the elevator is almost impossible, so you're relieved when the doors open up on your floor.

SMACK.

Oh god, your entire face is exploding. Squinting, eyes watering from the pain, you look up, from where you've collapsed on the elevator floor, to see who punched you.

Of course. It's Anthony, the IT guy.

"I thould have KNOWN you would try to take her from me, you thnake in the grath!" He screams, spit sprinkling down on you.

"Wait...what's going on?" Debby says, turning back and forth between the two of you. "What is he talking about, sweetie?"

Go to page 75 to continue.

48

No, you can't try to snake Anthony. You made a promise. Besides, you really want those vacation days back. Hopefully Debby's easy…

You forward her email, along with a quick note:

"I'll walk you there and introduce you if you want."

He replies almost immediately:

"Yes."

You look up at 1:10 to see the hulking, voluminous presence of Anthony looming over you. He's wearing a "C:/DOS C:/DOS/ RUN RUN/DOS/RUN" t-shirt over camouflage cargo shorts. Chubby cankles encased in tight white sweat socks disappear into generic black sneakers. You reflexively lean away a bit when you see how greasy his nothing-colored hair is.

Jesus, there's no way you're getting those vacation days back. Even Debby must have SOME standards.

Sighing, you walk with him to the elevators. Debby's waiting there, snort-giggling nervously, her eyelids screamingly electric blue.

"Debby, this is your secret admirer—"

"Anthony," she finishes for you.

"I…I didn't know you were…erm…aware of my ekthithtenthe," he mumbles, looking away, as though Debby's too bright a sun.

"I thought the same thing! SNRCK!" She squeals excitedly. The resemblance to a pig briefly becomes overwhelming.

But then you see him reach for her hands, and—pig or no— you can't help but feel a searing stab of jealousy.

Even evolutionary chaff like these two can find love, and you…well, you haven't slept with anyone since your ex moved out six months ago.

And you hadn't slept with her for at least a year before that.

If you want to try to sabotage Anthony's chances, go to page 77.
If you want to try to exit with some dignity, go to page 78.

WHEN YOU SHOW UP AT WORK, NO ONE IS WAITING AT YOUR DESK and, miracle of all miracles, you don't have any emails from your boss, asking you to join him in his office "to just talk for a few minutes."

But you know better than to rely on that. That IT guy was spiteful enough that he definitely logged the exact minute you first tried to log on, and when you finally called in. The paper trail is right there: you didn't come in for most of the morning.

As the afternoon wears on, nothing comes in. You head to the break room, even though that could mean bumping into your boss. Better to get it over with, right?

By 4:45 you've still heard nothing. Apparently no one cares whether you show up on time or not. In fact, even with a report filed, no one seems to have noticed your absence.

God, that's really just depressing.

The minute the clock turns to 5, you're out the door, on your way to the dive bar near your apartment (no point in forcing yourself to cab it home again). In fact, you should swing by the liquor store on your way. Just so you'll have something around in case you want a nightcap.

You're not planning to go *wild*, but even if you do have one too many, what does it matter? Now that you know nobody's really paying attention, it's hard to see the point in trying to be good just because it's a "school night."

Go to page 1 to continue.

50

THE COP SAID HE WASN'T THERE FOR YOU; BETTER TO RISK SOME annoyance than have your boss fire you.

"Sorry, I'm absolutely listening, and I wouldn't say anything if it weren't an emergency, but…"

"Yes?" The officer raises an eyebrow, clearly annoyed.

"I just really need to use the restroom." You wince in a way that you hope is somehow endearing.

"Oh. Of course," the cop's face relaxes. "Go on, then."

You turn, grateful to get away.

"In fact." Fuck. "I'll just tag along. I've gotta drop the kids off at the pool if you know what I mean."

You look over your shoulder, trying to repress your anger.

"Get it? It's like the toilet's the pool, and…"

"No, no, I understand. Right this way," you say. You have no other option.

You reach the bathroom, the officer following just behind you, and head into a stall. But you don't have to go. At all. Jesus, the cop is going to know you were faking it, and then you're gonna get hauled in for not paying the driver, or worse, ratted out to your boss…

If you want to try to fake pooping to maintain the ruse, go to page 79.
If you want to hide in the stall for as long as you can, go to page 81.

He's walking straight towards you.

"What's the problem, officer? Uh-uh-uh. Is this one causing you some trouble?"

"Well no, sir, that's not why we're here today. I was just explaining why you need to pay your cab drivers."

Your boss's face turns stony and his eyes narrow.

"Why would you need to explain that? Surely everyone understands how hard transportation professionals have to work just to make ends meet. I mean, uh-uh-uh, I thought we hired *smart* people in this office."

"Yes, well, apparently your employee was unable to pay the driver this morning and so simply abandoned the vehicle, and I was explaining—"

Really? Can a cop legally say that to your boss?

"Abandoned. The vehicle?" Your boss's voice is low. Dangerously low.

"It was a one-time thing," you say, "the cabbie didn't have a card reader, and he was getting upset—violent, even—and I didn't know what else to do, so…"

"The onus is on YOU to find a way to pay, not on your driver."

"I know, it was a mistake, but…wait, why does it even matter to you? I know it was stupid, but—"

"My father was a horse and carriage man, and my father's father before him. They toiled for years with just their horses, their landaus, and their hands. They're part of the same brotherhood as your 'cabbie,' as you so derogatorily put it, uh-uh-uh," he snorts derisively. "And they're deserving of your RESPECT."

"Okay, I'm sorry, like I said, it was a mistake, and—"

"You know what running out on a fare means? It means three little children forced to split just one Pop-Tart between them for breakfast. And it wouldn't even have FROSTING!" Your boss is red in the face, now. Maybe if you're lucky he'll have a heart attack and this will end. "Go pack up your, uh-uh-uh, desk. You're fired."

Fuck. Next time, you're definitely not owning up to *anything*.

"See how many Pop-Tarts YOU can afford this month," he

adds, turning on his heel to march out of the room.

On the plus side, getting fired over an unrelated cab fare seems like a pretty clear bid for unemployment…

It's not a total loss…
The End.

THE MORE YOU THINK ABOUT IT, THE MORE YOU REALIZE YOU HAVE to tell. Dear god, what if he's embezzling? What if he's running some sort of underground fight club out of the archives room?

What if the cops turn their attention towards you running out on a cabbie this morning?

You have to speak up.

"I think I know who it was you saw on the security footage," you say, turning towards the cop. You can see your boss widening his eyes, shaking his head, and drawing a line in the air in front of his throat…but that just proves you have to press on.

"IT WAS HIM!" you say, pointing at your boss dramatically. Man, this is just as cool as it is on TV.

"Is that true, sir?" the officer says, turning to your boss. He seems so…not as dramatic as you feel. "Were you the one who tripped the alarm?"

"Well, uh-uh-uh, yes, yes, that was me."

The cop looks bored. If the truth's going to come out, it's up to you.

"Why were you here so late? What could anyone possibly be doing here at 11 PM?" You realize as soon as you say it that he *could* have been working, but surely even your boss can't be that self-loathing, can he?

"The, uh-uh-uh, the servers were…down…"

"If there's a server reboot we're automatically sent an email, and I didn't receive one! You're lying!" you say triumphantly.

"It's true, I wasn't here for the servers," your boss says, looking down and sighing. "I was here because, uh-uh-uh, my wife kicked me out." He bursts into tears. Soggy, snotty, choking tears. "I have nowhere else to go!"

The officer looks at you in disgust.

In fact, everyone in the room is looking at you that way.

Go to page 83 to continue.

54

YOU GLANCE AT YOUR BOSS. IF HE'D JUST BEEN HAVING ONE OF YOUR average late-night-drunk-pee-at-the-office type incidents (you can't be the only one who's been there before, right?), he'll 'fess up and the whole thing will be over and done with.

"Hmmm, that's strange," he says, coming over towards you and throwing an arm around your shoulder. It seems especially heavy. "I wonder who that could have possibly been. Maybe we have an, uh-uh-uh, intruder, huh?"

He turns to you, staring intently and widening his eyes meaningfully.

It's pretty clear he knows that *you* know it was him. It's even clearer that he doesn't want you to mention that fact to the police officers.

What could he possibly be hiding?

If you're pretty sure you have to tell on him, now, go to page 53.
If you're no snitch, go to page 84.

"Sure," you say, smiling inanely to keep him calm. "Let me just call the people you'll be meeting with." You back up a few steps. "I'll be right back."

You dash to your desk and call security, then wait, hoping they'll show up soon.

A few minutes pass and then you hear:

"Get your nasty taint hands off me you dick-lickers. I have to look good for my interview! STOP FUCKING PAWING MY GRUNDLE!"

Eventually the noise dims and you hear a door slam. Apparently they managed to get him out of the building.

The way he reacted proves you did the right thing. Clearly the man was volatile. Deranged, even. You had no other option.

Go to page 86 to continue.

56

So he got the wrong idea. That's okay—you can just explain the situation calmly and clearly. Surely he'll understand.

"I'm sorry if I wasn't clear earlier; I'm going to be getting in touch with management soon in order to let them know about you as a potential candidate. There's no interview today, though I hope to have one lined up for you shortly."

"What the SHIT are you talking about, queef?"

You look around, but only Gina is in the room. She raises an eyebrow then turns back to her computer.

"I don't think you *understand*," you say in a fierce whisper. "I'm not even aware which openings we have right now, if any—you can't just come in for an interview that hasn't been scheduled. It's not—"

"Do you want me to tell these pube-burgers what you did? Hmm? Want me to explain to all your fart-porn friends around this place who you are?"

He's raising his voice. Gina's openly staring now.

"Please, just let me explain—"

"No, let ME explain motherfucker. You're going to GET me a goddamned interview right the hell NOW, or I am going to take you OUT. You think I don't know how? You think I can't fuck a tittiefuck like you up?"

Gina has picked up the phone and is whispering into it urgently. You try not to wither under the cabbie's continuing fury.

A few seconds later two security officers rush in, grabbing each of the cabbie's arms.

"Get off of me you moose cunts! GET YOUR FUCKING HANDS OFF ME!"

They drag him away to the elevator bank, still screaming.

Well *that* went terribly. But on the other hand, you no longer have to feel guilty about making exactly zero effort to get the guy an interview.

Go to page 86 to continue.

YOU SHOW UP A FEW MINUTES EARLY. IF YOU LOOK EAGER ENOUGH, maybe he won't even ask you to pay him back. Besides, it's not like you're actually doing any work.

"Aahh, there you are," your boss says, "thought you might have forgotten about our little meeting, uh-uh-uh."

"Of course not, I'm very interested in your financial planning advice." You try not to laugh aloud. You've rarely said something so absurd.

"Well tell me, how much do we pay you?"

"Ummm…" you say the number.

"And you don't find that sufficient?"

"No, it's more than sufficient. Like I said this morning, I just…" shit, what had you said this morning? "Lent my bank card to…um…a *friend*, who was…going through a rough time, and I didn't realize she'd charged so much on it."

"Well that's just preposterous, uh-uh-uh," your boss says, recoiling backwards as though someone's waving a butter knife in his face, loaded with a fresh pat of shit. "I would think you'd know better than to do something like that."

"Yes, well…I guess I just have too big a heart," you say. The words are so saccharine they almost make you gag.

"That," your boss says, staring intently at you, "or you're not telling me the truth. If I ask you a question, will you answer me honestly? I promise your job's not at risk, no matter what you say."

Jesus Christ, what kind of question is this?

"Of course."

"Well, uh-uh-uh," he says with his nervous tic of a laugh. God you hate that fucking laugh. "Is it cocaine?"

Well, is it? Go to page 87.
Of course it's not. Go to page 88.

58

YOUR BOSS SHOWS UP AT YOUR CUBE AT 2:15.

"So, didn't feel like making it to the meeting, I see, uh-uh-uh." He's doing that wheezy laugh thing, but he's staring at you with pure disgust.

"No, I meant to come, I just got caught up with this… presentation." You quickly close the listicle you were reading— even though you'd only made it to number 42—and try to make your face look innocent.

"Yes, well, I'm aware that you have a, uh-uh-uh, 'problem' with certain substances," he says.

"Wait, what are you…?"

"…and I was willing to be understanding. To try to get you the help you so obviously need, even. But after your failure to make even the most minimal effort to repair your situation, I'm afraid I can't see the point in investing in you further," he finishes.

"I'm so sorry, honestly, I just lost track of time, if you're available I'd be happy to talk about this now—"

"Your performance has been erratic, your personal habits are inappropriate for a professional setting, and you've failed to follow through on even the most basic requirements of your job. I'm sorry, uh-uh-uh, but I'm afraid I'm going to have to let you go," he says, smirking triumphantly.

"Please, if you'd just let me expl—"

"I'll have accounting deduct the $50 I lent you from your final paycheck," he adds, turning on his heel and stomping away.

The End.

YOUR BOSS STARTS POKING AT HIS KEYPAD.

"Erm, there's something I should mention," you mumble.

"Yes?" your boss says. "What's the, uh-uh-uh, non-emergency line? Maybe I should just dial 9-1-1? He was being very aggressive with you."

"Yes, well," you cough awkwardly, looking anywhere but at your boss. "That's probably because I hadn't paid the fare, yet."

"You…excuse me?" Your boss squints at you. But at least he's not trying to call the cops…on you.

"Well he doesn't have a card reader, and I didn't have any cash, so I was trying to figure out the best option…"

"There's an ATM just down the block," your boss says, pointing. "Though I admire you for attempting to go cashless, I'm thinking of doing the same myself. Cash is, uh-uh-utterly anachronistic in modern society, don't you think?"

"Are you going to pay the fucking fare, dick-sneeze, or not?"

"Yes, just…" you turn to your boss. "Could I borrow a few dollars for this and pay you back at the end of the week? I had a large…furniture delivery yesterday, and I'm low on funds." Jesus, that's possibly the stupidest excuse you could come up with.

But your boss seems to buy it, fishing out his wallet and pulling out a $50 bill.

"Here, you can consider this a freebie—"

"No, I couldn't, I'll pay you just as soon as—"

"As long as you agree to meet in my office later this afternoon to discuss financial planning. I want my employees to have a longer term vision than payday, uh-uh-uh."

"Sure, yes, of course," you say gratefully, passing the cash to the cabbie and getting out of the way as he speeds off, mumbling curse words. "I'll be there."

If you plan to show up, go to page 57.
If you'd rather skip it, go to page 58.

"I DON'T KNOW, I DON'T WANT TO MAKE A BIGGER DEAL OUT OF this than we need to," you say, but your boss is shaking his head vigorously.

"Uh-uh-uh, I won't hear of it. You have to press charges. Make an example of this man! He's a stain on the profession!" He shouts. "I wouldn't even let riffraff like him muck out the stables," he adds in a mumble.

"What?"

"Nothing," he grunts. "Make the call."

"Umm, okay," you sigh, as your boss dials the police station.

Minutes later, two cops pull up in a cruiser. They get out, sauntering up to the group of you around the cab as slowly as possible.

"You the one got assaulted?" the fatter one says, pointing a pen lazily at you and yawning. The way he's looking at you—aggressively bored and already half-smirking—makes you feel even more awkward. It's clear he thinks you're a waste of his time.

"Out of curiosity, why would you assume I'm the one who was attacked?" you stammer.

"You just look like the kind of person people would wanna punch," he says, shrugging.

"Let's get this over with. You wanna report an incident?"

If you want to confess to the cop that you didn't pay the driver, go to page 89.
If you want to file false charges, screw that guy, he was an asshole, go to page 90.

THERE'S BLOOD EVERYWHERE. THE SIGHT OF IT IS STARTING TO MAKE you a little nauseated. Though that could just be the hangover.

Either way, you're too embarrassed to call an ambulance, and you definitely can't afford it, anyway.

Obviously the only option is to cauterize the wound yourself. You try to tie a tourniquet above the gash, which is basically just like a really tight tummy-belt. Good enough. You look around for something metal to use to cauterize the wound.

The knife in your hand seems like as good an option as anything else. Unfortunately, only after you heat it do you realize that the metal runs through the handle, too.

"FUCK!"

Now you have a burnt hand and a bleeding, un-cauterized wound. Also, you think you tied the tourniquet too tight, and you're starting to feel dizzy. And like your toes aren't there. The numbers on your phone are starting to blur together.

If you want to run over to your neighbor's place and ask for help,
go to page 93.
If you want to wander outside in the hopes of encountering a good Samaritan,
go to page 92.

"WHAT DO YOU MEAN MY INSURANCE WON'T COVER SELF-INFLICTED knife wounds?"

You hang up the phone in frustration and walk back into the kitchen.

You never put the top back on the bottle of vodka. Good. You take a slug. And then another.

That scene in *The Shining* where blood gushes out of the elevators and fills the entire hallway has nothing on this back wound.

But at least there's an upside to blood-loss. You're barely two drinks deep, and already *very* drunk.

Go to page 1 to continue.

AND THEN THE SCREAMING STARTS.

"YOU!" Betsy shrieks, pointing a gnarled claw your way. "You're not supposed to be here. Go home!"

She pulls the end of her cardigan up over her nose, backing away rapidly, her arthritic hips banging into her desk.

Your boss emerges from his office. Great.

"What's going on here? Where's the fire? Uh-uh-uh." Your boss looks from you to Betsy, his smile even more forced than usual.

"The whole place will be infected! We can't have it! I said we couldn't have it! I don't have the strength for this!" Betsy crumples into her desk chair, eyes owlishly large through her bifocals, hand still covering her mouth.

"Okay," you say, using your rabid-animals-with-guns voice, pure soothe. "What if I just head downstairs to get my lunch, so that I won't bother you." You glance at your boss, eyes wide, and tilt your head towards the elevator. He nods almost imperceptibly.

"I'll have to Lysol THIS WHOLE PLACE!" you hear as the doors close behind you.

You head with your boss to one of the many open tables at the SaladXPress in the building lobby. Even with no other options nearby, people avoid the place.

"I'm sorry to put you on the spot, uh-uh-uh," he says, shaking his head nervously, "but I need to know what happened back there."

"Your guess is as good as mine," you say, shrugging dramatically. "I don't know why, but she seems to think I'm infected or something. Which I think I'd know."

"So you didn't call in sick this morning?" your boss says, squinting at you beneath his caterpillar brows.

"No. I was just taking a bathroom break and she lost it." You shake your head. "Honestly, it was a little scary," you add. That kind of stuff always helps.

Your boss sighs heavily.

"Uh-uh-uh," he says, shaking his head sorrowfully. "I thought it might have been something like that. Frankly," he says, leaning towards you, his voice conspiratorially low, "I don't think she's all there anymore."

"I didn't want to say anything, but…" you let the question linger in the air.

"Well, that ties it," your boss says brusquely, sitting up and slamming his hands on the table. It looks like it landed in some sort of greenish blob. Mustard? Salad dressing? "I'm just gonna have to cut her loose."

If you want to try to save Betsy's job, go to page 95.
If you'd rather let Betsy just get the axe, go to page 94.

"Bronchitis?" you say, raising your eyebrows dramatically. "That's strange. I definitely didn't mention bronchitis."

Your boss narrows his eyes at you. You can't tell if he's listening intently, or passing judgment. It's too late to go back.

"Of course I didn't mention the lump. It felt a little…personal. But I wouldn't have said bronchitis. In fact, I think I probably said 'going in for some tests,' which I guess she might have assumed was bronchitis, but…" Your mouth is dry, and your tongue feels like it might get permanently stuck to the roof of your mouth. "I definitely didn't say bronchitis. Huh."

You look down at your plate. How do you stab a mayonnaise-coated pea nonchalantly?

"I thought that might be the case," your boss says, his voice grave. "Frankly, I think Betsy's been, uh-uh-uh, slipping lately," he says, shaking his head mournfully. "She seems…confused."

"I've noticed that too," you say, nodding agreement.

"Well, this is the last straw. I mean, if you hadn't trusted me enough to tell me the truth about where you were, she might have tanked your career."

"Mmm." You gulp.

"There's only one thing to do. I'll have to fire her. Just as soon as we finish these desserts, that is! Uh-uh-uh! I just love how they manage to get the cheesecake bites INSIDE the Jello!"

If you want to try to backtrack to save Betsy from getting axed, go to page 95.
If you think Betsy's getting what's coming to her, go to page 94.

"WELL," YOU BEGIN. HOW CAN YOU PLAY THIS? WITH THE LEAST collateral damage? "I never said the word bronchitis—I don't know where she got that from."

The first target you have to protect is yourself, after all.

"But I admit I did keep the real purpose of the appointment from her. I just told her I was feeling under the weather and needed to go in for some tests. How she spun that into bronchitis is beyond me," you say, raising an eyebrow. "Maybe Betsy's getting a little less sharp in her old age."

"Why would you hide the truth, though?" your boss asks. Somehow he's managed to give himself a ranch dressing goatee. You try not to stare at it.

"I guess I thought…if I didn't say anything about it, maybe it…wouldn't be real?" Dammit, why can't you cry over this? You can cry over someone stealing the last zebra cake out of your desk drawer, but not this? You look down, grimacing as hard as you can to make up for it. "And I just didn't want people to pity me, you know?"

Look up at his eyes…now. Yes. Perfect. You may feel filthy inside, but you're nailing this performance.

"I do know, uh-uh-uh." He shakes his head, his weird exhalations somehow becoming mournful. "I know because… because I felt exactly the same way when Karen died!"

Your boss starts bawling. Oh, Jesus, you'd forgotten his first wife had cancer. But honestly, why would you remember that? He's been married to his second wife the entire time you've worked here.

His nose is starting to drip into his "tater-tot surprise," and even the other zombie-eyed, soul-sucked diners of SaladXPress are starting to stare.

Jesus, now what?

If you want to just try to wait this out, go to page 96.
If you want to try to cheer your boss up, go to page 97.

"I, ummmm…" you look around, frantic. You see your boss ahead of you, waiting at the elevators. "I just realized some really important issues with my presentation that I need to discuss with the boss. But I'd love to talk more about this later," you say over your shoulder, almost running now. You look back at Debby. Through the haze of your fear, she looks like a confused, permed sow.

You have no idea what she was talking about, and you hope you never, *ever* learn.

"Oh, did you change your mind?" your boss asks. "Or did Debby put you off your food? Uh-uh-uh." He brays to himself, obviously amused. "I'm kidding of course."

"I just realized this is still too…raw for me to discuss with Debby right now," you say, trying to look grave. "I'm afraid I'll upset her. You know how sensitive she is." Does he? Is she?

"That was incredibly brave of you," he says, taking your arm lightly. You try not to shudder. "And smart, since I've got a table with your name on it at the SaladXPress! Uh-uh-uh!"

Well shit. Whatever Debby wanted to do with that wheelchair couldn't be worse than the pathetic lobby restaurant, filled with dingy counters and washed-out customers.

It's too late now. You try to load up on the slightly suspect-looking potato-alfredo salad; at least if you wind up with food poisoning from the lunch, your boss can't blame you for going home sick.

You set your tray on the table, careful not to touch the strange, still-glistening blob of beige goo near the center.

"I meant to ask you," your boss says. A limp, brownish broccoli floret is stuck between his two huge front teeth. "How did you find out about the lump, anyway? I could have sworn Betsy said you were getting checked for bronchitis."

Shit.

If you want to sow doubts about Betsy's competency, go to page 65.
If you think you can somehow spin this back to cancer-fear, go to page 66.

YOU CAN'T IGNORE IT. SOMETHING ABOUT DEBBY'S SUGGESTION IS making your blood flow…southward.

That's when you remember…ish. There were texts. Late-night, vodka-fueled texts. You'd have to pull out your phone to fill in the details, but you're almost certain you told her you wanted her to "give you a fireside chat, if you know what I'm saying."

How could she have possibly known what you were saying? What were you even saying?

You let her drag you into the supply closet. Before you know it, she's plopped down onto what does, indeed, appear to be a rusty wheelchair. She pulls you towards her by your waistband until you're awkwardly straddling her…and the chair arms.

Then she starts wriggling.

"GRRRGGGGH," Debby moan-gargles, "oh, Madam First Lady, I love this saucy new getup. So androgynous. What WILL the press corps think," she says, thrusting her lower half—from this angle she looks like a sausage about to burst her polyester casing—up against your genitals.

Apparently she's gonna be FDR this time.

Still, it's kind of working for you. You would have been an awesome Eleanor.

"I thought it suited me," you say in falsetto, pushing downwards. Something in your hip twinges dangerously. "After all, I'm far too busy to get tangled up in a skirt."

Just as Debby is telling you to "alienate those constituents with your no-nonsense demeanor, GRRRGGGGH—"

…the door opens.

She only stands there for a minute before squeaking and slamming the door, but it's long enough for you to see who it is: Alex. Your secret love. The one you've wanted to be with since the moment you first saw her on your day-one office tour.

And she not only had to catch you getting it on in the office, it had to be with *Debby*.

If you want to try to explain, go to page 98.
If you want to send apology flowers, go to page 100.

OUTSIDE THE BATHROOM, YOU TAKE OUT YOUR PHONE AND START sifting through your contacts so it won't be so obvious you're waiting for the bathroom-sex-bandits to emerge.

You pace around the entrance, one eye on your phone, the other eye on the bathroom door.

"What are you doing?" you hear a voice ask from behind you.

You turn around. Of course, it's Alex.

"Who me?"

She nods, rolling her eyes.

"Nothing," you say, then proceed to immediately drop your phone, shattering the screen.

The bathroom door swings open. Out steps Morgan, your office nemesis. God, you hate that schmuck.

"Star performer, at it again," Morgan chuckles as you pick up the pieces of your broken phone.

"I knew it was you!" you scream from the floor. Alex looks at you pityingly, then walks away. God, Morgan is such a shit, always making you look like an idiot.

Clearly Morgan was fucking…or drug-using…or drug-using while fucking? Whatever, Morgan needs a come-uppance.

Whatever was going on in there wasn't work appropriate, anyway.

It's time to do the adult thing here and tattle on Morgan to your boss: go to page 101.

"Um, excuse me, do you need any help in there?" you ask, as you slowly approach the stall.

There's no response. The two depraved sex-bandits go absolutely quiet. Wait, what if they're drug fiends?

You knock loudly on the door. "Who's in there?"

Again, no response.

"Look, I'm not dumb. I know there's two of you!"

"How about you fuck off!" yells a nasal, pinched voice.

You'd recognize that weasel-sucking-helium voice anywhere! It's Morgan, the divisional manager…and your office nemesis.

Giddy at finally having one up on that piece of shit, you toss your wet shoes on and run out of the bathroom in glee.

Go to page 101 to continue.

"Barbara," you say, "do you mind if I call you Barbara?"

"What is it, Johnson?" she says swiftly.

"The thing is, I'm not actually Johnson. Unfortunately, you have me mistaken with another employee."

"It doesn't matter. As I said, cuts are looming, and…what on earth is that awful smell?" She grabs her nose, putting her coffee down on the desk.

There's no escaping this one. You have to come clean.

"It's puke. You see, a homeless man named Clancy vomited all over…"

"Stop it right there. You're clearly lying to me. 'Clancy'? That's rich. One of those 'so unbelievable that it's somehow believable' names?"

Damn. She saw right through your bullshit. No wonder she holds the reins at this company.

"This is classic addict behavior," she says, returning to her coffee.

"It's not…"

"Let me smell your breath," she says with supreme confidence.

"No, it's just that—" you start…but you have no idea how to finish that sentence.

"There's no shame in being an alcoholic. It's a disease," she says.

"But I'm not an alcoholic!" you protest.

"That's denial speaking! I would know, I spent half of the '90s dancing on top of bars. Look, I'm willing to let you keep your job, so long as you attend a few meetings…"

"Sure, I could do that…" you start.

"…with me."

If you want to admit to being an alcoholic, hoping it will help you cozy up with the CEO, go to page 104.
If you're pretty sure you're not an alcoholic, go to page 102.

72

"BARBARA," YOU SAY, "DO YOU MIND IF I CALL YOU BARBARA?"

"What is it, Johnson?" she says swiftly, swigging at her coffee.

"Oh, um, nothing, it's just that I wanted to compliment you on your pants suit."

"They're new slim fits! Good of you to notice," she says heartily. "Anyway, our staff really needs to be whittled down if we're going to boost our Q3 profits. I would say we need to cut every department in half by the end of the day," she says emotionlessly, reaching for her coffee again.

"Okay…"

"You'll draft up a list of redundancies within the next sixty minutes, yes?"

If you agree to fire half the company, go to page 106.
If you'd rather pass on the instructions to the real Johnson, go to page 105.

YOU PEEK INTO THE CONFERENCE ROOM. IT'S FILLED WITH SENIOR staff members. Are people actually standing in the back waiting to hear your presentation?

What are you going to tell them? That you didn't finish it because you got solo-shitfaced last night?

Your eyes dart around the hallway, looking for a way out. Anything.

You spot a fire alarm.

You walk up to the box and gently brush your hand against the white handle.

It would be so easy to just pull it down right now. They'd have to postpone the meeting to another day if it went off...

Should you do it? If you got caught, you'd certainly lose your job. Can they send you to jail for something like that?

You pace back and forth past it. You shouldn't...but it looks so inviting...

If you want to pull the fire alarm, go to page 107.
If you want to ignore the fire alarm and give the presentation,
go to page 108.

"WE'VE GOT ALL THE B-ROLL WE NEED, LET'S FIND AN INTERVIEW," the television reporter says to her cameraman.

At this point, you've been waiting around for nearly 35 minutes for the track to clear, and you've stopped paying attention to where you're pacing.

Whoops.

"Excuse me, but did you witness the accident?" The microphone is already in your face, and the light from the camera is blinding you.

"Umm…yes, I…" you blink rapidly.

"Go on," she says as the cameraman pulls in even closer.

"Well, I saw this person pacing erratically. I wanted to help and everything…"

Where the fuck is this coming from? If anything, you tried your best to create as much distance between you and the bizarro-you as possible.

"…but I couldn't get close before it…happened."

The reporter gives you a reassuring nod of the head.

"Did you recognize the city council member?"

"Um, no."

A short silence ensues.

"Do you know…is someone getting us cabs or something?"

The reporter stares at you, obviously disgusted, and walks away. You can't wait any longer, you're going to have to spring for a cab. After twenty minutes of unsuccessful attempts to hail one, you finally manage to get one to drive you to your office.

The minute you walk in you notice everyone huddled in the conference room, watching something on the wall-mounted television. It's…the news of the subway suicide.

If you want to run into the bathroom and hide, go to page 109.
If you want to toss the TV on the ground to destroy the evidence,
go to page 110.

You look back and forth between Anthony, who's shaking out his hand and wincing, and Debby, kneeling beside your exploded head. Jesus, who knew getting punched hurt this badly?

"It's a long story, Debby, but Anthony here…"

"I thaid I'd comp a vacathin day if you could be perthuaded to accompany me to lunth," Anthony wheezes flatly.

Debby's eyes narrow further. Which you would have thought was impossible, they're already so piggishly small, but there you have it: every day, a new mystery.

"I was going to tell you, Anthony, but I passed by the elevators on my way to the IT department, and Debby obviously got the wrong impression that I was putting myself forward…" you mumble thickly. You can't breathe through your nose. "It was all a misunderstanding."

Debby stands up, stepping away from you delicately, as though you were contagious. Or a spreading pile of shit.

"It was you who said all those beautiful things about me? But I never thought you even knew I existed," she whispers wetly.

"You're all I think about," Anthony says, turning to Debby. "I jutht couldn't get up the courage to approach thomeone tho lovely…" He grips her arms, and they stare into each other's eyes.

Great. Now you're jealous again. You had your shot with her and you just let it slide through your fingers!

"So…all's well that ends well, I guess," you sigh, trying to dust yourself off a bit.

"Well, not for you," Anthony says. "After the way you acted, you thnake in the grath, you'd better believe I'm going to report your abthenthe thith morning." He smirks triumphantly, a single greasy lock of hair falling over his fat forehead, grazing the tops of his oversized glasses. Debby grips his arm, nodding furiously.

"Then I guess I'm just going to have to tell HR that you punched me. In the face. Because you're pursuing an inter-office romance."

Anthony's face falls.

"Fine. You win. The deal thtandth."

"The extra days?" you plead.

"Don't puth it," he says, turning and leading Debby back to the bowels of IT.

Your whole face is throbbing…but it could be worse. Now that you're seeing her from below and behind, an angle that shows the lumps a too-tight velour skirt can't conceal, you're realizing you dodged a bullet. Definitely.

There are worse things than being alone, right? Totally, utterly, seemingly endlessly alone.

Right?

RIGHT?

The End.

YOU START HAUNTING THE ELEVATOR BANK AROUND TWENTY MINUTES after they've left, hoping to catch Debby as she's coming in.

Fully twenty-five minutes later they stroll in together, hand in hand, hanging around outside the elevators and whispering to one another for several minutes before they pull themselves apart, fingertips lingering until the last possible moment.

Jesus, fuck this guy. He doesn't deserve her.

"Debby, I was wondering if you had a minute to chat?"

"What? Oh sure," she says dreamily, staring off after Anthony's retreating waddle. "I'm very…free for the rest of the day. SNRCK!"

"Well, I wouldn't say anything if I didn't care about you, but you should know some things. About Anthony."

She tilts her head to the side, looking somewhat like a confused blob of silly putty.

"I don't know many of the details, but I hear that there was an…incident after one of the office parties. Gina the receptionist was passed out, and…" God, are you really going to do this? Debby's staring at you, her beady eyes slightly wider with worry. "Well, like I said, I don't know all the details, but from what I heard she was seriously considering pressing charges."

"What did he *do*?" Debby says, hanging on your every word.

If you want to accuse Anthony of something like date rape, go to page 111.
If you want to put this accusation train into reverse, go to page 112.

HOW CAN YOU JUST LET THEM RIDE OFF TOGETHER, INTO THE SUNSET-glow of the dropping elevator?

"Wait, Debby, there's something I need to tell you. About Anthony."

They look at you, Anthony frowning slightly, Debby's face open, like an especially trusting prized farm animal.

"What? Nothing bad, I hope. SNRCK!"

"It's just…" Can you really do this? Ruin the budding romance of two nerds, people who—even more than you—may not ever have another chance to find human companionship?

No, you can't.

"It's just that he's far too modest. He probably won't even tell you about all the amazing things he can do with code. It's way over my head, but from what I hear from people in the know, it's like something out of a movie." You avoid looking at Anthony's lumpy body as you say this, so it doesn't come out sarcastic.

"Oh, really?" Debby turns back to Anthony, rapt. "Tell me all about your sexy code. SNRCK!" He nods at you approvingly as they step into the elevator together.

The rest of the day, you wistfully think of those dawning moments of romance, the promise of a young…ish couple just setting out on the road to love and never-ending happiness together. No one knows how great your sacrifice was.

Sure, it was just Debby, but it was also the prospect of not being utterly alone, at least for a little while.

God, you wish you had someone, you think as you head out of the office. Anyone.

You don't. But at least you have alcohol. You head for the nearest bar and order a double.

Go to page 1 to continue.

I<small>F THE COP THINKS YOU WERE LYING</small>, things will go worse for you, you just know it.

Somehow, you have to *fake* pooping.

You look around the stall. What do you have that you can drop into the water? There's nothing but the toilet paper dispenser in the stall. Maybe if you roll up a big wad and just throw it at the water?

Fffffft. It dissolves soundlessly into the bowl.

You pat your pockets. Nothing. You've left everything at your desk, ever since the third time your phone dropped into a toilet. If only you had it now to drop into the toilet. That would splash. And you have a warranty now.

"Doing alright in there?" you hear from the next stall over. From the sound of it, the cop is having *no* trouble taking a big ol' dump. Ew.

"Yeah. Just…I should eat more fiber I guess, or…"

"We all should." The cop chuckles softly.

God. Weird.

You can almost feel the cop's heightened hearing trained on your toilet bowl, listening for the slightest proof that you are not, in fact, in an emergency pooping situation.

You look at the bowl. Splashback would work. You could use your hands, but you probably won't be able to scoop up enough water to make the right sound. Oh, but your shoe! That could easily hold a shit's-worth of bowl water.

Standing on one foot, arm against the wall of the stall to steady you, you work your other shoe off. You take a deep breath, close your eyes, and scoop.

Splaaaaaasssshhhh.

"Oooh. Careful in there," you hear from the sinks. "I'm just gonna leave you to it. Good luck."

"Yeah, thanks, I'll need it," you say, giggling with relief. It worked! The cop bought it!

And…now you're just stuck here with your soaking toilet-shoe and probably the most virulent case of toilet-rim norovirus the world has ever known. Charming.

You do your best with about a hundred paper towels and emerge.

"Oh, there you are," your coworker Johnson says. "We were starting to think you were going to skip the meeting. Alex was joking that you probably hadn't even done the presentation."

Alex was right. You'd entirely forgotten you had a presentation today. One you've done exactly zero work on.

"Oh…no, I just had a little stomach upset. I'm on my way," you say.

Fuck.

If you want to try to wing it with your presentation, go to page 114.
If you want to feign some sort of illness, go to page 113.

IF THE COP THINKS YOU WERE FAKING IT, THINGS WILL GO WORSE FOR you, you just know it.

But despite your hangover, and the ridiculous amount of greasy pizza you don't remember eating last night, you have nothing in you. It's dried up. Disappeared. You're a poop desert.

Dammit, you knew you should have ordered the extra-spicy mushrooms. Why are you so afraid of fire-poops? It always ends up working against you.

You'll just have to wait it out and hope the officer isn't the kind of person who listens for proof of other people's shits.

"Doing alright in there?" you hear from the next stall over. From the sound of it, the cop is having *no* trouble taking a big ol' dump. Ew.

"Yeah. Just…I should eat more fiber I guess, or…"

"We all should." The cop chuckles softly.

God. Weird.

After a few seconds, though, you hear a flush from the next stall. Apparently SOMEONE is getting some shit-traction.

"Good luck in there," you hear from the region of the sinks. "I'll just give you a little privacy while you finish up."

"Oh, um, thanks."

"Some people just have performance anxiety, you know?"

"Yeah…"

"And I get that, I do. Course I've had to discipline my mind to overcome those bodily reactions—that was one of our first classes at the academy."

Wait, specifically force-shitting? You shudder to imagine day two…

"But I don't expect civilians to be capable of that kind of resolve."

"Mmmm." You have no idea how else to respond.

"Anyway…see you out there, I guess."

"Yup. For sure."

You finally hear the opening and clicking closed of the door that indicates that the officer has left. Weirdly, the relief flooding your gut prompts a massive shit.

Go to page 115 to continue.

"No, no, of course not. I've never even tried cocaine," you say, shaking your head vigorously.

That one time in college doesn't count; you're pretty sure it was just cream of tartar mixed with some dried-up horseradish.

"There's nothing like that, it was just…really dim in there." Now that you're repeating it, it does sound a little flimsy. "Also, the sound was distorted. I have…tinnitus?"

"Really." Your boss scrunches up his forehead, half confused and half disgusted. "How…uh-uh-uh…disappointing."

He turns towards his computer screen and taps a few things on the keyboard.

"I see you've already used up almost all your allotted P.T.O." he says coolly.

"Not quite, I still have a couple—"

"You have one day left. And geez, we're only a couple months into the fiscal year. You'd better hope you don't get the, uh-uh-uh, flu."

"Yeah…I've been…unlucky this year."

"Well I must be honest, I assumed that for anyone your age to be such a total, uh-uh-uh, mess, there had to be a drug problem. Or do you maybe have some ongoing mental health issues you're dealing with?"

"No," you blurt before you can think. Fuck, you never thought you'd wish for tangible proof of depression.

"Mmmm. That's just…uh-uh-uh…just…hmmmm." Your boss is wrinkling up his nose, like someone's just smeared shit all over his upper lip with a butter knife.

"Is there…anything else? Or…"

"No, nothing. There's nothing more to be done for someone like, uh-uh-uh, you. Just…just go," your boss says, shooing you out.

Jesus, you didn't realize he thought you were *that* pathetic.

Hopefully you didn't completely kill that bottle of vodka last night; you need several drinks *immediately*.

Go to page 1 to continue.

YOUR BOSS IS WEEPING LOUDLY NOW. EVERYONE ELSE IS GIVING YOU disapproving glares before quickly and quietly exiting the room.

"There, there," you say, awkwardly patting him on the back. "It'll be okay. It happens to everyone…"

"UH-UH-UH WHYYYYYYYY," he wails. He's buried his face in your shoulder, which you can feel growing damp with tears and snot.

You continue to cradle him for the next twenty minutes, after which he abruptly gets up and leaves, shooting you a dirty look.

So now you're probably gonna take flak for his wife hating him, to boot.

God, happy hour cannot come soon enough today. Maybe you should even consider heading down the block to the liquor store so you can start early at your desk…

Go to page 1 to continue.

You turn to your boss.

"Maybe we do. We should…make sure the closed-circuit cameras are working tonight. It sounds like it could be dangerous." Your boss nods at you in feigned agreement. "Maybe he's after the…computers…or…something else. Someone should probably tell accounting."

"Oh, uh-uh-uh," your boss gulps. "Yes, certainly, we'll have to see if anything is missing."

"So you don't have any additional information for us?" the cop says, yawning. Clearly this is a *top* priority for the force.

"Afraid not," you say. "Gina must have been mistaken." You smile towards the reception desk. She scowls back at you. "Sorry I can't be more helpful."

"Well, if you think of anything, please be in touch," the cop says, already halfway out the door. "You know where to reach us."

Your boss pats you on the back chummily.

"Care for a, uh-uh-uh, coffee? This one's on me."

"Sure," you say. "We can discuss…*presentation* notes," you say meaningfully.

"Yes. PRESENTATION notes." He winks exaggeratedly.

You've barely ordered your cookie-supreme lattes at the CoffeeXPress when he grabs your shoulder, leaning in to whisper in your ear.

"It's not what you think," he says, steering you towards the corner of the shop. "I swear to you, I'm, uh-uh-uh, not doing anything illegal."

"Then what were you doing?"

He shushes you dramatically. "It's…well, it's my wife. She…" He sniffs. "She's kicked me out."

He bursts into loud, snotty tears.

You sip your latte, trying to ignore the scene he's making. You awkwardly pat him on the shoulder. He grabs your hand. God, this is so fucking weird and getting weirder.

"Thanks for being such a good friend about this," he says once he's finally quieted down. "Can I ask you a favor?"

"Sure…" you say tentatively. No, you won't keep this quiet around the office, but you'll certainly pretend to.

"Can I, uh-uh-uh, stay at your place for a while?"

Oh, HELL no your boss isn't staying with you. Go to page 116.

Sure, why not? Go to page 117.

OH DEAR GOD, THAT DAY JUST WOULDN'T END. LIKE, YOU KNOW, every other day since you've started at this fucking miserable job.

You walk into your apartment and slough off your messenger bag and coat at the front door, where they'll sit in a pile, wrinkling, until tomorrow morning.

Ugh, you already need a drink.

You pour a weak vodka soda and flip on the television on the kitchen counter. You turn to the evening news; you like to keep up with current events, after all. Plus, in the time it would take one of your co-workers to read some pointless *Times* op-ed, you can learn about at least a dozen stories.

The screen is staying on the same long shot of the suspension bridge downtown. If you squint, you can make out a little human shaped speck standing at the edge of the screen.

"Again, the gentleman hasn't offered any explanation for his intended dramatic action, but emergency services are standing by. For those viewers just joining us, traffic has come to a standstill downtown because of a would-be jumper on the Wilmington Street Bridge…"

That's what you should be doing with your evening.

The helicopter cam zooms in on the jumper.

Oversized, rumpled-looking suit. Greasy hair slicked back with about a pint of motor oil. And even though you can't hear it, a constant string of obscenities obviously contorting his mouth.

You're pretty sure you can lip-read, "Cocksucker. No fuckin' interview…"

But then you can't see anymore, because he's jumped, out into the air.

Oh dear god.

He'll land in the water, and they'll get him, right? He'll be fine, it can only be a…hundred foot drop from there? Maybe a hundred twenty?

You pour several inches of vodka into the bottom of your glass. It wasn't your fault, right?

Right?

Go to page 1 to continue.

You haven't done cocaine since that model UN party in college, and you're not entirely sure that wasn't just Adderall cut with flour. But it would be such a convenient out. And your boss is leaning forward in a strangely eager way...

"I suppose I thought I was hiding it well," you say, staring off into space thoughtfully. "It started because I wanted to perform better—burn the candle at both ends, you know?"

Your boss nods vigorously.

"...but before too long it wasn't something that was helping me control my life anymore. It was controlling *me*." Yeah. That's the stuff. "Lately I've even been doing it anally, to, you know... get it into my bloodstream faster. We call that...butt...bumping?"

"Oh, I read about that in *USA Today*. They caught that one country singer doing that before the country Grammys, right?"

"Yeah. I saw that story," you lie.

"Uh-uh-uh," your boss shakes his head, grinning ruefully. "What was it *like*?"

"Oh, you know..." No, you don't. And neither does he, apparently; he's raising his eyebrows at you expectantly. "It's sort of like...when you stick your hand in an electrical socket. But good? You're very...charged. And there's a lot of anal leakage of course. And...itchy?"

You've seen drug addicts scratch at themselves before, right?

"Like bugs are inside your...nails," you finish.

"I've heard that," he says solemnly. Apparently you hit near enough to the mark for him.

Weirdly, he looks almost...proud.

It's too late to turn back now, anyway. You have to go for this "pathetic cokehead" thing (although really, cokeass would be more accurate, now) full-tilt.

Go to page 118 to continue.

"No, no, of course not. I've never even tried cocaine," you say, shaking your head vigorously.

That one time in college doesn't count; you're pretty sure it was just a crushed up aspirin and a couple of Pop Rocks.

"There's nothing like that, I just…lent some money to a friend, like I said." Now that you're repeating it, it does sound a little flimsy.

"Really." Your boss scrunches up his forehead, half confused and half disgusted. "How…uh-uh-uh…disappointing."

He turns towards his computer screen and taps a few things on the keyboard.

"I see you've already used up almost all your allotted P.T.O." he says coolly.

"Not quite, though, I still have a couple—"

"You have one day left. And geez, we're only a couple months into the fiscal year. You'd better hope you don't get a flu."

"Yeah…I've been…unlucky this year."

"Well I must be honest, I assumed that for anyone your age to be so hopelessly, uh-uh-uh, incapable, financially speaking, there had to be a drug problem. Or do you maybe have extremely high student loans?"

"No," you blurt before you can think. Fuck, you never thought you'd wish your grandparents HADN'T paid for school.

"Mmmm. That's just, uh-uh-uh, just…hmmmm." Your boss is looking at you like he's just noticed you're drooling. Are you? No, you'd feel that, certainly.

"Is there…anything else? Or…"

"No, nothing. There's nothing I can do for someone like you. Just…just go," your boss says, shooing you out.

Jesus, you didn't realize you were that pathetic.

Hopefully you didn't completely kill that bottle of vodka last night; you need several drinks *immediately*.

Go to page 1 to continue.

You look at your boss, nodding eagerly over the cop's shoulder. Then you look back to the cabbie, spitting an endless string of curse words into the dashboard, rocking slightly in that abandoned-Russian-orphan sort of way. Does this guy really deserve to be arrested because you have less financial acumen than M.C. Hammer...and lamer pants? And will he come to hunt you down in your sleep if he *is* taken in?

"No, I'm sorry, there's nothing to report," you tell the officer.

He sighs exaggeratedly. "We received a call that—"

"No, I know that, I just—"

"I WITNESSED the attack. I can tell you, uh-uh-uh, it is absolutely worth reporting, this man *viciously* went after my—"

You raise your hands up to cut off your boss's tirade.

"I know, yes, he tried to punch me." The officer perks up, flipping his notepad back open. "But it's because I couldn't pay him. I hadn't paid the fare, then you came over and started yelling at him, and I guess...well, I'd have thrown a punch too."

"Me too," the officer says, snorting derisively at you.

"Oh," your boss says coldly. "I...see."

"Sir, filing a false police report is a jailable offense. You're gonna need to come down to the station with us," the police officer says, grabbing your arm. Despite his general appearance, something like a stubbly cream-filled donut, his grip is strong. Really strong. "So we can book you."

"But I haven't filed any reports yet," you plead.

"Are you resisting?" the officer says, gripping you tighter.

"No, no, I'll come," you say.

"Just one thing before you go," your boss says, taking out his wallet and paying the driver. The officer is starting to tug you towards the car, but you can hear his next words loud and clear:

"You're fired."

The End.

90

You look at your boss, nodding eagerly over the cop's shoulder.

It's too late to turn back now.

"I do want to file charges, but I think I'd like to do so at the station. I'd feel more comfortable there, seeing as how that's the man who just attacked me," you say, pointing at the cabbie. He unleashes a string of expletives in your general direction.

"Sure," the officer says, nodding towards the cruiser. "Hop in."

You head to the station, where the fat cop leads you into a dingy looking room with a table and two folding chairs. He points to one and leaves, returning several minutes later with a stack of paperwork, a pen, and one coffee…for him.

"So what happened?" He sounds supremely bored, and refuses to look you in the eye.

"Well, I was getting out of the cab, preparing to pay," you start. Nice, now if the driver says you didn't, you'll have laid that groundwork already. "When the guy just went berserk. Started swearing at me, and screaming about…the holy land…" Why not? This cop looks racist. "And then he just threw a punch. Luckily my boss was there to see it and to help pull him off me. It was really terrifying."

"So he's one of them dangerous Islams, huh?" You have his attention now. "They should all be deported if you ask me. They love nothing better than murdering the American dream."

"Ummm…yeah. I mean, it wasn't a *big* part of the whole thing…"

"Why even come here if you don't like the way we do things, you know? Taking good jobs from honest citizens—REAL citizens. It's enough to make you sick."

You just nod. You're starting to feel a little sick, too. From what you could tell (from the swearing) the cabbie's accent was from Chicago.

"Thanks for being a brave citizen, sir," the cop says, standing to shake your hand. "We'll file this right away and then we'll really fuck this asshole."

You're not sure, but you think you hear him murmur "raghead" as he walks away.

As you walk out of the station, you see that you have a new voicemail.

"Hey there, hope you're doing okay, uh-uh-uh. Such a traumatic event this morning, but you handled it so well. You should take the rest of the day off to recover; don't worry, I'll make sure HR doesn't dock you more than half a day, even though TECHNICALLY you're really taking more time than that! Uh-uh-uh. Anyway, just wanted to let you know that, and to tell you how proud I am of you. You did the right thing. Men like that deserve to be punished. Oh, and we've moved your presentation back to tomorrow, so just plan on doing it then. Alright. Goodbye."

You delete it immediately. The inside of your stomach feels grimy and you can't seem to unhunch your shoulders.

It's only noon, but you have nowhere to be. And you feel utterly disgusted with your race-baiting self. There's no better way to get rid of the self-loathing…

You walk as quickly as you can to the bar at the end of the block. It's dim and gritty inside.

Perfect.

"Excuse me, can I have a double vodka?"

Go to page 1 to continue.

YOU LOOK AT YOUR BACK; IT SEEMS LIKE GALLONS OF BLOOD HAVE poured out. You can see it starting to stain the top of your waistband. Probably half of your blood has leaked out. At least. Just the thought makes you start to feel cold.

You think back to kissing your dead grandmother in her coffin. Her corpse was definitely warmer than you are now.

At least you'll be seeing her soon.

You can feel your teeth chattering as you make your way out to the sidewalk. There has to be a Good Samaritan around here somewhere. You want to live!

"Help me! Please, help me!"

You think back to your self-defense class and remember that people are more likely to come to your rescue if you scream "fire" instead of "help."

"Fire!"

There isn't a soul in sight to witness this fiasco, slash help you.

"Fire! Please! Fire!"

Although you're not particularly religious, you decide to ask for help from Jesus just in case. But it's too late, even for Jesus. You collapse face first onto the pavement.

THUD!

Go to page 120 to continue.

BLOOD CONTINUES TO STREAM DOWN YOUR BACK. YOU FRANTICALLY speed walk through the hall to your neighbor Dylan's apartment.

You must look like something out of a Tarantino movie, and you haven't spoken to Dylan since that one incredibly drunken night, but that doesn't matter right now, you need help. You knock loudly on the door.

It opens.

Totally ignoring your massive back-wound, your neighbor immediately starts shrieking at you.

"What are YOU doing here? You think you can just show up here, never calling me back after that night of *passion?* That night of *love?* I'm not your prostitute-whore!"

"What? What's a prostitute-whore?" You clutch for the wall in an attempt to regain your balance.

You're certain you're as white as a ghost, and yet this person feels the need to berate you. You feel faint. You better resolve this quickly.

The only option is to play along.

"To be honest, I was worried that we are almost too compatible..." You can tell by that raised eyebrow that you're not selling this well. "I was just feeling so *many* feelings...that...I guess I was scared? It's my fault. I cared so much it terrified me."

Your neighbor slams the door in your face mid-sentence and storms back inside.

So...will anyone be calling an ambulance?

Go to page 121 to continue.

94

YOU SHAKE YOUR HEAD MOURNFULLY, TRYING TO MIMIC YOUR BOSS'S look of half-constipated sorrow.

"It's always tough to make these decisions. But sometimes you just have to. In the end, it's for the best," you say.

You take a sip of your Diet Coke to try to wash the taste of that particular brand of bullshit out of your mouth.

"Well, no point in delaying the inevitable any, uh-uh-uh, further," he says. You wonder if he knows he makes that sound. It has to be doing damage to his esophagus. "Let's go get this over with."

You feel sick the entire elevator ride up to the office, but that's probably just the hangover combined with old mayonnaise. Anyway, it's too late to change things now, you've already committed.

It *will* be for the best, though, right? You don't have to feel guilty about Betsy losing her job. After all, she's definitely at least half senile…

Go to page 122 to continue.

"OH, I DON'T THINK IT'S AS BAD AS ALL THAT, DO YOU?" YOU SAY. You gulp, trying to swallow a wave of bile rising into your mouth. Sure, she's an old nutbag, but you don't want Betsy to get *fired* for it. She's at the age where losing a job is a direct route to surviving off of cat food. Plus, there's something incredibly uncomfortable about the idea that it takes this little to get someone fired at your office. Somebody who *doesn't* really deserve it.

"Well, this is just the latest in a string of errors. Just last week she tried to tell me she caught some poor schmuck sleeping in the supply closet. Uh-uh-uh. Can you believe that? I mean, it's ridiculous."

"Yeah," you gulp again, trying to look innocent. And wakeful. "That doesn't seem very plausible."

"The fact of the matter is, we can't have the first point of contact for customers be someone unreliable. Her behavior today was frankly delusional. No, no," he shakes his head and smacks the table with an open palm. It barely misses a dried-looking crumble of what might have once been blue cheese. "It's time for Betsy to call it quits. So." He stands quickly, gesturing towards the elevator bank. "Shall we?"

Go to page 122 to continue.

You sit there, staring awkwardly at anything but your boss, trying not to actively think about how gray the mayonnaise on your salad looks under the stronger lights above your table.

Finally—thank GOD—his phone buzzes on the top of the table.

"Uh-uh-uh, I guess somebody up there wants me to stop reliving past miseries, eh?" He snorts loudly. His eyes look like a childhood illness.

"Mmm," you say, trying not to look as uncomfortable as you feel.

He picks up the phone, looks at it briefly, and turns to you, suddenly all business again.

"Whelp, I guess we should get back to the office," he says, stuffing one last massive bite of deep-fried alfalfa sprouts into his mouth. "Betsy's dead. Apparently she was spraying Lysol directly into her mouth when she just, uh-uh-uh, keeled over. They're saying heart attack, but it could be Lysol poisoning. We've all seen that before."

"Oh, umm…okay," you say. He slaps both hands on the table and stands up briskly.

You arrive back in the office just as the EMTs are zipping up the body bag. Your boss heads over to talk to one of them, and you wander a few feet away, unsure whether you're supposed to stay in the room, acting distraught, or whether you're allowed to go dick around for the rest of the afternoon, since obviously no one can be expected to get anything done under the circumstances.

From the corner of your eye, you can see Betsy's computer monitor, still glowing, a few dozen browser windows open.

The top one is titled "Bronchitis: The Deadliest Chest Cold?"

The one behind that reads, "What You Should Know About the Government's Bronchitis Kill-Plan."

The third says "Better Off Dead: One Woman's Struggle With A Disease More Horrific Than The Grave, Bronchitis."

Jesus Christ, who is even putting these sites up? And why is the internet so fucking afraid of bronchitis?

If you leave the screen alone so as not to tamper with potential "evidence,"
go to page 124.
If you want to close the windows to try to clear your name, go to page 125.

"I'T'S, UM…IT'S NOT SO BAD AS ALL THAT, REALLY," YOU SAY, TRYING not to stare at the dribble of snot streaming down your boss's face. "Buck up!" You slap his shoulder lightly, chummily. He winces dramatically.

"Don't, uh-uh-uh, hit me, uh-uh-uh," he gurgles. "I'm already in, uh-uh-uh, PAIIIIIN!" This provokes a fresh wave of mucousy wails.

"Sorry, I…sorry. Then what would make you feel *better*?" you say, a hint of desperation creeping into your voice. You're not sure you can handle watching a grown man—who happens to have power over your ongoing employment status—continue to weep for much longer. "What would help you take your mind off this?"

"Well," he says, hiccuping, "there is *one* thing. But I couldn't ask you to do it. It would be…" he looks you up and down. "Inappropriate. I couldn't even ask you, let alone expect you to agree."

"Try me."

"No, I'll offend you."

"You couldn't possibly! Look at me!" You gesture to yourself. "Think of me as one of the guys!"

He raises an eyebrow, then laughs. A little too heartily, actually, but at least he's no longer bawling.

"We could…" he looks around furtively, lowering his voice, "go to the strip club?"

Why would he think you, of all people…but he *has* stopped crying. And maybe you can earn some much-needed brownie points by agreeing.

"Sure, why not!" you say, your voice thin and high. "First time for everything, right?"

"Oh, good. I'll call the driver."

Go to page 126 to continue.

Maybe you can just explain things to Alex, then she'll understand…and you'll still have a chance with her (as long as she swings your way, that is).

> Dear Alex,
>   I just wanted to apologize for what you saw in the supply closet. I've been in a bad place lately, personally—on top of everything else that's going on, there was a recent death in the family.

Ooh, that's good. Not true, but good.

>   It's really been hitting me pretty hard. I've been making some bad decisions as I'm trying to work my way up through this ocean of grief.

God, you're a fucking POET.

>   That's what you saw—a bad decision in action. I don't even have feelings for Debby, but I guess I just needed to feel some human affection, no matter who was offering it. I should have said no, but she was coming on pretty strong, and it was easier—and I'll admit, filled some need that I think I've been trying to ignore—to let it happen.
>   I hope I haven't completely destroyed any relationship we have, or might someday have. I've always admired you, and I would feel terrible if something like this—a mistake made from a place of personal hurt—would ruin our chances of getting to know one another better.
>   All best,

You let it auto-fill your work signature. Don't want to sound too desperate, after all.

Minutes later, Debby waddles up to your desk, her face pink, eyes so narrow it looks like someone left her doughy cheeks out to rise for the last few hours.

"So I was a MISTAKE, hmm? You just 'let it happen'? That's not what I remember! SNRCK!" She snorts derisively.

"Debby, I don't know what you're talking about." You look around. People are starting to stand up in order to watch the scene over the tops of their cubes. "Could you please keep your voice down?"

"Am I just a warm body to you? Is that it? Because that's not what you said last night!" She's screeching, now.

"Honestly, Debby, I don't know where you're getting this from, but—"

"From ALEX, you dope! She forwarded me your EMAIL!" Debby starts bawling, in a snotty, glottal-stoppy sort of way.

Oh god, the entire office is watching you now.

Including your boss, who's on his way over to your desk.

If you want to try to escort Debby out of the building, go to page 128.
If you want to act confused and hope your boss deals with this,
go to page 130.

100

WHAT CAN YOU DO TO TRY TO MAKE THIS BETTER? WHAT WOULD smooth over witnessing…well, mostly it was humping, but Debby was going for a reach-around, so it seems like you must have rounded third base. Anyway, witnessing something she shouldn't have?

Duh. Flowers. What woman doesn't like to get flowers? You of all people should know *that*.

You actually smack your forehead, which seems to reactivate your sleeping hangover.

You get online and look for the nearest florist that will do same-day delivery. Jesus CHRIST, it costs that much to carry some flowers…a block?

You opt for the carnations, and start filling out the note section of the online order form:

> Alex-
>   I'm so sorry you had to see that; it was a mistake that, without going into too much detail, I'll say I made out of grief. I'm not even interested in Debby.

Should you risk it? Why not, it's on flowers; flowers soften any heart, right?

>   I'm interested in *you*. I hope you'll accept these as an apology…and maybe as a chance at a new beginning?
>   Yours,

You type your name in the "from" box and click "place order" before you lose your nerve.

Hopefully she'll come over to thank you in person. You watch the clock, counting down until the order is set to arrive…

Fifteen minutes after the delivery time you get an email. The subject line is "flowers!"

> Please report to the HR department to discuss a recent breach of the employee code of conduct.
>   -Sharon
>   Head of Human Resources

Fuck.

If you want to try to get out ahead of this, go to page 134.
If you want to just keep your mouth shut and hope this ends quickly,
go to page 132.

You head straight to your boss's office to explain what you've seen. Which you might have embellished *just* a titch.

"These are some pretty serious accusations you're bringing to me, uh-uh-uh," your boss says, with his strange laughing tic.

"Let me be the first person to say that I fully understand the gravity of the situation," you say with your most concerned-looking frown.

"Good," replies your boss. "Then you'll have no trouble going into a meeting with Morgan and Sharon in HR. Tina will probably want to sit in on this one, too, since she's the head of workplace safety. I would imagine we'll also have to bring in…"

You mind starts to race; shit, this is escalating fast. You thought Morgan might get a little slap on the wrist, not a full-frontal attack by HR.

"And the lawyers, of course, that'll cost, uh-uh-uh…"

You start to dig your nails into your chair. You don't actually have the foggiest idea what really happened in that bathroom stall, other than there being four legs.

"But you'll be fine with that, right? After all, you've already been so brave to come forward with this, uh-uh-uh, information."

If you want to stick to your guns and let the process unfold, go to page 136.
If you want to backtrack before it's too late, go to page 138.

"I REALLY DON'T THINK THAT'S NECESSARY. I HONESTLY DON'T EVEN drink that often…"

Well THAT'S a load of horseshit. But so is admitting to the boss of your *entire company* that you're a miserable drunk. And it hasn't gotten that bad, has it?

"Denial. I appreciate that. It took me years to admit I had a problem." The CEO clicks her fingernails rapidly along the side of her coffee cup and takes another massive gulp.

"I swear, I don't have a problem!" you scream. Oh god, are you about to cry?

"Ahh, it's worse than I thought. Listen, I don't think you're ready for meetings, yet. You need more help than that." She squints thoughtfully, then seems to make up her mind. "I'll call my friend Jim over at Happier Trails. It will be the best thing for you."

"Happier Trails, but isn't that a rehab center?" You gulp.

"The very one I went to in '96, after I blew that member of the Motley Crue cover band right on stage. It saved my life. Now it'll save yours."

She picks up the phone. Jesus, she's dialing. Is this really happening?

"But…I can't afford to take that much time off. I have bills, and…"

"Oh, don't worry about that. You'll be taking paid leave, and the company will pay for treatment. People like us need to help each other out. After all, the same impulse that makes us alcoholics is the one that drives us to succeed, Johnson—or wait, that wasn't you, correct? Here, write down your name so accounting knows where to keep sending your checks."

You write it down.

"How long will I be there?"

"I'm thinking…90 days." She turns slightly in her chair and begins barking into the phone. "JIMMY! It's Barbara Houseman. I have a pickup. Yes. Exactly. Alright, see you in twenty."

Three months without a drink. On the one hand, that sounds awful.

But on the other hand it'll be three months you don't have to be here, mindlessly going through the motions every single day while the last shred of you that you think of as actually *being* you coughs and hacks away on its deathbed.

It'll be like a really long, paid vacation. Hell, all your meals will be paid for, and you won't be wasting money on booze and dinners out…you might actually MAKE money on this prospect.

You turn back to the CEO, shoulders back.

"You're right. I've been crying out for help for months now, and I couldn't even admit it to myself."

"YES! Precisely. I knew you were a go-getter," she says, nodding rapidly.

"Thank you for giving me this opportunity to turn my life around," you say. "You won't regret it, I promise you."

"I know I won't. They'll be here in a quarter-hour, so go power down your machine. And while you're at it, send Johnson in here. I need his help on those redundancies."

You turn to leave, buoyed by the first joy you've felt in months.

Three months away.

Surely that's long enough to find a different job.

The End.

YOUR FIRST MEETING GOES FANTASTICALLY...UNTIL THEY ASK IF you'd like to share your experience of addiction.

The CEO is nodding at you furiously from across the circle, so hard, in fact, that her coffee is spilling out over the rim of the cup and onto the floor.

"Well, yesterday I really had a wakeup call, with the help of Barbara, of course," you say, nodding in her direction. "I woke up with very little memory of the night before, and I'd...well I'd wet myself overnight," you say, coughing. Most of the folks in the circle of plastic chairs nod in recognition.

You continue.

"And I was so hungover—usually it's not so bad, but this time it was just horrific—that I vomited on myself in the cab to work. Which I couldn't afford, since I'd apparently ordered food before passing out and tipped the delivery boy everything in my wallet. And that was just a normal Wednesday. No reason to be that way. I hadn't even been drinking with anyone."

"Mmmhmmm," the group leader looks at you, nodding pityingly. "And that's when you realized that other people—non-addicts—don't have 'normal' days that look like that, right?"

Wait, surely this story can't register as fully alcoholic in a room of alcoholics, can it? The CEO is watching you with the kind of intensity only a daily diet of 72 cups of coffee can bring.

"Right," you say, swallowing convulsively.

Go to page 139 to continue.

YOU RUN UP THE STAIRS IN SEARCH OF JOHNSON.

"Hey, Johnson!"

"Why doesn't anyone around here call me by my first name?" Johnson asks impatiently.

"So, I have a funny story," you say with a slight chuckle. "I was in Barbara Houseman's office…"

"The CEO?"

"The very one…and, funnily enough, she thought I was you."

"Hmmm…" Johnson ponders this information for a few seconds. "But you corrected her of course…right?"

"Well, not exactly—it's a bit of a long story, she was on such a tight schedule, but the takeaway is…she wants you to fire half of the staff."

"What?"

"I don't know, it has something to do with Q3 profits, I really wasn't paying close attention. But what I *do* know is that it needs to be done in the next fifty-five minutes."

Johnson's mouth drops open in disbelief.

"Thanks, Johnson," you say taking a step backwards.

"Just one second," Johnson says, clicking open your employee file on his computer. "That's you, right?"

"Right."

He taps at his keyboard for a moment.

A large red "TERMINATED" blots out your details.

"Thanks for passing on the message," Johnson says. "You twat."

The End.

YOU AGREE, AND HEAD BACK TO YOUR DESK TO GET STARTED.

But *where* should you start? Do you even know half the company?

Well there's Debby.

For some reason it gives you a little pang, which is strange, since Debby's aggressively weird, and always wearing those upsettingly ugly velour outfits.

But someone's gotta go. You write Debby's name on the firing list. And Martin has always been kind of boring. It would be nice not to listen to him drone on about the benefits of wheatgrass every time you see one another in the break room. Oh, and Gina. Gina hates you, ever since you agreed with her that she *does* kind of look like her dog. She's definitely got to go.

After a few more minutes of furious scribbling, you decide to tally things up.

You've got 45 names written down so far.

You've officially eliminated everyone who has so much as given you a dirty look in the past five years, but you're still 55 people short and time is ticking.

> *If you want to start flipping a coin to decided who loses their*
> *livelihood and who gets to keep it, go to page 140.*
> *If you want to hand in the list incomplete, go to page 141.*

YOU TAKE A DEEP BREATH AND QUICKLY PULL DOWN THE FIRE ALARM.

Black ink jets everywhere, the bulk of it going directly into your eyes, blinding you temporarily, as the alarm starts to blare.

The conference room empties out into the hall.

"Where's, uh-uh-uh, the fire?" asks your boss, obviously puzzled.

"I...I thought that..." You can't think straight with all this ink in your eyes.

"Clearly you're the one who pulled it. So, uh-uh-uh, what happened?" your boss says.

You can't think of a lie fast enough. Shit, you can't even see. There's only one option: the truth.

"Because I didn't finish the presentation..."

Your boss approaches you and places his hand on your shoulder.

"I think you better, uh-uh-uh, pack up your desk," he says in a quiet, dignified manner.

A tear starts to roll down your cheek.

"Settle down everyone," your boss says to the large crowd of people pouring out of the conference room. "There isn't a fire... just someone FIRED!"

The hallway bursts out into collective laughter.

God, it wasn't *that* funny.

The End.

YOU WISTFULLY WALK AWAY FROM THE FIRE ALARM. WHAT COULD have been…if you weren't such a total pussy.

You can't see any other escape-routes. Sighing, you walk into the conference room, where everyone is chatting and enjoying coffee and croissants. You, too, were once so carefree.

You place the shitty loaner computer down on the table next to where your boss is standing.

"What do you call an accountant with an opinion? An auditor, uh-uh-uh!"

Everyone around him erupts into laughter. God, his jokes are truly terrible.

You grab yourself a coffee and sidle up to the gang.

"Oh wait, have you heard this one? What's an actuary? An accountant without a sense of humor, uh-uh-uh."

Jesus. Your boss clearly just "discovered" some shitty accountant joke website. You can't bear to hear another one of his "zingers," so you turn around to find another, less obnoxious group.

Your boss, seeing he's losing an audience member, turns to grab your arm…

…and spills his coffee all over the computer. Dear god, he's finally done something USEFUL.

You try not to let that thought show on your face as you dab with deliberate ineffectualness at the spill.

You sigh as melodramatically as possible.

"Even a bowl of uncooked rice can't help this," you say mournfully.

If you want to cancel the presentation because of the spill, go to page 144.
If you want to try to wing the presentation, go to page 142.

You run down the hallway towards the bathroom, hoping nobody will notice you.

Nothing bad can happen to you in the bathroom. It's the only retreat in this shithole. Ironic.

How long can you feasibly stay in here?

You sit down on the toilet and wait.

Fuck, you forgot your phone. At least if you had it the time would pass—you could play with your favorite app, the "What's Near Me" GPS pizza locator.

Gross—someone in the next stall over is shitting. You don't want to marinate in a stranger's poop molecules all afternoon.

It's time you get out of this bathroom.

Go to page 145 to continue.

No one can know that you were away from the office for so long. You run up to the wall-mounted television and yank down on it as hard as you can.

It comes crashing to the floor, making an extremely loud THUD in the process.

The room goes dead silent. It's as though someone has hit the pause button on your life. Everyone in the office is staring at you in disbelief, mouths wide open.

How the hell do you un-shitstorm this? Do you claim Tourette's? Would Tourette's make a person smash a TV? Probably only while screaming "cockfuck" or something. Too late for that.

"I'm sorry everyone, it's just that…I have the migraine of the century."

You just Hulked out on an incredibly expensive TV. But you're supposed to be crippled by your headache right now. Nice. Plausible.

"Again, I'm really, really sorry. It just hurts so much…"

In strolls your boss, smartphone in hand, fixated on his screen.

"Jeez Louise! Did you hear about that, uh-uh-uh, city council member's suicide? It's on the news right now."

He stares a few seconds longer, then looks up and sees you.

"Hey, we have a television star in this place! Why didn't you tell us you were going to be on the…"

He looks around, noticing the smashed television, and the circle of stunned employees, for the first time.

"What the hell happened in here?"

If you want to confess everything to your boss and hope he's merciful,
go to page 146.
If you want to play it cool and pretend like nothing happened,
go to page 147.

"Well," you say, trying to meet Debby's eager stare, "I don't think they tested her blood afterwards, but the rumor was he slipped her something. And then of course…no one knows what happened after that."

"Well. SNRCK!" Debby sounds like she's choking on something big and wet. "Wouldn't there be evidence? Tests or …something?"

"Maybe, maybe not. I'd wager he would be smart enough to use something that doesn't leave a trace. Presumably there wasn't any evidence that was strong enough to prosecute him. And I think Gina was just so shaken up by the whole thing that she tried to pretend it never happened. But just…be careful around him. I wouldn't have said anything if I weren't really, really worried about his character."

"Thank you," Debby says, nodding frantically, her wattle wobbling above her too-tight collar. "I'm so glad you said something."

She scurries away to her desk and you try to swallow the bile flavor in your mouth. Ugh. That felt dirty. Do you even want Debby?

Luckily, you don't have much time to dwell on it before Anthony, eyes narrowed and gut heaving, shows up at your desk.

"What, EK-THACT-LY, did you tell Deborah?"

"I don't know what you're talking about, man. I set you guys up like I promised, that's it."

"That'th obviouthly not 'it, man,'" he sputters mockingly. "If it were, thee wouldn't be thending me emailth about how you told her 'what I did to JTH-ena at the offith party,' whatever that'th thuppothed to mean."

Huh. You'd kind of hoped that implied date rape would keep her from contacting the source.

If you want to tell Anthony to fuck himself, go to page 148.
If you want to admit you acted out of jealousy, go to page 150.

Seeing her intense stare makes you realize both the fact that you're planning to accuse a man of something prosecutable and the fact that you're doing it over *Debby*. Come to your senses, for Christ's sake!

"Well," you say, trying to force some levity into your voice. "Apparently he was *criminally* heavy-handed when he poured her drinks. Ooof, she was not happy the next day. So, you know… if you guys get cocktails or whatever, make sure you're mixing your own."

You can feel your forehead sweating, but wiping it will just draw too much attention. You look away from Debby's confused stare.

"Okay," Debby says. "That's…well, honestly, I thought you were going to say something much more serious. SNRCK!" She laughs nervously. "The way you framed it, I almost thought you were going to accuse him of ra—"

"NO! Of course not, god no!" Your armpits feel like two polyester swamps. Why in the fuck did you ever buy a shirt with so little breathability? "Geez, Debby, what do you take me for? I mean, I set the two of you up in the first place! HA!" You sound manic. You *feel* manic.

"Is everything…okay with you?"

"YUP! Great! So good! You?"

"I'm alright…but I think maybe you could use a visit to Frieda." She pronounces it Free-yay-dah. "She's my crystal healer."

"Oh, no, that's alright, I'm sure I don't need any…"

"Please, I insist. She's especially good with…well, neurotics! SNRCK!" Debby smiles apologetically.

"No, honestly, I don't even believe in…"

"I insist. After what you did for me and Anthony, helping you with your ongoing life issues is the *least* I can do."

"Ongoing life issues?" Jesus, you thought Debby kinda wanted to sleep with you. Still, it will get you out of the office for the afternoon…

Go to page 152 to continue.

"WELL HURRY UP, WE'RE ALL WAITING ON YOU!" JOHNSON POINTS towards the conference room.

"My stomach is still feeling a little off…"

"Suck it up—the boss has been telling everyone how important your presentation will be to the future of the company."

Apparently half-measures won't be enough to get you out of this one. You have to go big. And you haven't been able to vomit on command since college.

There's only one option.

Most people don't really go for it when they fake a faint. They try to cushion the fall somehow, or go down too slowly, or ease back in a way that just doesn't look like someone pulled the plug on their brains for a moment.

Not you. You know better.

Without warning, you roll your eyes back into your head and deadweight yourself.

As your eyes swing skullwards, you see Alex, your office crush, emerging from the conference room.

Dammit, she shouldn't see you this way. The fake faint was too risky of a move.

Your skull cracks hard against the edge of the filing cabinet— you misjudged the angle! AMATEUR HOUR!—and you can't think, or see, all that there is are explosions of red, razor sharp pains rippling from your head out through your entire body.

Oh, great, *now* you can vomit. In a puddle on the floor that immediately spreads around your face, and which you're too weak to move away from. You can feel a matching puddle of toilet water leaking out of your shoe.

At least you sold it?

Go to page 158 to continue.

114

"I SHOULD ADD, THOUGH…" WHAT COULD PLAUSIBLY KEEP YOU FROM the meeting? "My laptop has been having…issues. This morning before I left for work, the files were all garbled. I sent an email, but maybe Outlook was acting up, too."

"Oh. Alright, so do we need to cancel?" Johnson asks.

Realistically, you're not going to get a better opportunity to totally suck at this. If you reschedule any further out than the afternoon, you'll have to have a fully functioning, actually planned presentation. But if you do it today, everyone might buy the story about you losing your data.

"No, we're on too tight of a deadline. I have my laptop with the IT folks already, they should be able to figure it out by lunchtime, or at least let me know what to expect."

"Well, I suppose that could work," Johnson says, shrugging. "You're lucky today's 'Marketing your Project to the Marketing Team' meeting got canceled. There should be an opening in a couple hours."

"Perfect. Do you mind passing along the new time to everyone else? Obviously my email's been a little spotty." And you don't remember who's attending this meeting. "I need to check in with IT about this now if I'm gonna get those files recovered."

"Sure. I'll call a new meeting."

"Great."

You head back to your desk, hoping to crap out some sort of presentation between now and then…

…but your laptop isn't there. Because idiot you thought you'd actually work on this thing last night, as if you've ever *once* actually worked on anything you've brought home.

Your laptop is sitting on your kitchen counter. And without it, your lie is going to be obvious to everyone in the room.

If you want to run home to pick up the laptop, go to page 45.
If you want to head to IT and beg for a loaner computer, go to page 44.

FINALLY, SEVERAL MINUTES LATER, YOU EMERGE, JUST AS A FLOOD OF your coworkers is exiting conference room B.

"Where were you? We waited for half an hour," Johnson sneers. It should bother you, but it's hard to get upset by someone as forgettable as Johnson.

But then you hear it.

"That's right, uh-uh-uh, it's just like Johnson says." Your boss sidles over and lays an arm heavily around your shoulders. "We were all waiting for your presentation, and we looked around, and checked your desk, and even paged the front desk to see if you'd, uh-uh-uh, snuck out, but poof! It was like you'd vanished." He's keeping a chummy smile on his face, but your boss's arm is like a lead weight, and his eyes are narrowed.

Fuck. You totally spaced on the fact that you had a presentation today.

"Sorry about that, I've just been in the bathroom. I think I may have a touch of food poisoning or something. But I can do the presentation later today, if that's…"

"There's no way everyone can come together again on such short notice," your boss says shortly. "I'm afraid that's not an option."

"Okay," you say tentatively, looking away from his too-close face. You can't seem to shake your shoulder loose. "What would you like me to do?"

"I'd like you to set up a meeting with me tomorrow so we can talk about your recent performance," your boss says, smiling falsely. "That is, if you think you'll be able to squeeze it in to your busy schedule of hiding in the bathroom."

"Sure," you gulp.

Who would have thought you could dread tomorrow even more than you dreaded today?

The End.

"Don't get me wrong," you start, coughing awkwardly, "I'd love to help out, but I just…I can't."

"Why not? I, uh-uh-uh, I need someone right now, and you already know, I—"

"I just can't. It's too…" You can't think of anything but the truth, "it's too likely to reveal all the horrible things about me as an employee," which doesn't seem like something you should say out loud.

"No, no, I, uh-uh-uh, understand. It was too much to ask, anyway. Just…if you don't mind not saying anything to the rest of the staff."

"Really, I *would* let you stay with me in a heartbeat if I didn't…have a girlfriend?" That's a good out. Then it won't seem personal, but it will seem final.

"Really, you? A, uh-uh-uh, *girl*-friend?"

"Yeah," you say, a little defensively. "Why wouldn't I have a girlfriend?"

"No reason, no reason," your boss says, shaking his head back and forth. "I just hadn't heard, I guess."

He sighs heavily. His eyes look infinitely tired. "You're so lucky, you know? You have, uh-uh-uh, everything. A nice place. A woman you love. Those stylish khakis you're wearing." He sighs again. "Just…everything."

You'd like to leave, but the look on his face is so lost, so morose. Can you really leave him like this?

More importantly, wouldn't you gain a few much-needed brownie points with him if you didn't?

Go to page 153 to continue.

"WELL…" GOD, YOU CAN'T IMAGINE ANYTHING WORSE THAN YOUR boss staying at your house. The single happiest moment of your day—sometimes the only happy moment of your day—is leaving the office. If he were to tag along with you, though…you shudder. This too is hell.

"Um." You gulp back the bile that involuntarily rose in your throat. "Sure, yeah. You can stay with me while you get things sorted."

"Oh, *thank* you. You, uh-uh-uh, don't know what this means to me." Your boss leans across the table and throws his arms around you. You stiffen awkwardly. Oh god, are you starting to feel aroused?

"Of course, it's no problem at all," you say, squirming out of his embrace.

It's only when you're halfway back to the office that you realize your house is devastatingly filthy—enough so that even you're starting to get skeezed out touching the surfaces, and that pile of toenail clippings in the bathroom is getting really big—and you only have one set of full-on crusty sheets.

So much for earning some points with the boss.

If you want to rush-order a maid service to marginally improve your sty,
go to page 156.
If you hope the state of your place might evoke some sort of pity-help
from your boss, go to page 154.

"I'VE ALSO HEARD THAT IF YOU HAVE SEX ON COCAINE, YOU'LL NEVER orgasm again during normal sex," your boss says, eyebrows raised. "Is that…uh-uh-uh, well, is it true?"

You're pretty sure this constitutes sexual harassment. But you're also pretty sure admitting to a coke habit, real or fake, isn't going to sit well with HR, either.

"No, that's an urban legend," you say. It has to be, right? "But your orgasms are so much more intense—I mean, I've personally experienced some that I could actually see AND feel at the same time…like sexual synesthesia? Anyway, it definitely feels less exciting when you're 'down,' as we…users…say…"

"Mmmm, that makes sense," your boss says, nodding gravely.

"But even with the awesome sex—and it is awesome, your depth perception increases, and if you…see a jar of marbles—or anything, jellybeans, gumballs—you know exactly how many are in the jar? Which is really…awesome."

"I KNEW that guy at the carnival was high! My guesstimating skills are near-perfect!"

"But I know I need to stop. I've just got this monkey on my back, you know?" you say, sighing. Oh god, you may have stolen that line from an after-school special. "I need help."

"I want to give you that help," your boss says, leaning across the desk. "What would you say to a three-month, uh-uh-uh, 'sabbatical.'" He pulls his eyebrows up and his mouth down in a kind of facial silly putty. "Of course we would pay for your treatment at the clinic; it could come out of the employee welfare fund. That's what it's there for, after all."

You'd always thought that was supposed to be for standing desks and retreat days, but a three-month vacation at a spa— because really, if you don't have a drug problem, isn't that all rehab is?—sounds pretty good…

"I'm not sure I can afford to take that much time off…" you say. Please disagree, you think at your boss, please disagree.

"Of course you can. Uh-uh-uh, you'll get disability leave, of course," your boss says. "We just want you to get *better*."

"Thank you," you say, "I really needed this."

And you did. The tear sliding down your cheek is 100% genuine.

The End.

YOU COME TO WITH SOME SORT OF LIQUID BEING SPLASHED INTO your eyes and mouth. It's soothingly warm.

You open your eyes to see a massive Irish Wolfhound penis streaming hot piss all over your face.

You're too dizzy to yell at the dog, let alone shoo him away, so you just take it, gently rolling over onto your stomach under the stream.

You're covered in blood and piss, lying out in the street in broad daylight.

Awesome.

At least your wound seems to have stopped gushing. Ever so slowly, you stand up. The dog scampers away to a smoking hipster couple on the street corner, deliberately looking away from you.

You slowly shuffle back towards your house. You grab a beer and get into the shower fully clothed. It's kind of like doing laundry.

Whoa, you must have lost even more blood than you thought. That beer is already hitting you pretty hard.

Go to page 1 to continue.

You wake up…in the hospital?

A tall, burly mustachioed man in a ripped t-shirt is looming over your bed. Since when have hospitals been employing Hooters bouncers as nurses?

"If you ever visit Dylan's apartment again…"

"Who are you?"

"Dylan's brother, you piece of shit."

"Oh. Um, hello," you respond, somewhat confused.

"After the way you treated Dylan you better stay away from that apartment—"

"It's just that I was losing a lot of blood—"

"I don't give two fucks what you have to say. Just stay away from Dylan or you won't be waking up in an emergency room, you'll be waking up in a morgue! Do I make myself clear?"

"Yes," you say, nodding with a diplomatic half-smile, even though no one could actually *wake up* in a morgue. "You've made your point," you say eagerly.

The brother Hulks away, and a nurse approaches your bed.

"How are you? You know, you lost a ton of blood," she says sympathetically.

"I've been better," you mumble.

"Look, there's no easy way to put this. I've got some bad news for you…I'm gonna need you to go down and talk to the insurance people," she says with a condescending smile.

"Of course you do."

"I meant now. They need to see you now."

The End.

You walk into the office. Somewhere or other, Betsy's managed to find a facemask. Her slight wail at seeing you is in no way muffled by the layer of blue gauze over her mouth.

"Betsy, would you come into my office, please," your boss says quietly. "I'd like to talk about what, uh-uh-uh, happened earlier."

"No! Not when…" she flings a gnarled hand in your direction. "I'll have to walk right past THAT, and the Lysol's in the other room, and—"

"I can just move out of the way, if that will—" you start.

"Betsy," your boss says, his voice louder, "let's not do this here. Just come into my office, and we can—"

"I SAID NO!" Her voice is getting higher, thinner. Her breathing is starting to sound ragged, like she's sucking the air through a narrow straw. "I said earlier, I said on the phone, I can't HAVE that foul disease here, my constitution can't…" She starts coughing wetly. "I can't…"

"Well if you refuse to do this privately, Betsy, I'll have to do it here. Frankly, this kind of behavior is exactly the issue—you've become erratic. Unreliable. Delusional even. Disease? Look at this fine colleague of yours. Is that really what you see?"

A small crowd of your coworkers has gathered around the edges of the room to watch the scene. Judging by the way they're looking at you, that's exactly what *they* see…

"I'm sorry, but, uh-uh-uh…I'm afraid we're going to have to let you go."

Betsy leans over in her chair, pulling at the facemask. Oh god, if she vomits in here, you're going to vomit, too. Your stomach is still too…

Thump.

She's fallen on the floor. And she isn't moving.

A coworker runs up to Betsy, grabbing her liver-spotted wrist between two fingers.

"Someone call 9-1-1! I think she's dead!"

Everyone turns to you. Your boss points your way.

"I told you she wouldn't be able to handle the shock of getting fired. Still, you were probably right. We needed to axe her!" He makes a throat-slicing motion. "No pun intended, of course. Uh-uh-uh."

Go to page 189 to continue.

124

YOU CAN FEEL YOUR HAND TRYING TO FLOAT TOWARDS THE MOUSE, close all those damning windows…

…but you can't. God, if this really is your fault, someone should know. Your hangovers kill old ladies. You need to be punished for that. With more than a hangover.

Your boss finishes up his conversation and sidles over to where you're standing, hands clenched behind his back. Nope, you were wrong, you should have closed all those windows. Fuck.

"Sad day, uh-uh-uh," he hangs his head, shaking it back and forth. You notice all traces of his tears have completely disappeared. "I just can't imagine how it happened. She seemed healthy as a horse."

"Yeah," you say, moving your body a few inches to the left, so that you maybe block the screen a little. "It's just so sad."

"What's that?"

Oh god. He's leaning in towards the computer.

Go to page 160 to continue.

KEEPING YOUR EYES ON YOUR BOSS AND THE EMTS, YOU INCH A BIT closer to the computer.

If you can just get these windows closed, no one will know you're the one responsible for Betsy's freak-out and, therefore, her death.

Indirectly, though. It could have been *anything*, it's not like you should get hung up on this.

It's impossible to find the little "x" in the corners of the windows without looking at the computer. Glancing up one more time—they're talking about where she'll be taken, surely this will take a few minutes—you start closing the windows.

God, there are dozens. Frantic, you click browser window after browser window—"Bronchitis Linked to Brain Cancer," "Is the Illuminati Using Bronchitis to Control Your Actions?" "Bronchitis Pain Scale: It's Always at a 10." She must have spent the entire morning diving further and further down the crazy hole.

"What are you doing there?"

CLICK CLICK CLICK!

Okay, at least they're all down. But your boss is still standing at your shoulder, and he seems to be expecting an answer.

"I was just…uh…I was…"

"You wouldn't be going into Betsy's files, would you? Uh-uh-uh. What possible reason would you have to…"

"I was looking for contact information. For her relatives."

You click the address book icon, finally visible on the cleared desktop, and see three numbers. God, that's depressing. Especially since one of them is for "PODIATRIST: Dr. Cody Blakey."

"Oh, of course. Thank god you're so good in a crisis, I'd almost forgotten about Betsy's daughter. Which is surprising, since Laura is even more beautiful than her mother, uh-uh-uh."

You try not to grimace. There are many things you would have called Betsy, but "beautiful" was never one of them.

"Why don't you call her now," your boss says. "The sooner they hear about this, the better, right?"

If you want to call Betsy's daughter, go to page 161.
If you want to get your boss to call, go to page 162.

YOU PUSH THROUGH THE DOOR. IT SMELLS LIKE UNWASHED CROTCH and tears in here. You try not to make eye contact with the glassy-looking stripper sitting next to the bouncer, taking entrance fees.

"Isn't this GREAT?" Your boss's face is bright, almost manic. You try to smile, but it probably comes out as a grimace.

"Yeah. Totally. Great."

You can see three c-section scars from here, and the second stage isn't even in sight from the door.

"Well, if we're gonna play hooky, uh-uh-uh," your boss turns to you, grinning mischievously, "we may as well go all out, right? What are you drinking?"

"Oh, just soda water is fine, I…"

"First round's on me!"

"Okay, I guess a…vodka tonic?" you say.

"Excellent choice. Excellent. Find us a, uh-uh-uh, table, and I'll get us some BEV-erages," he winks at you leeringly. The inside of your skin feels dirty.

But after the first drink it feels a little better.

After the second, you don't even push away the stripper trying to grind against your lap. She goes at it for a few seconds, then looks at you, half-confused and half-disgusted, and promptly gets up and walks away.

You order another drink.

By the time you've downed half of it, you're feeling expansive.

"Really, I'm *lucky* to have you as a boss. DAMN lucky."

"No," your boss waves his hand in your general direction. You try not to stare at his boner. "I'm lucky to have *you*. Uh-uh-uh. We need more like you. Willing to just…go out and get wild!"

"Yeah?"

"Yeah."

"Wanna hear something *really* wild," you say, leaning in, grinning widely.

"Yeah!"

"I didn't even *do* that presentation." You start laughing wildly. "Haven't even started it!"

"You didn't complete the presentation?" Your boss has set his drink down and is squinting at you, his face blank. You look down. His boner's gone.

"Well…no, but I had a good outline…" You gulp down more of your drink. Maybe there's an answer to this in the bottom of the glass? "I like to…let ideas flow more freely."

"How many days have you been out of the office this year?"

"I mean, you could ask Betsy, it can't have been more than…"

"And despite your continued absences, and an overdue presentation you, uh-uh-uh, admit you haven't started, you're spending your afternoon drinking. Heavily."

"Well…wait, what?"

"I'm sorry, but I'm afraid I'm going to have to let you go."

"You can't be serious."

"Please don't make a scene. This is a place of business," he says, frowning at you scornfully.

Well, at least you might have a shot at a settlement.

The End.

"DEBBY, I UNDERSTAND YOU'RE UPSET. LET'S GO TALK ABOUT THIS somewhere else."

"Why not here? SNRCKKK," she blows her nose into a handkerchief that's appeared out of one of her velour folds. "Are you too EMBARRASSED by me?"

"No, Debby, I just don't want you to regret saying something that could hurt you professionally," you say, putting an arm around her back and grabbing a puffy elbow. You start leading her towards the lobby door. "Let's go grab a latte and we can talk about it more, okay? My treat?"

"Oh—SNRCK—kay," she says shakily, sniffling wetly. "It's probably the only chance that you'll be straight with me, anyway."

You say nothing. It seems pretty obvious to you that you're not going to discuss your weird, presidential-themed hookup at your cube.

You head down to the cafe on the corner and order two frothy lattes, "six pumps peppermint chocolate chip" in Debby's.

"Debby, let me first just say I'm sorry."

"For what, sending the email or doing anything with me in the first place? SNRCK," she sniffles loudly, in a way that borders dangerously on tears.

"For the email. I didn't want to hurt your feelings, honestly, I just…" How are you going to play this? Clearly Debby's filter between "office-appropriate" and "totally mortifyingly embarrassing" conversations is pretty thin. "I was trying to do… damage control. I thought that if I smoothed things over with Alex, she might not report what she saw to HR. The last thing I want is for you to get in trouble because I was so overcome by my…desires…that I couldn't stop myself."

Ew. Especially because you have a sneaking suspicion that you're telling something very near the truth.

"Oh, that makes sense," Debby says, looking up at you. The puffy redness around her eyes makes her look sort of like a stress ball with conjunctivitis. But she's stopped crying. She's even smiling a little. "I thought you were disgusted by me."

She takes a huge swig of her peppermint-chocolate latte. Your teeth hurt a little watching her.

"No! Of course not, no. The exact opposite, in fact. I just wanted to protect us. That's why the letter was so...blunt. I wanted to convince Alex that it was an isolated incident, so she wouldn't try to get us—get *you*—in trouble."

"But it doesn't have to be, you know. SNRCKKK!" Debbie's smiling softly, like a coy, spikeless puffer fish.

"Doesn't have to be...what?"

"An isolated incident."

"Oh, I see."

"In fact, Mr. President." Apparently this time around you're FDR. The power and gender dynamics in this roleplay seem extremely fluid. "I'd love to show you how much I appreciate your taking the time to calm a woman's tears. Maybe at your place?"

She puts a hand on your knee.

You feel a rush of blood to your groin.

"Excuse me, waiter?" you call loudly, unable to meet Debby's beady stare. "Could we have the check, please?" You turn to Debby. "Bring my chair round, Ellie."

Go to page 291 to continue.

"I'M SORRY, DEBBY, I DON'T KNOW WHAT YOU READ," YOU SAY, taking a step back, "I'm sorry whatever it was upset you so much."

Debby lets out a gurgling wail that sounds like a geyser sneezing.

"What's, uh-uh-uh," your boss puts one arm on your shoulder heavily, the other on Debby's, "going on here, guys?"

"I...Alex sent me...SNRCK!" Debby chokes wetly. "The email said I was a MISTAAAAAAKE!" Debby starts snort-sobbing again.

"Let's discuss this somewhere more private, hmm?" Your boss herds the two of you forward. "Like my office."

By the time you've settled in, Debby's sobs have subsided to an occasional dim honk. Unfortunately, that means she has a chance at being coherent enough to be understood. You do your best not to blush visibly as she explains how you two "couldn't fight it anymore, we had to give in to our raging flood of desire," then details the email that followed.

"Well, I haven't, uh-uh-uh, seen this email, but it sounds to me like a straightforward attempt to apologize for a frankly inappropriate scene. Is that right?"

You could be wrong, but it looks like your boss is winking at you.

"Yes, that's exactly what happened," you say slowly.

"But you said, SNRCK, that I was a mistake, and, SNRCKKKKK."

"I may have worded that poorly," you break in. "I meant that what we did was a mistake. It was against company policy, and against my own moral code."

"Well there you have it. Well said. I'm not going to take any, uh-uh-uh, disciplinary action at this time," your boss says, looking back and forth between you and Debby, "that is, as long as you two promise this won't happen again?"

"Absolutely not," you say immediately. "No way will this ever happen again."

Debby sighs pitifully.

"It won't—SNRCK—happen again," she says.

"Wonderful. Debby, you're free to go." You start to rise, too. "Uh-uh-uh, one minute if you don't mind."

Dammit. You were so close.

The door clicks behind Debby.

"So, finally joined the club, eh?"

"I'm…excuse me?"

"Oh come on, you had to know we've all been there already." You frown.

"With Debby? Uh-uh-uh," your boss shakes his head, grinning slightly. "We all have. Even Alex. It's like an initiation rite around here."

"So you're saying you…"

Oh god, have you had sex with the same person as your boss?

"Oh, sure. Dozens of times. I keep telling myself I'll stop, but there's just something so…fascinating about her. Like a sideshow. You don't want to stare, but you just can't seem to help yourself." He chuckles softly. "But she's good, right? I mean, the things she comes up with? It's like visiting a German bathhouse for the afternoon. Don't you think?"

If you want to try to bro down with your boss over Debby's weird sexual preferences, go to page 164.
If you just want this to end as soon as possible, go to page 163.

YOU STEP INTO SHARON'S OFFICE, WHICH SMELLS A BIT LIKE STALE Parliament cigarettes. Sharon maybe-smiles—at least her face, tanned to a rich walnut-y shade by years of smoking, briefly crinkles in a few more spots around the mouth and eyes.

That's encouraging-ish, right?

"Do you know why you're here?" Sharon asks. Her voice sounds like a buzz saw on concrete.

"I think I have an idea," you murmur, looking down as though you're embarrassed. How much did Alex tell her?

"Yes, well, while I think the gesture probably came from a good place," Sharon begins, lacing her leathery fingers together, "it crossed a line."

"I understand," you say. You seem to be getting off pretty lightly, actually.

"We want to encourage employees to develop friendships with one another, and I'm sure that's what you thought you were doing."

"Yes…" you say slowly.

"But I think Alex here feels that your…display was perhaps a bit too…personal."

You glance over at Alex. She's resolutely staring at the floor, her cheeks bright red.

"So while the flowers certainly brighten up the office, I'm going to have to ask you not to send them to a coworker again, unless they're expected, or celebrating a special occasion. As you know, we frown upon inter-office relationships of a…*romantic* nature."

You're here about the *flowers*. Not the closet—well, it was more than humping, but less than sex—anyway, not that whole debacle. Just the flowers.

God, you wish you hadn't spent so much on the stupid things.

"Of course, Sharon, I see that now. Alex, I'm so sorry I made you uncomfortable. It won't happen again. Seriously. Never again."

"Well, good then," Sharon says, looking down at her report.

You take the opportunity to mouth "thank you" to Alex. Alex

looks away, disgusted.

"That's all, then," Sharon says. "You're free to go back to work."

You step out, light on your feet. It's like you just had a death sentence commuted to parole…

Then you see your bouquet. On J.J.'s desk—that douchebag in PR—with a handwritten note stuffed in the base in what looks like Alex's handwriting. God, you would have never thought Alex would be into someone like *that*.

Why were you so happy again? You just wrecked things—probably permanently—with the person you've had a crush on since the day you started, you're still in a job you hate, and you still have three hours before you're allowed to go home and wash off the smell of Debby (vanilla lip balm and moth balls).

God, you need a drink.

Or five.

Go to page 1 to continue.

WHEN YOU STEP INTO SHARON'S OFFICE, ALEX IS ALREADY THERE. She's standing, staring straight ahead at Sharon, a thin, pinched-looking smoker whose face is most of the way towards its goal of becoming beef jerky. You stand next to Alex, crossing your arms behind you.

"Sharon, before you say anything, I just want to apologize for what Alex saw," you begin. "I've been going through a hard time, lately, and Debby has been such a good friend, and things just got out of hand."

Alex is looking at you, eyes wide.

"Of course it will never happen again—that goes without saying—and there's really no excuse for it. But I will say, the loss of my…" think fast, who's died? "grandmother," she's already dead, it can't hurt, "with whom I've always been so close, has really shaken me up.

"But like I said, that's no excuse for having inappropriate relations with a coworker. Though I will add we were both on our lunch breaks," those are federally mandated, right? That has to be in your favor. "So please, Sharon, and Alex, accept my apology. I know I was in the wrong."

"What, ex-*act*-ly," Sharon says slowly, "are you referring to?"

You frown.

"My…tryst. With Debby. In the supply closet?" You turn to Alex, who looks at you with a mix of disgust and pity. "Isn't that why we're here?"

"It *wasn't* why we were here," Sharon wheezes. It's hard to tell, since her exhalation sounds like a bag of rocks falling down a flight of concrete stairs, but she might be laughing. "We were here because Alex felt uncomfortable when you sent flowers. And we were going to discuss appropriate boundaries between colleagues. Which I guess we still *should* discuss, actually."

Now you know she's laughing. The sound grates against your ears, almost physically painful.

You can feel your armpits starting to get damp. Great, it smells like metabolized vodka. That's *definitely* gonna help the situation.

"But considering the severity of the breach that Alex chose to omit from the initial report, I think my recommendation for ongoing action items is going to change."

"Ummm…" you gulp, "what do you mean?"

"I mean you're fired, hon," Sharon wheezes. "Go and pack up your desk."

The End.

136

You head back into your boss's office at the appointed time and find yourself face to face with the accused. You're also surrounded by various employees you've seen before, but don't really know, as well as your boss.

"Well. Uh-uh-uh. Why don't you tell everyone what happened."

"I heard…" you look at your feet. It's too late to go back on this now. "I heard loud orgasms coming from inside the stall!"

"What are you talking about?" Morgan says, clearly shocked.

"Loud moans of pleasure! It was like I'd walked into a brothel."

You slam your hands down onto the table for emphasis.

Everyone in the room has their eyes focused squarely on Morgan. It looks like it's checkmate. You've got this one. You can almost taste the win.

"Um, are you referring to my insulin injections?" Morgan asks coolly.

Oh, shit. You slump into a chair.

"I inject into my, well, my buttocks, because of the slow absorption rate. Are you familiar with adipose tissue?"

Of course you're not fucking familiar with "adipose tissue."

"I'm sorry if I'm making anyone here squeamish, but from time to time, I get help injecting from other diabetics around the office. We all help each other when we can."

Now everyone is staring at you. In disgust.

You should have known Morgan would have the ultimate trump-card: diabetes. Who can argue with diabetes?

"Well, I'm glad that's clarified. Shall we get back to work then?"

"Uh-uh-uh, not so fast, there," your boss says, looking around the room, a look of faux shock on his face. "I think you owe Morgan an apology." The entire room nods in agreement.

"Right. I'm terribly sorry, Morgan. It won't happen again."

"Come see me after work. We need to, uh-uh-uh…talk," your boss says as the room clears out.

That can't be good.

The only two people left in the room are you and Morgan.

"In case you're wondering, the fuck was amazing," Morgan says softly.

"I knew it! I *knew* it!" you yell, seething with anger.

Morgan gives you a condescending little pat on the shoulder, turning to leave.

"I'm sure they'll believe you if you tell them. Go on, try," Morgan says, chuckling softly.

Great, you've managed to alienate yourself from just about everyone important at your company. Worse, if Morgan wants to use you as a personal piñata—which is all but a guarantee, now—there's basically no recourse.

That flask has to be around here somewhere…

Go to page 1 to continue.

138

"Well, here's the thing," you say, "maybe I actually only saw one pair of legs in the stall. The lighting is just so fucking...*dim* in there. I just can't be sure what I saw."

There's a long pause as your boss stares deeply into your eyes.

"So you're changing your story just like that?"

"Yup." It's not very persuasive, but you really can't think of anything else to say.

"Are you, uh-uh-uh, okay?" your boss asks.

"Fine. Just fine...Perhaps I'll gather more evidence and bring it to your attention at a later date," you say, squirming in your chair.

"You'll do no such thing," your boss replies sternly, rising from his chair.

"Oh. Okay then. We'll close the book on this case right here and now and get on with our lives," you respond, tapping your foot nervously on the floor. "Onwards and upwards!"

"Is there anything you, uh-uh-uh." You can tell he feels awkward. He won't look you in the eye. "...want to tell me?" he asks.

"Nope."

"Because you've been acting very erratically recently."

"Nope. Nothing I can think of."

"Be honest, is it, uh-uh-uh, cocaine?"

Is it? Go to page 87 .

No, of course it isn't. Go to page 82.

AT LEAST THE CEO HAS BEEN TRUE TO HER WORD. YOU STILL HAVE your job, and in fact, you've been getting a lot more leeway on deadlines since she's told your bosses that you're "reorienting yourself towards a healthier, more productive lifestyle."

But every time you tell a story in AA meetings to keep Barbara thinking you're committed—like the time you had so many martinis you answered that ad in the alt-weekly paper to be a middle aged long-haul trucker's adult-baby-fetish partner, or the time that you tied a camelback around your thigh and threaded the hose through your shirt so that you wouldn't have to sit through that colleague's funeral without a drink—you get a little more worried. *Are* you an alcoholic?

Of course you don't tell them that your first stop post-meeting is the bar. Because you still know you don't have a problem, even if the group seems to think you're lucky to still be standing. That's ridiculous. You're fine.

And you need a double.

The End.

140

You walk into the CEO's office with just seconds to spare, but with the list fully compiled.

The coin was a ruthless decider, but fair, you tell yourself.

"No, no, no," Barbara cries, nearly spitting out her coffee all over your list. "Anderson has had far and away the best sales figures for the past ten years!"

"He's shown, um, signs of complacency…"

"And why would you cut Carman? He's wanted by all the major firms. Frankly, he's one of a very few people around here who knows what's going on!"

"I have it on good authority that Carman is often… insubordinate?"

"He's the HEAD of the IT department, there's no one to be insubordinate *to*! How did you even go about making these cuts?"

"I um, analyzed…recent performance reviews…"

"We don't even do those. I'm starting to think that this list is completely arbitrary!"

Barbara gives you a death stare. You try to hold it, but quickly wither under its intensity.

"You're fired for gross incompetence!" she yells as she jots Johnson's name down on the top of the list. "Now go and pack up your desk at once, Johnson!"

Go to page 1 to continue.

DESPITE YOUR BEST EFFORTS AT BEING A DICK, YOU JUST DON'T HAVE it in you to fire another 55 people.

In fact, you don't want to fire anyone! Someone should be fighting for these employees, Barbara Houseman and the shareholders of this company be damned! You can be that person, the person who stands up to corporate greed. Or, well… you as Johnson.

It's your chance to be the Madeline Albright of the office. *That* was someone who fought for the underdog. The woman was a true hero.

You turn towards the CEO's office. Are you really going through with this? You are! You're really going through with this!

Unfortunately, just as you reach the door, the *real* Johnson exits the office.

"Oh, it's you," Johnson says. "Can I ask you why you're walking around pretending to be me?"

Gulp.

"About that, it's a funny story…"

"I'd love to hear, but as you know, I'm under a tight deadline," Johnson responds dryly. "Apparently, I have to cut quite a bit of dead weight around here."

You laugh nervously. "You don't say?"

"Yeah, and I think I know exactly where to start," Johnson says, looking you squarely in the eyes. "With you. In case that wasn't obvious."

Dammit, you'll never be an Albright.

The End.

"STILL," YOU SAY, TURNING TO LOOK YOUR BOSS FULL IN THE FACE, "the show must go on."

"Bravo. That's the, uh-uh-uh, spirit!" your boss says.

"Of course without my presentation notes I'll just be working from memory, you say. "I can't promise it will be as well-rehearsed as I'd hoped."

"Of course, of course," your boss says, taking a seat. "We all understand."

"Alright, then," you say, looking around. Fuck, you really expected him to tell you not to do it. "Here goes."

• • •

You look at your watch. Shit. You've only been speaking (and wildly gesticulating) for four and a half minutes and you're pretty much done. Everyone in the room looks thoroughly unimpressed. And if you're honest with yourself, it's probably better than you would have done *with* the computer

"So, does anyone have any questions?" you ask.

Your boss starts talking.

"Well, I for one would like to know about the actual *sales* our competitors are making. Uh-uh-uh. You spent a lot of time going into…"

You're trying to focus on what your boss is saying, but you still feel so hungover that just looking attentive is taking up most of your resources. You should have ordered poutine on the way into work—that stuff is like a toilet snake plunging through your intestines. Is there anywhere around here that would sell that, though?

"What would be your recommendation on that, uh-uh-uh?" asks your boss.

Fuck, you totally missed whatever he was talking about.

"Interesting question. I'd like to make this presentation more…interactive? So why don't we open it up to the floor. Does anyone have any thoughts on the matter?"

Silence. You can almost see the tumbleweed bouncing by.

"I'll have to get back to you on that one…" you say to your boss. "I wouldn't want to be too…hasty on such an important topic. If you want to drill down into the numbers, don't hesitate to reach out to me…once IT has recovered my notes, of course."

This is a fucking disaster. You've yet to say anything of substance.

"But really, our ROI on this should be pretty good. There's a lot of…CMS at stake, and the COB should be a good metric for our OC…" God, you hope the rest of the room is as clueless about what all these acronyms mean as you are. "So…work on those deliverables, everyone!"

Your boss excuses everyone in the room…everyone but you.

So much for winging it.

If you want to blame your poor performance on another employee, go to page 168.
If you want to blame your poor performance on the non-existent death of your non-existent second cousin, go to page 166.

144

"LOOKS LIKE WE'LL HAVE TO TAKE A RAINCHECK ON MY PRESENTATION," you say to no one in particular, tilting your computer up so that the coffee cascades over the table. Nice visual reinforcement.

"I've always been a bit of a klutz, uh-uh-uh," your boss says.

"Don't worry," you say, trying your best to mask your excitement. You try to think of one of those Christian Children's Fund starving kids, the ones with flies on their eyeballs, to keep your expression appropriately somber. "Things like this happen. I may need a few days to rebuild this presentation though." Awesome. Another bonus.

You begin to walk away from the table with the coffee-soaked laptop in hand.

"How about I make it up to you over lunch? I have a 2-for-1 coupon for SaladXpress. It sure beats eating Al Desko, uh-uh-uh!"

You wince at your boss's attempt at a joke.

"Um, I did just eat there yesterday..." you're really not thrilled about the idea of spending your precious half-hour of freedom with your captor.

"Come on, I'd love to get a sneak peek at those Q4 projections anyway, uh-uh-uh."

"Oh..." you say, caught off-guard. Didn't you just make it clear that you won't have any of those?

"And I hear they have a new chipotle Yucatan chicken coleslaw served hot in, uh-uh-uh, a bread bowl."

You shouldn't—at your last physical the doctor said your mayonnaise levels were off the charts. But you DO really love creative coleslaws...

If you want to take your boss up on the lunch offer, go to page 170.
If even free lunch isn't worth eating it with your boss, go to page 171.

You poke your head out of the bathroom and look up and down the hall to make sure no one's there to see you sneak back to your cubicle. Though you always just think of it as "the pit of despair."

Just as you're about to slide into your chair and blissful obscurity, you hear him:

"There's our television star, uh-uh-uh," says your boss.

Fuck, how did he creep up behind you so fast? Can he shape-shift into office plants or something? You try not to shudder visibly. He continues:

"Can you imagine, a city councilor just jumping in front of a train like that? Crazy! Uh-uh-uh. Did you see it happen?"

How are you going to play this in a way that doesn't get you in trouble for being late?

If you want to play up the difficulty of seeing this, go to page 172.
If you want to just downplay the whole thing, go to page 187.

"IT'S THESE HORRIBLE MIGRAINES…" YOU SAY.

Your boss looks at you in disbelief. Obviously he isn't buying your bullshit.

It's time to come clean.

"Okay, I'll admit it, I was running late, and then the subway just wasn't coming, you know how that is," you say, hoping your boss will agree with you. He doesn't.

"Well anyway, I was just waiting for, I don't know, easily an hour. I left the house by 8:45—" they can't have reported the exact time of death, can they? "—but I was…unlucky…and then this guy jumped in front of the train."

"Right," your boss says flatly. "That's what we were all watching before you decided to, uh-uh-uh, *punish* the television."

"I just didn't want everyone to see me on television. Because… that's *why* I was late, and I don't really have any vacation days left, and I thought if they saw me getting interviewed on the subway platform…"

"Yes?" your boss prompts.

"That I'd be in trouble. For my lateness."

That wasn't so bad. It's like a weight has been lifted off your chest. Maybe you should start telling the truth to people more often.

"Is there, uh-uh-uh, anything else you'd like to tell me?"

"I'll be honest, I'm a little hungover."

"That's lovely. You can tell security all about it as they escort you out of the building," your boss says sternly. "You're, uh-uh-uh, fired."

So much for honesty.

The End.

"...AND THEN HIS FEET WERE PLACED SEPARATELY INTO LITTLE plastic bags, and they finally let me go find a cab." You shrug. You feel even emptier than you usually do. "I wonder if they'll reimburse me for the cab."

"Ugh," your boss exhales, visibly shaken by your gory recap. "It must have been, uh-uh-uh, really difficult to see…foot bags."

"Yeah, I guess," you say. "Anyway, I'll be sure to replace the TV before tomorrow morning. Like I said, I just didn't want to have to answer everyone's questions about this and I suppose I overreacted."

"It's not the television that I'm worried about," he says. "It's *you*." He pinches his face into a constipated approximation of concern. "You know I hate speaking in platitudes, uh-uh-uh, but in my opinion employees really *are* the most important asset. And right now, I'm worried that you're devaluing your emotions."

You try not to think about your most recent pay cut, nodding instead.

"It means a lot to hear you say that."

"I say it because it's true. And right now, I'm concerned you could be suffering from, uh-uh-uh, shock. I mean, I know if I saw a person's skull crack open as easily as a soggy fortune cookie, I'd be more upset than this."

Would the brains be the message part of the cookie in that analogy, or the cookie part? You nod again.

"As far as the presentation you had scheduled for today, I don't want to force you to 'perform' so soon after a trauma. The important thing here is that *you* process this. Would you rather postpone it?"

If you want to soldier on with the presentation, go to page 173.
If you want skip the presentation, go to page 174.

ANTHONY LEANS HIS PENDULOUS GUT FURTHER OVER YOUR workspace, squinting at you. Is that supposed to be a threat? Usually nerdy Pillsbury doughboys try to slice you up verbally, not intimidate you physically.

Though given Anthony's "thpeaking difficultieth," maybe that's not an option.

"You know what, Anthony?" you say, suddenly too angry to be cautious. "Fuck yourself. I only told Debby what everyone here whispers behind your back, anyway. You're creepy."

Anthony looks at you, stunned, and briefly speechless.

"I mean, for Christ's sake, you only got the date with her in the first place because I basically acted like her *pimp* for you."

You can almost see something snap in half in his head.

But not for long, because your face is soon full of Anthony's fist.

SMACK.

Oh god, you think your nose may have exploded. You didn't think this headache could be worse.

When you open your eyes, one of your cube mates is pulling Anthony backwards, and a few others are clustering around you, obviously concerned.

You're hustled off to talk to Sharon, the head of HR. Blood is seeping down your face into your mouth. Awesome—at least that's gonna help your case.

"What happened here?" she asks, her voice rattling and dry from years of smoking. She looks a little like old boots, and the room smells like somebody's been smoking your late grandfather's old clothes.

"He..." Anthony stops, flummoxed. He can't tell on you without indicting himself.

"Anthony had some personal issues with me," you jump in, looking at him meaningfully, "but I think we've resolved them now."

"Would you like to file a formal complaint?" Sharon asks with a hacking cough.

"No, that's not necessary, but if you could spare some petty cash funds to help cover the painkillers I'm going to need, and the deductible at my doctor's—I think it's $150 per visit?—that would be really helpful."

Sharon smirks at you, her face twisting with more wrinkles than a strip of dried meat.

"Unless you'd prefer I take this through outside channels," you add, smiling as serenely as you can manage, "which I'm happy—and totally prepared—to do."

"Yeah, yeah," she mutters. "Take this paper to Kathy in accounting. She'll get you your blood-money." She chuckles to herself, making a shooing motion towards the pair of you. How …official.

Well, you have at least one day of vacation back—Anthony wouldn't dare try to take it away now—and you'll soon have cash in hand.

It's just a matter of which bar you'll hit up first on your way home…

Go to page 1 to continue.

Anthony leans his pendulous gut further over your workspace, squinting at you. Is that supposed to be a threat? How threatening can someone whose entire body is the color of a particularly wan fish's underbelly be?

You know what, it doesn't matter. You're tired, and the idea of *any* sort of confrontation is too much to handle right now.

"I'm sorry, Anthony, I just wanted Debby to have second thoughts about you…because…"

"Well?" He leans in, so close his spray of spittle hits your mouth. "Thpit it out."

"I was jealous. You guys just clicked so instantly, and you're right, she's a really amazing person, and I just…I want that in my life, too."

He leans back, smiling lightly.

"Well I thuppothe I can underthtand that," he says, folding his arms across his jello-mold gut. "But you're going to have to tell her tho yourthelf. Otherwithe thee'll never thee me again."

Oh Jesus, how much debasement can one person go through and still live?

More than you would have thought before you woke up this morning.

You head to her desk, staring at your feet, and recite the fastest version of the apology you can think of.

"I'm sorry, Debby, I lied to you about Anthony."

"Becauthe?" He's standing right behind you. The scene is drawing a few whispering onlookers. Awesome.

"Because I was jealous. And I was hoping to drive a wedge between you."

"BECAUTHE?"

"Because you're a catch." You look at Anthony, who's making a "go on" motion with his hand. "And I suppose I wanted you for myself."

You hear snickers break out all around you, though whether it's because you admitted to wanting the office-party-mistake or because Anthony and Debby have begun groping each other's back folds, you can't tell.

Yup. Even now, you'd say yes to Debby if you had the chance.

This day has left you needing a drink. Or seven. Immediately.

Go to page 1 to continue.

You walk into a room that smells like patchouli and is lit almost entirely through draped scarves.

Oh Jesus, what did you sign up for?

"Free-yay-duh will be waiting for you in the sanctum," Debby says, awkwardly lowering her velour-encased bottom half onto a beanbag chair. "I'll just wait for you here. Have fun, and make sure to open yourself up to the healing! SNRCK!"

There's nothing for it but to go through.

Inside, a woman wearing what looks like a tablecloth, and with piles of blond dreadlocks, stands waiting, hands folded rather stiffly in front of her.

"I'll just, hmmmm, step out while you get undressed," she murmurs softly. "You can leave your underwear on if you like, then just lie down under this sheet, hmmmm."

Of course you're not wearing any underwear, thanks to last night's bed-wetting "accident," but maybe she'll just take it as you being really open to the healing.

Frieda steps out and you strip.

She returns and starts laying crystals all around your back and shoulders.

You feel nothing, but laying down in a dim room isn't terrible.

"Feel the energy flows moving through your muscles, hmmmmm," she whispers from somewhere around your hip. "I'm going to move on to your legs and lower back now," she says, pulling the sheet a bit lower.

Dammit, you really need to keep a pair of emergency underwear in your desk. Which is possibly the most disappointing thought you've ever had.

You feel the coolness of crystals being placed on your butt, and the tops of your thighs, and...

Whoa. Something just touched your genitals.

Were you imagining it? Maybe it's just the energy flowing through—

Whoa, no, that's definitely the crystal therapist, touching your naughty parts. Kinda hard, actually. And a little haphazardly.

Is this part of the "healing?"

If you want to just take it, go to page 175,
If you want to call out this rape-happy hippie, go to page 177.

"I'D LOVE TO HAVE YOU OVER FOR DRINKS, THOUGH," YOU SAY, TRYING to salvage the situation. "I know you need a friend right now, and while I can't offer up an extra bed, I can offer my services as a great listener."

Wow, what an awkward thing to say.

But it seems to work on your boss.

"That would be great. Uh-uh-uh. That's so nice of you."

"Why don't we hit up this one bar near my place. They have an amazing shot of Jäger," you say, hoping to sell it. Boss plus bar has to equal free drinks, right?

"Actually, if it's all the same to you, I'd prefer something a little quieter. Maybe just a nice bottle of wine at your place? I think a bar would, uh-uh-uh, stress me out right now."

"Oh, sure, that's fine," you say. It's not, but you've already gone too far, now. "We can pick one up on the way."

Of course, when you roll in after work, there's no girlfriend in sight. And there's plenty of evidence that you're not living with a partner...or like an adult.

"Is your girlfriend, uh-uh-uh, out of town?" your boss says, narrowing his eyes at you.

"No, she...must be out. Let me call her and see what she's up to while you crack open that bottle of wine," you say, herding him toward the kitchen.

If you want to order a temporary "girlfriend," go to page 178.
If you want to pretend your girlfriend just isn't around tonight,
go to page 180.

YOU KNOW WHAT, HE'S THE ONE WHO ASKED TO STAY. AND BESIDES, you're pretty sure one look at your place will convince him he needs to go easier on you. It's like a depression diagnosis written in empty bottles and sticky-dust.

When you walk in the door, though, you wonder if this was the best decision. Piles of half-empty food containers cover most surfaces, including the couch you said he could sleep on.

"Oh, how, uh-uh-uh…Bohemian," your boss says, picking his feet up daintily and scrunching his nose. "It's like a place out of some college…movie."

"Yes, I'm sorry about the mess. I just…I don't know. I get so…sad."

"Good thing I picked these up, then," your boss says, flourishing a case of craft beer with a forced smile. "We'll get a little, uh-uh-uh, happy before we go to bed." He looks at the couch warily, setting the beers on a mostly-free patch of the coffee table.

A few beers later, though, and you're both happy to sit on the stained, lumpy couch.

A couple more and you're laughing. Almost like you *like* each other.

"…and so I told her 'fine, I'll be Grover Cleveland, but, uh-uh-uh, only if you ride my mustache!' And she *did*." Your boss wipes a tear from his eye.

"Man, that Debby. What a hoot." You say, standing and yawning conspicuously. "Well, I should probably hit the hay if I'm gonna be able to make it into the office tomorrow." There aren't any beers left, anyway. "See you bright and early?"

"Sure," your boss says. "See ya, uh-uh-uh, pal!"

That was encouraging, you think as you drift off to sleep. Maybe this could work even better than you—

You hear a knock at the door. Fuck, you never told him the trick to get number twos to flush.

"Are you, uh-uh-uh, awake?" Your boss sounds quiet. Almost meek.

"Yes, what's going on? Can I help with something, or…"

He opens the door and creeps into the room. Okay, you didn't actually invite him in. This is getting strange…

"Sorry about the state of the room, I didn't…"

"I don't care. I just, uh-uh-uh, I wanted to ask…" He pauses. You try not to fall asleep. "Could I sleep with you? It's just been so long since I've slept alone."

If you're too tired and miserable to say no, go to page 182.
If there's no fucking way, go to page 181.

"ALSO, IS IT POSSIBLE FOR YOU TO BUY A SET OF CHEAP SHEETS ON your way over?"

"New sheets?" the woman from the cleaning service rumbles. She sounds like a pack-a-day smoker with a cold. "That'll be an extra $150."

"WHAT?" God, this "rush-ordered" maid service is already costing more than your rent. "I'm not talking anything fancy, just like, a $30 set of sheets."

"That's just the convenience charge. The sheets will cost extra."

Fuck.

"Fine, just the cleaning then." You can throw your sheets in the wash the minute you walk in the door and play it off as the one thing you'd been "caught off guard" by. And then you can sleep on a bare mattress while he uses them, because everything about this plan is making it abundantly clear that saying yes was the stupidest fucking thing you've done this week.

"Someone will be by for your keys within the hour," the woman says, then promptly hangs up.

Probably they'll steal something from you, too.

A few hours later, you walk in the door, your boss trailing behind you with a bottle of "break the ice" wine in hand. Will the place be empty? Or worse, just the way you left it?

No. It's...it's miraculous. This must be what it's like inside a real person's home. You can see surfaces. And the original color of the carpet. And things don't smell vaguely of retirement communities and rotting cheese.

"Sorry for the mess," you say immediately, "I didn't know I'd have guests."

Bam. You nailed that.

"No, it's, uh-uh-uh, lovely!" your boss says, sitting down on the couch. You almost cringe—he can't defile your home, this perfect, pristine, sure-to-be-gone-tomorrow home. "Let's celebrate the end of the work day with some of this wine, eh?"

He starts unscrewing the top, leaning over towards the coffee table as he's doing so to check out a stack of decade-old news mags you really do plan to get around to eventually.

He's not paying attention to the wine, frowning as he tries to find the date on the cover.

So he doesn't realize he's pouring it onto your couch—beigey-clean for the first time since you bought it back in college—until it's too late.

"Ooops, looks like I've wet the bed, uh-uh-uh," he says.

Fuuuuuuuuuuuuck.

If you want to offer him your bed, go to page 186.
If he's just gonna have to deal with sleeping in the wine mess,
go to page 183.

158

YOU WAKE UP IN A HOSPITAL BED, YOUR HEAD THROBBING PAINFULLY. You try to remember what happened—you can piece together not doing a presentation, and taking a dive, and everything hurting… but how did you get here?

"Uh-uh-uh, looks like Sleeping Beauty's finally awake!" You turn—a motion that makes it feel like an axe is thrusting into your forehead—to squint at your boss.

"Whuh…?" Your mouth feels funny, too thick. You move it around and try again. "What happened?"

"You fell pretty hard. We thought we'd lost you there, uh-uh-uh."

"I'm in…the hospital?"

"Just for a couple days, for observation. You've got a doozy of a concussion."

"I…my sick time this year…" it's hard to focus, what with the light ice-picking your eyeballs. "I've had a lot of…colds…"

"Right, 'Irish colds.' No, no, uh-uh-uh, I'm just kidding. Don't worry about that," your boss says, waving a hand in front of your face. The motion immediately nauseates you. "We've got you on a paid leave of absence for the next month so you can recuperate."

"Oh…that's…" Everything hurts, but you realize this is a NICE gesture. "Thank you."

"Our pleasure. We care about our employees. You're going to remember that, aren't you? If anyone comes by to ask a few questions?"

You're not sure what he's talking about—it's too painful to think—so you just nod. Which hurts explosively.

"Great. Well then, you, uh-uh-uh, rest up. We need you in tip-top shape ASAP!" Your boss gets up to leave, thankfully allowing you to close your eyes, diminishing the pain very slightly.

For the next month you do nothing more strenuous than sit on your couch watching Netflix. Unfortunately, the concussion makes it impossible to enjoy. It also makes it impossible to pursue a claim against your office for what the lawyer has told you is "clear and criminally improper maintenance of restroom facilities." It could have a sizeable payout...if you could even handle the pain of a ten-minute phone call with your attorney, let alone maintaining even the simplest of lies in front of a jury.

Oh well. At least it's better than going to work.

The End. Until next month...

YOU TRY TO STEEL YOURSELF—HE'LL PROBABLY FIRE YOU ON THE spot; he must have liked Betsy to keep her on for so long. And you...killed her. You killed her with your lies.

"Hmmm. Uh-uh-uh, *this* is certainly troubling."

"Oh? What is?" You look towards the screen, squinting to show that you've never seen it before.

"She seems to have been, uh-uh-uh, *obsessed* with bronchitis. What could have..." He trails off, squinting at you for a moment before shaking his head. "I should've seen this sooner."

"What?" You swallow convulsively. Don't throw up on your boss.

"She must have been...senile. I mean, what else would have even planted this idea in her head?"

"Yes. Definitely. Okay, yes." You can feel your stomach untying itself. A small crowd has gathered at the edges of the room.

"I should have known I could trust your, uh-uh-uh, instincts," your boss says loudly. "I probably wouldn't have seen it for years—maybe ever—if you hadn't let me know she was slipping. But I guess now it doesn't matter. Uh-uh-uh. She's gone on to that great secretarial pool in the sky."

"Oh, ummm...yeah."

The entire office is staring at you. Great. Now they all think you ratted out the sick old lady.

"Frankly, that kind of insight is something we could use more of around here."

And now you're getting *congratulated* for it. You didn't know stares could burn that hard.

Go to page 189 to continue.

YOUR BOSS LOOKS EXPECTANT.

"I'm just gonna write down this number and call from my desk. It's too hard for me with…" you can't say "you over my shoulder" so instead you settle on "Betsy right there. Too…raw."

"Of course, uh-uh-uh," your boss pats you on the back. "It's good that you're so sensitive."

You're not really sure what he means by that, but you nod, jot down Laura's number, and quickly scurry back to your desk.

The phone rings. And rings. Shit, no one's answering. You're going to have to leave a message.

"Ummm, hi, my name is…well, you don't know me, but the point is I work with your mother, and unfortunately…I don't know how to say this, even, but…well, she died today. We're all so sad, she was such a fabulous addition to the office…"

You're starting to hit your stride, eulogizing someone nothing like the Betsy you knew.

"Anyway, we're so sorry for your loss. Please call your mother's office if you have any questions. You can ask for—" Just because you're nailing this doesn't mean you want her to ask for you. "—the general manager."

You hang up the phone abruptly. Job well done. You're realizing, now, you didn't really have a chance to actually eat your lunch, what with Betsy's sudden demise. But what options do you have? You certainly didn't remember to bring anything from home.

If you want to see if Betsy left any snacks in her desk, go to page 190.
If you want to try to take Debby up on her previous lunch offer, go to page 191.

162

"WELL, I'M WONDERING..."

"Well? Spit it, uh-uh-uh, out." Your boss raises his eyebrows, obviously exasperated. "We can't let the family find out from someone else."

"That's exactly it. I thought maybe it would be best if it came from someone who knew Betsy...better. You obviously know Laura, maybe you could..."

"Me? Call Laura? With this?" Your boss shakes his head, laughing bitterly. "Uh-uh-uh, I don't think so. That would be disastrous, with all the...*history* between me and Betsy."

"What are you talking—?"

"I'm sorry, you're just going to have to call her yourself," your boss says, frowning at you forbiddingly.

Go to page 161 to continue.

"UM, YEAH, SHE'S DEFINITELY…SHE'S FEISTY," YOU SAY QUIETLY, looking down at the floor and folding your arms in front of your body.

"Alright, I get it, uh-uh-uh," your boss says, slapping a meaty paw onto your shoulder. "You're not one to kiss and tell. Especially when those secrets are a matter of 'national security,' if you know what I'm saying."

Dear god. But this will probably end faster if you play along just a *little*.

"I do, Mr. President," you say. Your boss chuckles indulgently.

"Alright, I'll let you get back to work. Let me know if you want to grab a drink sometime—and sorry we had to make a 'thing' out of this, I just have to keep up appearances, you know?"

"Oh, absolutely."

"Part of being 'Commander in Chief' around here, uh-uh-uh."

You leave and try to pretend it didn't happen.

Except you can't, because your boss has never been chummier. You've become the obvious favorite in meetings, his go-to conversation partner in the break room, and he's started calling you "Prez" around the office.

There are perks, of course. It never seems to matter anymore if you knock off a bit early, or show up a half hour or so late…

…but it's a constant reminder of what you did in that closet. Of your shame.

Of what you can't help fantasizing about doing again…

The End.

164

Clearly he's trying to find common ground here, and that German bathhouse reference immediately made you jump to "human shit is involved." Anything you can say will seem tame by comparison. You decide to go for it.

"Did she do any…like…roleplay with you?"

"Uh-uh-uh," your boss grins wolfishly. "OH yeah."

You raise an eyebrow encouragingly. You're not going first.

"Let's just say Debby likes to be the first lady of the boudoir, if you know what I mean."

"I thought that was just for me! Did she ever switch it up and make you the first lady?"

"YES. Uh-uh-uh. She's a kinky little minx."

You both sigh contentedly. This whole "fucking Debby in a supply closet" thing is really working out better than you'd expected.

"So, uh-uh-uh," your boss smirks, leaning towards you conspiratorially. "Who were you?"

"Well, let's just say that Debby got a 'New Deal' with me."

Go to page 192 to continue.

You leave Barbara's office and return to your desk.

You feel shitty for maintaining the Johnson ruse, but it *did* help you dodge the unemployment bullet. If anyone else had been drawing up that list, after all, there's no way you wouldn't have been on it.

The real Johnson walks by your desk, nodding a quick hello.

Poor schmuck.

You wonder how Johnson will spend the next few months— applying furiously for similar jobs, presumably. God, how depressing. To be seeking this *out*.

You dump your face into your hands and remain motionless for several minutes.

Then you start to rifle through your desk drawer furiously.

Success!

You've found your "emergency" flask. Surprisingly, it feels kind of heavy.

Looking around to make sure no one's paying attention, you open it up and down everything in one gulp.

Go to page 1 to continue.

"Is everything okay?" asks your boss.

"How do you mean?" you respond, playing dumb.

"Your presentation, uh-uh-uh, well frankly it was TERRIBLE."

This can't be good. You've never heard your boss speak so candidly before, even that time he was accusing someone on your floor of being a toner thief. Apparently "winging it" only buys you so much understanding around here.

You'll have to go for something more aggressively pathetic.

"I didn't want to say anything…but I've been coping…with a…loss. In my family."

"Oh…I'm, uh-uh-uh, so sorry to hear that," he says sympathetically. "Did one of your parents pass away?"

"No, my second cousin."

"Your second cousin?"

Fuck, why didn't you say grandma? Or at least just *regular* cousin. Now you have to go with this, though.

"It was so unexpected. She flung herself onto the subway tracks yesterday morning." Jesus. That's a bit dark, even for your standards. "My aunt—my *second* aunt—thinks it was depression."

Your boss seems to be buying it. And why wouldn't he? Who in real life lies about a family member committing suicide?

You start biting on the inside of your cheek, hoping to produce a few crocodile tears.

"Owww…" Shit. You can taste blood. You completely overdid the bite.

"Owww…?"

"Um, that's the pain talking. Owww! Why did you have to jump?!" You look around the room in search of a name. Oddly enough, you see a framed photo of Madeleine Albright hanging on the wall. "Madeleine!"

Tears start rolling down your cheeks as the blood begins to pool on your tongue. Dear god, are you crying for real? Where did this come from?

"Are you bleeding from the mouth?" asks your boss.

You ignore his question, in part because you can't think of a good lie, but also because these tears are really picking up steam.

"Come on now, buck up! What if, uh-uh-uh, oh, I know! What about an office happy hour? We can all have a couple beers, say around ten to five?

You're too busy crying to respond.

"Or we could just go get some lunch. My treat!" His face is frozen in a rictus smile.

Tears stream down your cheek into your mouth, mixing with the blood into a weird, iron-flavored tongue marinade.

If you want to take him up on the office happy hour idea, go to page 193.
If you want to go to lunch, go to page 194.

Everyone files out, shaking their heads in disgust.

"Congratulations" says your boss once they've all gone.

Wait a second. Did he actually like your presentation? Maybe you…

"Congratulations on the WORST presentation I have ever seen!"

Ahh. He was being sarcastic. Good to know.

How can you get out of this? Maybe it could be someone else's fault? It'd have to be someone who isn't here…

"I'll tell you something, that's the last time I ask—" you imagine the faces you saw around the table, "—David to help me with anything," you say.

"What? What on earth are you talking about?" your boss asks.

"Ah, you know, I asked him to do some research for the presentation," you lie. "He's a good enough guy, but his methods… are so…unconventional."

"What do you mean? Uh-uh-uh, unconventional?"

"Well, I was expecting hard quantitative results and he came back to me with all of this flaky qualitative fluff." What else can you add that's completely nonspecific? "I fully admit, I should have been clearer with him about my needs. I guess I just expected that he'd understand what I meant by 'competitive research.'"

You're not a professional decoder of body language, but it looks like something you've said is making your boss angry.

"You mean David Blanton?"

"Yes."

"Mr. Blanton in the marketing department."

"That's the one."

"Mr. Blanton who has been home sick for the past month with acute renal failure?" he says, "uh-uh-uh"-ing bitterly.

What does that even mean? How do you have renal failure for a month? Best not to ask right now, judging from the look on your boss's face. You can Google it later—it might be morbidly interesting, like Siamese twins or that disease where your body always smells likes rotting fish.

"Right," you finally say, when it becomes clear your boss has nothing else to add. "I imagine that probably has a lot to do with it…"

"So, uh-uh-uh, you're now blaming your ongoing poor performance on a guy who's gravely ill?"

Your boss looks disgusted, like he just found out his girlfriend was actually his second cousin or something.

He storms off, leaving you standing there to stew in your own guilt-juices, which might work if you weren't trying so hard to picture what acute renal failure actually smells like. Ewww. Gross.

Go to page 195 to continue.

170

"I should probably check to see when this, uh-uh-uh coupon expires," your boss says as he pulls it out of his wallet. "Looks like today just isn't my day. This isn't for SaladXpress, it's for *Sushi*Xpress."

Oh, god, not SushiXpress! The last time you ate there you got violently ill.

"You don't have a problem with that though, do you? Uh-uh-uh. Can't get enough omega threes at our age, you know."

You're so appalled at the idea you don't even process the insult—anyway, your boss is nowhere near your age.

Raw, most likely spoiled, fish, with a stage-ten-vodka-hangover.

Oh god, don't think of vodka.

"No, no, that sounds great." You're in too deep to turn back now.

You can feel the alcohol surge through your veins, futilely attempting to remind you that your body is fed up with being treated like an amusement park.

You need something like the aforementioned bread bowl to absorb the alcohol that's still splashing around in your system, not squid sashimi.

Just try to power through it?

Go to page 195 to continue.

"Thanks for the offer, but I'm brown-bagging it today."

"Really? Uh-uh-uh. That's not like you at all. Not to be a nosy nelly, but what's on the menu? I always like hearing about other people's lunches."

"Um, herring." What? You've never eaten a herring in your life. "It's a…Danish thing. I got the idea from…social media?"

"Suit yourself!" your boss replies. "But after you give the presentation tomorrow, I insist on treating you to that new slaw down at the ol' SaladXpress!"

"I can't wait," you shoot back, somewhat disgusted that you're actually telling the truth.

You can hear your stomach growl. Of course you haven't actually brought anything in to eat. You need to find something quick, cheap, and if possible, nutritious. That way you won't have to feel guilty about tomorrow's mayonnaise binge.

The vending machine upstairs will hit two out of the three…

Go to page 197 to continue.

172

"SO HOW ARE YOU HOLDING UP? YOU KNOW, AFTER SEEING THE, UH-uh-uh, the suicide? What was it like?"

"It was…actually, it was incredibly disturbing," you say, looking away. If you play this up a little, you can at least expect a pass for the rest of the afternoon.

"I can only imagine," your boss responds.

"I can't stop seeing it in my head. The look on the council member's face. The moment the train hit. It was just…it was horrible." Actually, it *was* pretty awful. You've seen that look, the crazed look just before the leap. You've seen it in the mirror. Yesterday. Also this morning.

"Oh, I'm, uh-uh-uh, I'm so sorry. Is there anything we can do, or…"

You close your eyes mid-conversation and just sit there in silence. The idea of more words disgusts you. You just need to …not.

Of course it's pretty awkward for your boss, and anyone else around, completely checking out mid-conversation. But you can't see their faces, so fuck 'em.

"I think I need help. Professional help," you add, eyes still firmly shut.

"Oh, of course…" he says. "We're, uh-uh-uh, here for you."

"Thanks. I'm going to just lie down, now."

You slither out of your chair and onto the floor, never opening your eyes. You can feel some sort of crumbs or rocks or something under your cheek, but you don't have the energy to move your head. Or brush them off. Or do anything, really. You didn't realize all of this could possibly seem *more* pointless than it had yesterday, but it does. It really, really does.

Go to page 198 to continue.

"Don't worry about me. If anything, this event has made me want to grab life by the balls, and that starts with this presentation," you say, forcing yourself to grin.

"That's the spirit, uh-uh-uh!" your boss shouts, slapping you on the back chummily.

Having idiotically closed off a perfectly good escape route, you head into the conference room and dive straight into your presentation.

It goes horribly.

Even to you it seems as though several of your Power Point slides are just…missing. You start injecting French phrases at random, and you don't speak French. Your pie charts only add up to 59%, or less.

And your copious sweat smells like a mix of metabolized vodka and bus farts.

"Can marketing *really* do less with more?" Tina asks after a pause so long everyone has to assume you're done.

Oh yeah, you're just remembering you planted Tina in the first row with a scripted question.

"Well…" Shit. You're drawing a blank on your rehearsed response.

Say something. Everyone is staring at you.

"Um…Nope!"

"Well, apparently that's, uh-uh-uh, all we have for today, folks." Your boss motions for you to sit down. "I suppose we'll just have to chalk up this…*different* approach to trauma," he says.

He turns to you.

"Stay here just a, uh-uh-uh, moment. I'd like to talk to you about what just happened."

Fuck.

Go to page 200 to continue.

174

"WELL, IF IT'S ALL THE SAME TO YOU, MAYBE I WILL HOLD OFF ON giving the presentation," you say.

"Oh…alright. I suppose that won't, uh-uh-uh, be a problem," your boss says, furrowing his brow.

Just two seconds ago he sounded genuinely concerned about your mental health, but maybe you misread him. It's like the time you thought your mom *actually* wanted to hear about what happened at school that day back in second grade. You never made that mistake again.

"It's just that my…second cousin died in the same way," you lie, hoping to milk a bit more compassion out of him.

"Really?" your boss says, incredulous.

"Yeah. I still have flashbacks to that day."

"You saw your second cousin jump as well?"

Shit. Now that he mentions it, that doesn't sound plausible at all.

"Flashbacks to when I got the call, I mean. I'll never forget it, I was just about to dig into a Peanut Buster Parfait. It used to be my go-to DQ order," you say, shaking your head nostalgically.

"Okay…"

"You know, I still can't mix peanuts with ice cream without getting a little bit choked up?" You raise an eyebrow, hoping this is going over.

It doesn't look like he believes you in the slightest.

Go to page 200 to continue.

IT MUST BE. AFTER ALL, ALL BODIES HAVE DIFFERENT ENERGY FLOWS, and the genitals probably channel a lot of stresses, and...

Whatever, the point is it's no big deal if this crystal therapist decides to give you a quick pat down. Or, you know, a lingering one. Should you ask her to do it again? Honestly, it's the first time in months anyone has touched you in a way that even approaches intimacy. Unless you count that time you hugged the pizza guy and started crying, but even if you did, it's not like you hugged him with your genitalia.

Eventually, she folds the sheet back up over your butt and lower back. Part of you feels relief...and part of you is swamped by regret.

The session ends soon after, so you dress yourself and exit to the lobby.

Debby is waiting for you, grinning a little manically.

"So? How was it? SNRCK!"

"Great," you say. You don't feel any different, unless maybe you're a little less hungover? Though that's probably more to do with lying in a dark room than magical crystal powers.

"I knew you'd love it," Debby says. "Free-yay-duh works *wonders* with your auras."

"Mmmm." That's not the only thing she works on.

You head over to the counter to pay.

"That will be $53.24," Frieda says, looking at you blankly. Maybe you imagined the whole thing? Surely if she'd been deliberately fondling your genitals there would be some sign. It had felt pretty accidental.

You hand over your card.

"If you'd like to buy a 10-pack of sessions up front, you can save 20%," Frieda says as she runs your card. "With regular clients I can really develop a plan to help them...release," she looks you dead in the eye, raising her eyebrow ever so slightly, "bad energies," she finishes.

Right, like you're going to pay this woman to randomly bang into you between the legs. Just because you haven't had sex in...

Jesus, how long was it before the breakup? And that was how many months ago?

But still, what kind of sicko would agree to that deal? You don't need human touch *that* badly, do you? You have standards. Morals. You could still find someone on your own.

"That sounds like a great deal," you hear yourself say. "I'd love that—sign me up."

The End.

No, no way. This is assault. Awkward, haphazard assault, but still.

"Hey, what are you doing?" you say loudly.

"Well currently, I'm placing some quartz on your lumbar vertebrae; your chakras need to be, hmmm, *redirected* so you won't carry so much extra weight around the middle…"

"No, that's not what I meant. Extra…I mean, you KNOW what I meant!"

"Sorry?"

Oh, classic. Of course she'll make you say it—just another power play. Well you're not gonna back down.

"I mean you…*groping* me."

"If you feel like my touch is too heavy I can attempt to…"

You spin around, clutching the sheet to your chest as rocks fall off you to the floor.

"My JUNK. You're touching my junk, and it's inappropriate! It's ASSAULT!"

Frieda looks like you've slapped her.

"I'm so sorry," she says softly. "It's just…I can't help it, I…"

"Oh right, I'm sure sickos like you love to believe it's out of your control. Let me tell you something—"

"No, I mean I can't help it—I have a prosthetic hand."

Frieda holds out her right arm. The hand at the end does kind of have an unrealistic, plasticky sheen.

"I used to do large-animal massage therapy, at least until the thresher accident. Usually it doesn't get in the way, but I can't feel anything with it, so sometimes…oh, I'm so sorry."

Frieda bursts into tears, holding both hands, one immobile, over her face.

Well shit.

If you want to apologize, go to page 201.
If you're not buying the poor-me-I-lost-a-hand act, go to page 202.

THERE MUST BE AN ESCORT SERVICE WITH LAST MINUTE AVAILABILITY. You call the first one in the search results, but they don't have any girls. The second wants $1,000 for the night—which you couldn't pay even if you wanted to, considering all the "emergency" Taco Zone meals you've been charging this month.

But this one several listings down, "Cheap 'N Easy Escorts," might pan out.

You call and a man that sounds like a sentient ball of phlegm answers.

"Could you maybe send someone over who looks a little classy? I just need her to pose as my girlfriend for an hour or so."

"Got it. Your ass-play willing girl will be there in twenty minutes."

"No, I didn't say ass-play, I said—" but he's already hung up.

Your boss appears, two glasses in hand. "What was that about, uh-uh-uh?"

"Oh, I just wanted to check in with my girlfriend. Turns out she's on her way home, so you'll have a chance to meet her," you say, trying to force a grin.

"That's great. I always love to learn more about my employees' lives," your boss says, handing you a glass.

You guzzle wine nervously on the couch as your boss begins to detail all the ways he failed as a husband—which are actually pretty extensive; you would have never taken him for a sink-peeing type—and start to realize how ill-advised it was to rent this hooker. It's not like your boss even seems to care about the presence or absence of a partner in your life, at least not now that he's gotten going.

You're just about to call back and ask to cancel the reservation when the doorbell rings.

You open the door on a haggard, leathery woman of indeterminate age—she could be sixty-eight or a meth-faced thirty-two—in dark lip liner and ripped fishnets.

She is the most comically stereotypical hooker you've ever

seen. Except there's nothing funny about this; at $75 for the hour, she's about $75 more expensive than you can afford.

If you want to kick her out immediately, go to page 205.
If you're strangely aroused by the whole "beef-jerky in booty shorts" vibe,
go to page 203.

YOU QUICKLY TUCK AWAY THE MOST EGREGIOUS SIGNS OF SOLO habitation—the pile of maybe-re-wearable clothes covering the ottoman, the stack of dating-site profile printouts on the coffee table—while your boss pours the wine.

You'll just have one quick drink, then he can go home, and you can…well you probably *should* clean up this shithole you call an apartment. But you're much more likely to watch reruns in your underwear.

After the second glass of wine, he's still here. And still talking.

And there's no more wine.

"Oh, man, I'd love to chat more, but I think my girlfriend has some plans for later…"

"I thought she, uh-uh-uh, was out tonight," your boss says, sipping daintily at his still miraculously full glass.

"Yeah, I thought that too. But I'm thinking I got the schedule switched. She sometimes works days and sometimes nights…" Why would that even make a difference? You're painting yourself into a corner!

"Is she a nurse?"

"Yes…" you say slowly.

"So you're expecting her soon, or is she…I'm sorry, I'm still not quite, uh-uh-uh, understanding."

"You should probably get going," you say, desperate enough now to just come out with it.

"What's going on here?" your boss says sternly, his voice suddenly boss-ish again.

Fuck, you really should have just endured the rest of the gab session.

Go to page 207 to continue.

Y<small>OU LET HIM INTO YOUR HOME, YOU'VE PLAYED NICE OVER DRINKS</small> (though the fact that they were free *did* help with that), you even gave him the least-crusty blanket.

He can*not* sleep in your bed. There are limits. You still have some limits, right?

"Um, I'm sorry you're having a little trouble falling asleep, but I'm just really, really uncomfortable with that idea," you say. He whimpers. "Because of our working relationship. It's important to me that we maintain a level of professionalism."

You see his silhouette nodding rapidly.

"Yes, uh-uh-uh, of course," he says, "I'm so sorry for asking." Then he closes the door and you hear him retreating to the couch. You're gonna pretend you're not also hearing the sobs of a broken man.

The next morning, the entire way into the office, your boss doesn't make a peep, though he does call you both a cab and refuse to let you pay for it.

Later, when you mention that you need an extension on a presentation, he nods and says, "That's fine, just take, uh-uh-uh, however long you need."

And after work, he makes you stop into a grocery store, where he buys non-condiment food for the two of you. "It's, uh-uh-uh, the least I can do while I'm staying with you."

If things keep going like this, who knows what could happen. A clean toilet? Fewer flies? The sky's the limit.

Of course you are putting up with nightly sob stories from your boss.

But then, you were dealing with solo nightly sob-fests before you agreed to let him stay over, anyway…

The End.

"I MEAN. THAT'S REALLY WEIRD…" YOU MUMBLE, ROLLING OVER SO you can see his silhouette in the door.

"You're right. It's, uh-uh-uh, too much to ask." He turns, sighing miserably.

"It's fine," you say. "There's room, we can just sleep head to toe. But there's only one pillow," you add.

"Oh, no problem." Your boss's voice is embarrassingly eager. God, you're already regretting this. "I'll grab a, uh-uh-uh, couch cushion."

Seconds later he's back, a 3'x3' cushion in hand. He nestles in at the foot of the bed. Just before you fall asleep you swear you hear, "Love you, uh-uh-uh, sweetiecakes." Jesus. You should have let him get a hotel.

The next morning you wake up to someone gripping you from behind.

Somehow your boss has flipped over, presumably in his sleep—if he didn't, can you file some sort of complaint for this? How would you explain it so it doesn't sound like some sort of lover's quarrel?—and now he's full-on spooning you.

Oh god, you can't move. If you do, you'll find out for certain whether that hard thing in your back is his knee or…well, not his knee.

"Mmmm…morning," he mumbles. You assume he'll pull away in embarrassment any second, but he doesn't. Maybe he still hasn't realized he's not home with his wife?

He nuzzles his nose into your hair. God, you have never experienced a more painfully awkward moment. And now you're becoming mildly aroused. Jesus fucking Christ.

"Hey, I, uh-uh-uh, forgot to ask you last night." Oh god, please don't mention some sort of wifely sexy times. "Have you finished that presentation?"

The End.

"Really, though, I'm so, uh-uh-uh, sorry," your boss says. "I'll clean this up." He gestures with the wine bottle, managing to splash entire new sections of the cushion in the process.

"Let me just grab you some towels to mop that up." You should offer to clean it, but fuck that. You just went even deeper into debt and he immediately fucked up your couch? Your expensive—at least the way you remember it, college is kinda hazy—couch?

"Here," you say, depositing a pile of rags into his lap. "I'm gonna go to bed, though please feel free to stay up as long as you like."

"Oh, really? I, uh-uh-uh, thought we could unwind a little."

"Yeah, I'm just really tired. Maybe some other time."

"Sure," your boss says, his face falling a little. It almost makes you feel bad; then you remember every single thing that has happened since you started this job. Jesus, why did you let him come over? "See ya, uh-uh-uh, pal!"

You didn't become besties, you think as you start to drift to sleep, but frankly, it wasn't all that bad. The couch is a worthwhile sacrifice if it means you might get a clean slate on sick days. Hell, maybe he'll even feel indebted to you, and you'll wind up getting a promo—

You hear a knock at the door. Fuck, you never told him the trick to get number twos to flush.

"Are you, uh-uh-uh, awake?" Your boss sounds quiet. Almost meek. And a little drunk. You can't remember the last time you noticed someone else sounding drunk when you weren't.

"Yes, what's going on? Can I help with something, or…"

He opens the door and creeps into the room. Okay, you didn't actually invite him in. This is getting strange…

"Sorry about the state of the room, I didn't…"

"I don't care. I just, uh-uh-uh, I wanted to ask…" He pauses. You try not to fall asleep. "Could I sleep with you? It's just been so long since I've slept alone."

Go to page 182 to continue.

184

YOU ROLL OVER AND GAZE ON TAYLOR'S BEAUTIFUL, SLEEPING FACE. Who would have thought you would ever wind up with someone so gorgeous? And that your someone would supplement part-time modeling income with work as a consulting rocket scientist? What amazing hours you're able to keep together. What fascinating conversations you have over the gourmet meals you whip up as a couple in your rustic farmhouse-style kitchen. And occasionally in the backyard—at the time, you didn't think you should spend the money for the handmade old world-style brick oven and custom seating area, but you definitely get a lot of use out of it. And you weren't using those 10 acres for anything, anyway.

You're the envy of literally every single person you've ever met.

Once again you thank your lucky stars that fate put the two of you in the same cab that night. You're more in love with Taylor every single day. According to Taylor, at least, the feeling is mutual.

In fact, being with Taylor, you can feel *yourself* becoming more appealing—more interesting, wittier, more upbeat. You're even more physically attractive these days—who would've thought you'd love hot yoga so much?

Of course it's easy to stay in love, what with all the new adventures you keep taking together. You almost still can't believe that quitting your desk job and following your lifelong dream of becoming a travel writer worked out so spectacularly well. With Taylor at your side—organizing the occasional international photo shoot to help pay the bills on your first class airfares (sure, the magazines only cover you for coach, but why not live a little?)—you've been able to visit dozens of amazing locales, and sell your brilliant stories, insightful essays, and occasional novelizations based on your own experiences, for a tidy six figures annually.

If November goes well, next year it might be seven figures. But who's counting—you barely spend half the year in the three homes you own as a couple as it is!

Taylor's eyelids flutter open.

"Hi, honey. I love you."

"I love you too, sweetie."

You make passionate love on your king sized bed.

Life really is perfect. So much so that you sometimes wonder how you even got here.

How *did* you get here? It's almost like you just woke up one morning with everything in your life magically slotted into place.

Weird.

But you're not questioning it. Especially not now, when Taylor's starting to feel you up like it's time for round two...

The End. You cheater.

186

GOD DAMMIT. ARE YOU REALLY GONNA DO THIS? YOU'RE NOT gonna do this, are you?

"Oh, well you should take my bed," you hear yourself saying.

GOD FUCKING DAMMIT.

"No, no, I, uh-uh-uh, couldn't do that."

"I insist. You've been going through a rough patch, you deserve a good night's rest."

"Are you sure?"

Fuck, you'd really been banking on him protesting one more time, so that you could reasonably back out of the offer.

"Yes, of course. Make yourself at home," you say. Hopefully the sound of your teeth grinding against one another isn't too distinctive.

After you share a strained glass of wine, your boss yawns extravagantly.

"Whelp, time to, uh-uh-uh, hit the hay. Another day tomorrow after all, am I right?"

You eye the remaining wine mournfully. Who leaves wine in a bottle? But if you drink it all, he'll notice.

"Yep," you squeeze out. "Gotta be fresh for tomorrow."

"Great, well, I'll, uh-uh-uh, see you in the morning."

Your boss retreats to the bedroom as you look around your mystery house—where did the cleaning ladies put all your stuff?—for blankets.

Finally you manage to scrounge up a beach towel and an old winter coat. That will have to do.

But you don't have a pillow.

Screw that, he can have your bed, but he can't have the only pillow in the house. You have *limits*, after all.

You grab a couch cushion and head to the bedroom.

Go to page 209 to continue.

"I DID. IT WAS TERRIBLE, OF COURSE," YOU SAY, EMOTIONLESSLY. YOU actually feel a bit numb, now that you think about it. "But that's just how it goes, I guess. Some people can't handle the pressure."

Your boss nods at you, a slight smile on his face. He's obviously impressed.

"I didn't realize you were so level-headed. That's a real asset in this place. In fact, uh-uh-uh…" He pauses, thinking for a second. "Yes, I think you're just the person to take over as our new Second Associate Accounts Manager, Western Region. If you can cope with seeing a person in the prime of life ripped apart like wet toilet paper, uh-uh-uh, then you can definitely handle the stresses of the Bornstein account!"

"Oh, well…thank you…for your confidence in me. I'm excited to get started," you mumble.

You should be happy about this, but you still feel nothing. Nothing whatsoever.

• • •

It's been two weeks since the incident, and professionally, you've never been doing better.

But that's only because diving into the minutia of the western region's current email reply template system is the only thing that can momentarily drive the horrible memory from your head.

You're haunted by the blood-soaked subway tracks, the council member's screams, the eerie resemblance to you. At the time, you thought it hadn't affected you, but you were wrong. Since that day, you haven't slept for more than 45 minutes at a time.

It's 3 a.m. and you have a big presentation in only a few short hours. But you've already rehearsed it ten times tonight.

After ingesting a handful of Ambien, you're finally managing to nod off…

"Don't take my teeth!" you yell, waking up in a cold sweat from yet another night terror.

If only you could tell someone at work about the fragility

of your mental state. But if you do, you'll lose your shiny new promotion, if not your job.

The Ambien doesn't seem to be working. Maybe if you added some vodka you'd pass out?

Go for it. After all, what's the worst that could happen?

The End.

THE EMTs ARE FINISHING UP, AND ARE NEARLY READY TO TAKE Betsy away. Your boss walks over to you.

"You know what, I'm just going to go with my gut on this one, because it's never steered me wrong before, uh-uh-uh," your boss says, clapping a hand on your shoulder. "What would you say to—"

"Before you do anything rash, I just want you to know that I didn't actually—"

"—a promotion?"

"—say anything about Betsy getting…wait, what?"

"We need your kind of thinking at the top of this company! The kind that says, 'Forget sentiment, we can't be carrying around dead weight if we're going to succeed!' No pun intended of course, uh-uh-uh."

You glance over to where the black bag containing Betsy's body is being hoisted up onto a stretcher. You can almost feel her ghost staring at you in disgust.

Though that could just be the rest of the office.

"Well…thank you sir," you say, sticking your hand out awkwardly to shake his. "I won't let you down."

You have an actual office, now, with a door, so no one would know whether you're working or just dicking around on BuzzFeed.

And yet, every day, you feel compelled to focus on the teeth-grindingly tedious tasks on your plate. The marketing analyses, the competitive research, the not showing up to work *quite* so hungover.

Every time you stop, you're reminded of how you got here.

By killing an old lady. A shrieking, generally horrible old lady, but an old lady nonetheless.

So you go back to work. It's your reward. It's your punishment. It's what you deserve.

The End.

It seems like everyone's cleared out from the area around Betsy's desk. You pull open the bottom drawers. Files, a tangle of scarves, a bottle of lavender water, denture cream.

No lunch.

You check the top drawer.

Jackpot, $5 is sitting right there, practically begging you to take it. After all, it's not like she's gonna miss it. And it will go a long way at the vending machine in the break room; the prices haven't been updated since before you were born.

You grab for it.

"Ahem. What are you, uh-uh-uh, *doing?*"

Your boss is right behind you, but your body is between him and the drawer. If he saw you take the money, it's all over anyway. You decide to risk it.

"I was just looking for something to…remember her by," you say. "It's been so hard for me, today," you start tearing up. God, how is this happening? It's definitely not about Betsy. "Her dying was just so…so…" You start full out bawling.

Your boss squints at you. It almost looks like suspicion.

Then the phone rings.

He picks it up. You can hear the shouting from where you're standing.

"Laura, I'm so sorry, I'm sure it was a mixup…Well, how would your daughter have even intercepted the message in the… Well, I agree, it was idiotic to leave a message about such a thing, but I'm sure no one knew it was a land line…Yes, I understand you'd like to speak to…"

He points at you, mouthing "LAURA" exaggeratedly.

As though you couldn't tell who he was talking to.

If you want to take the phone from your boss, go to page 210.
If you want to let your boss deal with Betsy's daughter, go to page 211.

"DEBBY," YOU SAY, PANTING AS YOU RACE TO CATCH HER AT THE elevator bank. Who knew they made leopard print pencil skirts in velour? Still, beggars can't be choosers. Maybe if you play nice, she'll pay for the lunch. "Debby, wait up. Are you still up for lunch? After all the crazy stuff that's been happening this morning, I could really, REALLY use someone to talk to."

She turns. When she smiles, her face looks sort of like a ball of beigey clay with eyes poked into it. And neon eyeshadow scratched onto those eyes. You work hard to maintain what you hope is a casual grin.

"Sure," she says throatily. "I'm definitely...*hungry*. SNRCK!"

"Great..." You try not to flinch. Something is off here. "Maybe we can go to..." Anywhere but SaladXPress, anywhere but SaladXPress. "SandwichXPress?"

"Oh, I was more in the mood to sample the menu you were telling me about last night..." She chuckles wetly to herself.

"Oh yeah, that..." What is she talking about? And why are you suddenly thinking of World War II...and simultaneously feeling incredibly horny?

She grabs your hand and starts pulling you out of the room.

"This way, Mr. President. Or do you want to be Madam First Lady today?"

"Uh...either. Whichever."

"We'll figure it out when we get to my...oval office. SNRCKKK!!"

Go to page 68.

"WAIT, UH-UH-UH, YOU WERE FDR?" YOUR BOSS NARROWS HIS EYES and frowns at you.

"Well, yeah...why, were you someone else?"

"Of course I was someone else," he spits, scrunching up his nose in disgust. "There's sick and then there's *sick*, you know."

What the fuck just happened?

"I'm sorry, do you have some sort of problem with my role-playing FDR?"

"No, I mean, uh-uh-uh, far be it from me to judge your... *proclivities*. I just didn't take you for someone who would be into something as debased as cripple play." He takes a step backwards. Away from you.

"Wait, but...but FDR was one of the greatest presidents to have ever lived," you sputter.

"If you call that a life, uh-uh-uh," he says, sneering. "I call it a travesty. Disgusting," he mutters under his breath.

You're at a loss.

"Well, who were you?"

"Woodrow Wilson, obviously," he says with a snort. "We've never had a better leader. Oh, by the way, the more I think about this, the more I feel it's imperative that you and Debby both be suspended for the rest of the week without pay. We have to make an example."

"But you said we'd all been there. I thought—"

"Yes, well, some things cross a line," he strides out of the room, refusing to look you in the eye.

"But Woodrow Wilson was incapacitated by a STROKE!" you yell at his retreating form.

The End. You sick, sick fuck.

By the time 4:50 rolls around, you've stopped crying. Well, at least on the outside.

The appearance of half a dozen bottles of cheap wine and a couple of cases of generic ice beer is helping. Oh, look, there are even a few sleeves of Oreos lying around.

Luckily, your boss is too busy demonstrating his golf swing to a few uninterested IT types to ask you how you're dealing with the death of your non-existent second cousin.

Relieved, you head to the drinks table and pop the cap off a room-temperature beer, taking a swig. You notice Johnson also standing alone, at the fringes of the group. You could go up and try to strike up a conversation. But Jesus, Johnson is so *boring*.

You take a second swig from the bottle. Almost immediately, you begin to feel tipsy, as though last night's dormant drinks are sudsing up in your system, revived by the merest hint of alcohol. You down the rest of your beer, doing your best not to look in your boss's direction.

No one else is on their second beer yet, but should you maybe just go for it? Who knows, tonight could be a good way to make some inroads on an office friendship or two, or at the very least allow you to put some names to faces come tomorrow. Although you don't remember anything about the last office happy hour beyond the point when you got up on the copy machine and started that interpretative dance expressing your emotions about the Insurance Brokers Liability Union account…

If you want to get to know your coworkers over several more free beers,
go to page 212.
If you want to leave after this drink, go to page 213.

194

You're still crying by the time you reach the SaladXPress in the lobby.

"It's, uh-uh-uh, it's not so bad as all that," your boss says. You can feel snot streaming down your face, but you're too distressed to even wipe it away. "Buck up!" He slaps your shoulder lightly, chummily. You wince dramatically.

"Please don't...hit me," you gurgle. "I'm already in, in, PAIIIIIN!" This provokes a fresh wave of mucousy wails. You're starting to suspect this isn't about your bloody cheek anymore. It was never about your fake dead cousin.

"Sorry, I...sorry. Hey, but I know something that might, uh-uh-uh, make you feel better," he says, a hint of desperation creeping into his voice. You almost feel bad about how incredibly uncomfortable the situation is. He frowns, shaking his head. "But I probably shouldn't even suggest it. It's inappropriate, forget I said anything."

"No, I'll," you snort, trying to dam the tears. It helps a little. "I'm up for anything."

"No, no, I'll, uh-uh-uh, embarrass you."

"As though I," you snort back more snot and tears, "could possibly be more embarrassed."

He raises an eyebrow, then laughs. A little too heartily, actually, but at least it's better than "obviously appalled."

"We could..." he looks around furtively, lowering his voice, "go to the strip club?"

Why would he think you, of all people...but you realize you *have* stopped crying. Maybe you can earn some much-needed brownie points by agreeing to this. You could have an in-joke. Or blackmail material.

If you want to take him up on the offer, go to page 126.
If you want to just head back to your desk and suffer through the rest of this fucking miserable day, go to page 214.

SEVERAL HOURS LATER, YOU STILL HAVEN'T RECEIVED ANY EMAILS from your boss. Which, now that you think about it, might not be a good sign.

You manage to zombie through the rest of the day, nervous, and feeling like a complete asshole.

Worst of all, it turns out acute renal failure isn't even a little bit cool. And it doesn't have a signature smell.

Oh well, at least you can look forward to that family-sized lasagna in the freezer. Silver linings, right?

It would probably taste even better with one crisp, refreshing vodka tonic alongside. That sounds really nice—you should definitely stop by the liquor store on the way home to pick up a bottle.

Maybe you'll even let yourself have two drinks. It's been a hard day, after all.

Go to page 1 to continue.

196

"Sorry that, uh-uh-uh, coupon expired. But on the bright side, at least most of the sushi we ate was reduced to clear!"

You feel incredibly nauseous.

"You can give me the $14.75 back in the office," your boss adds.

Like, truly fucking terrible.

"I tell ya, they sure didn't hold back on the mayo in those mackerel rolls, did they? Uh-uh-uh."

Sweet mother of mercy, here it comes!

"Blaaaaaaaaaaaaaaaagggggghhhhh."

You've just puked all over your shoes.

"Help. I can't…Blaaaaaaaaaaaaaaaagggggghhhhh…breathe…Blaaaaaaaaaaaaaaaagggggghhhhh!"

Your boss looks like a deer frozen in the headlights.

You splash hot chunks of undigested squid everywhere.

If there's a silver lining in all of this, hopefully it's that the vomit-covered sidewalk can serve as a warning to others against the dangers of SushiXpress. At least you're a good Samaritan.

"Hang in there!" your boss yells.

Blaaaaaaaaaaaaaaaagggggghhhhh!

You drop down to your hands and knees.

"Those squid rolls *did* look a bit rancid. I should have said something," your boss says.

"I'm going to…Blaaaaaaaaaaaaaaaagggggghhhhh…head home…once I stop…Blaaaaaaaaaaaaaaaagggggghhhhh!"

"Of course. By all means," your boss says.

Tears and snot are running all over your face. Your boss is doing his best, lightly patting you on the back as you heave.

As far as office lunches go, this is pretty brutal. Not the worst one you've ever attended, but pretty bad.

But you're already starting to feel better, like you've just left your hangover behind on the sidewalk. And your boss would totally understand if you were still a little off tomorrow. A little recovery-pizza—and recovery-vodka—is definitely in order.

Go to page 1 to continue.

BUILDING MANAGEMENT HAS NEVER RAISED THE PRICE ON CHEEZ
Doodles, either. For what you'd pay for a half-slaw combo down
at the SaladXPress, you can buy three…no, four bags.

That decides it. You scrounge up all the change in your desk
drawer and head upstairs to the machine.

You're just about to type in your third selection when you
hear a characteristic snort behind you.

It has to be Debby, from HR. At least she's nice to you, even
if she is kind of annoying.

"Hey, Debby," you say, turning around to nod at her. She's
stuffed into a too-small velour skirt and a puckering sateen blouse,
her pasty flesh squeezing out the edges like an overfilled human
eclair. "How's your day going?"

"Pretty good. Though I can't stop thinking about last *night*,"
she says, stroking a stubby finger along your upper arm. "SNRCK!"

You have no idea what she's talking about, but this is much…
friendlier than Debby usually is.

"Oh, umm…that's good. So you had a nice evening?"

"I did after I heard from you. SNRCK!" Debby looks down
and starts fluttering her eyelashes. You can feel your armpits
starting to go damp with nervous sweat.

"From…me?"

"Oh, that's right, I suppose you weren't really texting as *you*,"
she smirks. "You were texting as the commander-in-chief. And
you had me *saluting* if you know what I mean. SNRCKKKK!"

If you want to try to explain these apparently lewd texts, go to page 215.
If you want to just run away, go to page 218.

Three Days Later

You're at home, surfing OKCupid in your pajamas on the couch, when an email from your boss lands in your inbox.

Shit. Your unannounced extended leave from the office is going so well. You almost feel capable of seeing a human again. Hopefully he doesn't do anything rash, like ask you to... do something.

You're simply not emotionally equipped to...do...things...at the moment. You haven't even finished the third season of *Doctor Who*. No, it's just too soon.

> This letter confirms our decision to terminate you effective immediately. Please return your swipe card, office key, company laptop and cell phone or you will be charged for their full replacement value...

Looks like the Doctor is going to have to enter time stasis for the moment.

But surely they can't fire you for being emotionally distressed? Not after you indicated as much to your direct superior? You know what, screw that, you're calling your cousin the employment attorney. Now. That's not only a proactive option, it won't require you to put on real pants.

Actually, though, maybe you'll just find his number now, then call him after this episode's over. After all, this could be the one where the Daleks succeed in their plans to take over the earth. You can't be expected to focus until you know what happens there...

Four Months Later

You're at home, surfing Match.com in your pajamas on the couch, when an email from your boss lands in your inbox.

> You will receive the severance payment and back pay amounts listed below once you have signed and returned

the enclosed release of claims document. Your signature constitutes a formal agreement to withdraw all previous claims in re: your wrongful termination suit...

Success! Well, kinda. With the settlement they're offering, you might actually break even, despite not having worked in four months. Screw spending the rest of the afternoon looking for a job. You've earned a few hours off.

The End.

200

"I'M SORRY, IT WAS JUST THAT SEEING SOMEONE CHOOSE TO END their life that way was so…" you feel your stomach churn. You can't believe you're going to use a suicide to get you off the hook for weeks—months—of poor planning. "Traumatizing. I just haven't been able to focus properly since that moment. My own mortality flashed before my eyes, and…"

Ugh, you feel so nauseous. Shame-nauseous.

"The whole thing really made me reevaluate my…oh, god."

"What?" your boss says, his face contorted in disgust.

"I think…I'm going to be sick."

"You're going to…"

But it's already too late. You push your boss aside on your way to the only receptacle in sight, a half-full recycling bin.

"Blaaaaaaaaaaaaaaaagggggghhhhh."

Vomit ricochets off the empty plastic bottles in the bin, splattering back onto you.

Tears run down your cheek as you continue to vomit. You can't be sure, but you don't think the tears have anything to do with the strain of your violent puking.

Finally, you seem to be finished. You look down; it appears that about 25% of the vomit stayed in the bin and the other 75% fountained up onto your shirt and pants. Oh well, at least they weren't clean to start with.

Your boss just stands there, staring in disgust.

"Jesus. Go home." He actually pinches his nose, slowly stepping backwards, away from you.

"Really, I could…"

"Just go."

He leaves you alone with your filth.

Is there somewhere near here that you can buy new clothes? It would be great not to have to stop home before you drown out the memory of this at the bar.

Go to page 1 to continue.

"Oh, I didn't…" you gulp awkwardly. "I'm so sorry, I wasn't aware of your handicap. Handicap. Please," you continue, turning back over on the table and laying down. It's slightly easier not having to look at her mottled, weeping face. "It was just a misunderstanding. I'd love you to continue. The rest of the session has been going so well," you lie.

"Really?"

"Absolutely. My…chakras really feel more…aligned."

"Oh, hmmm, that's so wonderful to hear!" Frieda murmurs. "That's what we want."

At random intervals throughout the rest of the session, your genitals get brushed, or a few times, almost fondled, but you try to ignore it. How hard would it be to lose a hand? For all you know it was Frieda's dominant hand—you can't even brush your teeth left handed.

Finally, the session is over. If you really think about it, you might be feeling a little bit better. Though that might have more to do with lying in the dark for a half hour than with the cluster of rocks that rested on all the different parts of your ass.

You get dressed and head out to the counter to pay.

Wait a second, neither of those hands looks prosthetic…

You try not to stare but…okay, Frieda just *cracked her fingers*. And it sounds like she's typing on a keyboard—prosthetics technology can't have advanced THAT much in the last few years.

"Would you like to save 20% by buying a ten-pack of sessions?" Frieda asks casually.

"No, that's…no thank you," you say, trying to peer around the monitor for another glimpse of her fingers. Are they moving or not?

What the hell? Well you're not tipping, that's for sure.

Go to page 237 to continue.

You stand up, wrapping the sheet around you awkwardly, trying not to look at Frieda, standing at the end of the table, weeping, as you storm out of the room.

"I'd appreciate it if you could collect my things, Debby," you say, with as much dignity as you can muster. "This session is *over*."

"Why? SNRCK!" She makes a gasping, choking sound. "What happened?"

"Well…" how can you put this? "Frieda's trying to claim she has a prosthetic hand, and…"

"Yes, of course. That threshing accident. So terrible. She's still relearning how to live."

Okay, so maybe the hand issue is real. But then why not use your other hand? It's not like these crystals are so heavy you can't lift them with one arm.

"It's a long story, but I'd like to leave," you say.

"Well, of course, just as soon as you tell me what happened," Debby says, staring at you expectantly.

Go to page 219 to continue.

"I'm Patti," the woman croaks to the two of you. "I'm here for a…lemme just check the name, one second," from somewhere between her navel and genitals she produces a phone and, somewhat surprisingly, a pair of reading glasses that she puts on to peer at it.

"Well of course I know that, hun," you say, trying to force a smile. "Since we live together. But it's good of you to introduce yourself to my *boss* over here."

"Is that, uh-uh-uh. Did you just call, uh-uh-uh," your boss's face is turning extremely red, and he's frowning.

"Okay, I can't find the name," Patti wheezes. The whole room is already starting to smell like stale smoke and something pungently acidic that you can't really put your finger on. "But either way, you gotta sign this receipt right now, otherwise I'm leaving."

"Oh my god, why wouldn't you just tell me you didn't have a girlfriend?" Your boss is wrinkling his nose up in disgust at you, now. "This is ludicrous. And frankly, uh-uh-uh, rather disappointing."

"Can we do this later?" you mutter to Patti.

"Sign the receipt, please," she barks, thrusting a pen and a mini-clipboard with a receipt attached at your gut. For a prostitute, this Patti is extremely organized. Seeing no other option, you sign and hand it back to her.

"Alright, so now you got an hour. Would you like for me to dance a little first, or do you just want to get right down to the—"

Your boss lets out something between a snort and a shriek and begins gathering his things.

"Strictly speaking, I can't discipline you for this since it's an, uh-uh-uh, off-hours activity, but you should know, I will be watching you *extremely* closely in the days to come," he sputters. "And to think, I thought my love life was pathetic," he mumbles as he walks through the door.

At this point you *feel* pretty pathetic. Like no one has ever loved you. Like no one will ever love you again. Like you just dropped more money than you budget for the entire week on a single hour with a walking piece of old leather.

Fuck it, the money's gone; you might as well get what you paid for.

"You can, um…take off your…stuff," you say, pointing to the mostly-mesh outfit Patti's wearing. Desultorily, she pulls off her tatters.

"I don't do anal," she says, releasing her empty sacks of breasts from a weirdly frilly bra.

You try to caress her, but you feel nothing. Not just no lust, nothing at all. Like a dried out husk of a person with no meaning, and no purpose, and nobody.

Soon, your weeping is too loud and wet to ignore.

"You know, even if we don't fuck, I still get to keep the money. You know that, right?" Patti is edging away from you, clearly uncomfortable. The thought that you're enough to make a hooker back away only makes you weep harder.

"Just…just go," you choke out between sobs. "Just leave. Everyone should just…leave me."

"I still gotta charge you," she says under her breath.

"Fine, whatever. Just GO," you wail.

"I'll have 'em give you a discount next time," she says, throwing on her netting outfit and running out the door.

If you want to just cry yourself to sleep, go to page 220.
If you need the strongest drink you've ever had in your entire life,
go to page 221.

"I'M PATTI," THE WOMAN CROAKS TO THE TWO OF YOU. "I'M HERE for a…lemme just check the name, one second," from somewhere between her navel and genitals she produces a phone and, surprisingly, a pair of reading glasses that she puts on to peer at it.

"Well of course I know that, hun," you say, trying to force a smile. "Since we live together. But it's good of you to introduce yourself to my BOSS over here."

"Is that, uh-uh-uh. Did you just call, uh-uh-uh," your boss's face is turning extremely red, and he's frowning.

"Okay, I can't find the name," Patti wheezes. The whole room is already starting to smell like stale smoke and something pungently acidic that you can't really put your finger on. "But either way, you gotta sign this receipt right now, otherwise I'm leaving."

"Oh my god, why wouldn't you just tell me you didn't have a girlfriend?" Your boss is wrinkling his nose up in disgust at you, now. "This is ludicrous. And frankly, uh-uh-uh, rather disappointing. Strictly speaking, I can't discipline you for this since it's an off-hours activity, but you should know, I will be watching you *extremely* closely in the days to come," he sputters. "And to think, I thought my love life was pathetic," he mumbles as he walks through the door.

At this point you *feel* pretty pathetic. Like no one has ever loved you. Like no one will ever love you again. Like your boss thinks you like to buy hookers. Grandma hookers.

"Sign here, please," Patti says, thrusting her receipt at you, "or I'm leaving."

Well, that's the first piece of good news all night.

"Perfect. Leave," you say, holding open the door. Patti looks slightly abashed. At least you think that's the expression her face is going for; parsing out the meaning in the lined piece of old leather is like reading Sanskrit.

"But wait a second, you ordered…"

"You must be mistaken. And you've already caused enough trouble, seeing as that was my *boss*, so please, leave."

"Well…I…" Patti's face wrinkles even further. You take it for a frown. "Next time you call, you're getting one of our B-list girls."

Oh dear god, you can't even fathom what that could mean. Probably full-body boils, or maybe prosthetic boobs. The kind that are just hooks.

Either way, you hope to never, EVER find out. You'd resort to weird, doughy Debby in HR before that, any day.

God, what a depressing thought. It's so brutal it makes you start to cry.

Go to page 221 to continue.

"NOTHING, NOTHING AT ALL, I JUST…I THINK I WAS WRONG ABOUT my girlfriend's schedule is all."

"So she'll be home soon?"

"Yes. Maybe. I…"

Wait, you have a brilliant idea. The old "pillow girlfriend" ruse. It's genius.

"In fact, I think she may have just snuck in the back door. I know she wasn't feeling well earlier today, she probably went straight to bed. One moment, I'm going to go check on her and see if she's okay."

"Wait, you, have a, uh-uh-uh, back door?" you hear your boss mumble as you dash into the bedroom.

Fuck, you only own one pillow. Quickly, you pick up all the dirty clothes from off the floor and start tucking them under the covers, smashing them into the general shape of a body.

You ignore the part of you—the LARGE part of you—that just wants to lay down with the dirty-clothes-girlfriend and spoon. God, it would be so nice to be held, even if it is just by last week's stained button-down shirt.

But there's no time for that now, you can hear your boss coming down the hallway, and your girl-pile still doesn't have a head. Would a brown turtleneck look enough like hair if the lights were off? Fuck it, you don't have time to find a better solution. You pull the comforter up as high as possible over the piles of clothing. From the doorway it kind of resembles a sleeping person. With leg goiters.

You step away from the bed just as your boss opens the door a crack.

"Shhh," you say, finger to lips, "she's sleeping."

"No she's not," your boss says loudly. "She's, uh-uh-uh, made of pillows."

"What? How did you—I mean, that's ridiculous."

"You think I don't know a pillow girlfriend when I see one? Uh-uh-uh," your boss chuckles ruefully. "I've seen my share of pillow girlfriends, that's for certain. In fact, I'd guess that this

208

is actually a clothes-pile girlfriend." He walks over to the bed, flipping down the sheets. He turns to you, a triumphant smirk on his face. "Yes, a week-old, filthy clothes-pile girlfriend."

The jig is up! Admit that you tried to pull the old "pillow girlfriend" trick and try to salvage your remaining dignity. Go to page 222.
No, it's not over till it's over! Surely you'll learn how to spin this. Go to page 223.

209

You knock at the door softly.

"Hey," you say, "just forgot a couple things in there."

No answer. Oh god, what if he's already asleep?

You push inside. You're *getting* that pillow.

Your boss is sitting up on the bed, his back to you, facing the nightstand on the far side of the room. What the hell is he looking at on your nightstand? Usually it's just a pile of used tissues and the occasional half-full beer you meant to drink "while reading."

Fap-fap-fap-fap-fap.

He turns, obviously horrified, and tries to scramble under the covers.

"Oh, god, I'm so sorry, I just came to get my—"

No, there's one more thing on the nightstand. How could you have forgotten?

It's a framed picture of your ex. And judging from the sheet tent near his midsection, your boss was masturbating to it.

If that's the last straw, go to page 224.
If you want to try to use this to your advantage, go to page 225.

210

Hoping to contain at least SOME of the damage, you grab the phone from your boss.

"Hi, Laura? I called earlier and left the message. I'm so sorry there was a problem, I just wanted to make sure you heard about your mom as soon as possible. I know if it were my mom, I would want to know sooner than later," you add. Maybe that will make you seem human to her. You have a mom, too, dammit.

"Yes, well, my daughter would probably disagree with that sentiment," Laura says. Her voice is throaty and dark, a whiskey-voice. Even though you can tell she's angry, her words sound a little like a come-on.

You've gotta go all in on this one.

"I'm so, SO sorry she intercepted the message. It didn't even occur to me that I was calling a landline—digital-era side effect, I suppose. But that's no excuse, I absolutely should have been more thoughtful about how I conveyed the message."

"Well, I suppose you couldn't have known," Laura purrs.

Your boss gives you a questioning thumbs-up sign, and you give him one in return. You're totally handling this. If you're lucky, you'll be handling even more of this soon. Appeased, he walks back to his office.

"I just want to tell you how sorry I am, truly. I've lost people close to me, too." Your paternal great-uncle counts, right? "… And I know just how hard it is to process. Please, let me know if there's anything I can do to help. I'm sure we could spend hours sharing stories about your mother!" You laugh softly. Take the bait…take the bait…

"That's so sweet of you to say," she says, sounding genuinely touched.

This is your moment. She's like putty, softened by grief, ready to latch on to even the smallest amount of human kindness.

It's a perfect time to go in for the kill.

If you want to ask her out, go to page 227.
If you don't think you can ask her out right now, go to page 226.

YOU PRETEND NOT TO SEE YOUR BOSS'S INCREASINGLY OBVIOUS gestures indicating you should be taking this call.

"Well, uh-uh-uh, I'm sure grief played a part in that decision, because I can't imagine why else," he glares at you icily, "anyone would have left this news in a message."

You did your part. If he didn't want you to leave a message, he should have said so then.

He's clearly not agreeing with you. Eyes buggy-wide, he thrusts the phone towards you.

You jump back, physically, hitting your hip against Betsy's desk. Well, at least you won't have to try to sift through vodka non-memories to find the origin of *that* bruise.

At this point, it's a struggle of wills. You won't take the call. In fact, you don't think you can. Something inside your brain feels like it's snapped, and the idea of having to deal with someone else's grief and anger right now is just too much.

How are you going to get out of this? What can you possibly do that will make him leave you alone, already?

If you want to go straight-up psycho and punch yourself in the face, go to page 228.
If the stress of this makes you feel like you're going to burst into tears again, go to page 229.

212

YOU MIGHT AS WELL STAY AND ENJOY A FEW MORE FREEBIES. PLUS, you're so charming after a few drinks! Your coworkers will definitely realize that.

In an attempt to look busy, you take out your phone and pretend to read text messages as you sip your fourth drink.

As you glance up from the screen, you spot Alex walking in.

God, she's so radiant, even in this awful conference room lighting. Look at the way she moves; it's as if she transcends effort, floating through the air like some cartoon angel. What a gait she has. So…smooth.

That gives you an idea; surely no one could feel offended by having her gait complimented. You'll sneak in under her creep radar. Before she knows it, she might actually like you slightly. It's perfect.

Full of liquid courage you start meandering in her direction.

Go to page 230 to continue.

STAYING HERE LONGER CAN ONLY GET UGLY. PLUS, NO ONE IS TALKING to you. You decide to head for home.

Feeling proud of your good sense, you decide to stop by your favorite bar and celebrate with a couple beers.

You half-watch the game they have on as you nurse the first beer. By the end of the second, you're starting to feel antsy. You want to do something better than this. Something more interesting.

Something like Debby.

Debby? Really? Debby, who's always puffing out of too-small velour skirts that would have looked dated in 1985? Debby who snorts every time she laughs, so intensely that she sprays you? Debby who's always winking at you when she talks about presidential history, as though you're supposed to understand whatever weird in-jokes she has about FDR?

Well, sure, but why not? There's something about her. You should just call to see what she's doing. Maybe she'll even want to hang out! You'll invite her over!

That's a great idea.

Go to page 291 to continue.

You could go and only have one drink…but no, it's a terrible idea. Your boss believing your "dead second cousin" lie was already lucky; you shouldn't push this.

"If it's all the same to you, I'd just like some time alone," you say, drying your tears with the sleeve of your shirt. "But I appreciate the suggestion."

"Of course, of course," your boss replies. "Whatever you, uh-uh-uh, need."

You head back to your cube. Unlike most of your colleagues, you don't have a framed photo of a spouse or your kids push-pinned to the wall. You don't have any "hilarious" plastic bobbleheads. You've never even taken down the worker before you's picture of Antigua.

The thought of spending the rest of the day here is just too depressing. You have to leave.

Things will look better tomorrow. Or maybe after a couple drinks at the BeerXPress…

Go to page 1 to continue.

"OH, YES, OUR TEXTS…OF COURSE," YOU SAY SLOWLY. YOU HAVE absolutely no memory of these. They sound…unnerving.

"I must say, they were rather unexpected, but very, *very* welcome. I never knew you were as big of an FDR…*enthusiast* as I am. SNRCK! And of course I loved taking a turn at the helm of state."

Oh Jesus, what in the hell did you text her?

"Listen, Debby, I had a few drinks last night, and I really crossed a line. I'm sorry about…" what, exactly? "Those things I said. They were…unprofessional."

"Who cares about professional," Debby says, smiling coyly. "I want to take things to the—SNRCK—next level."

"The next—"

"Do you want to *do* all those things we talked about? Like, tonight?"

If you're too intrigued not *to dive into the swampy depths of Debby,*
go to page 232
If you want to make up a previous engagement and get the hell away from here,
go to page 233

You roll over and gaze on Taylor's beautiful, sleeping face. Who would have thought you would ever wind up with someone so gorgeous? And that your someone would supplement part-time modeling income with work as a consulting rocket scientist? What amazing hours you're able to keep together. What fascinating conversations you have over the gourmet meals you whip up as a couple in your rustic farmhouse-style kitchen. And occasionally in the backyard—at the time, you didn't think you should spend the money for the handmade old world-style brick oven and custom seating area, but you definitely get a lot of use out of it. And you weren't using those 10 acres for anything, anyway.

You're the envy of literally every single person you've ever met.

Once again you thank your lucky stars that fate put the two of you in the same cab that night. You're more in love with Taylor every single day. According to Taylor, at least, the feeling is mutual.

In fact, being with Taylor, you can feel *yourself* becoming more appealing—more interesting, wittier, more upbeat. You're even more physically attractive these days—who would've thought you'd love hot yoga so much?

Of course it's easy to stay in love, what with all the new adventures you keep taking together. You almost still can't believe that quitting your desk job and following your lifelong dream of becoming a travel writer worked out so spectacularly well. With Taylor at your side—organizing the occasional international photo shoot to help pay the bills on your first class airfares (sure, the magazines only cover you for coach, but why not live a little?)—you've been able to visit dozens of amazing locales, and sell your brilliant stories, insightful essays, and occasional novelizations based on your own experiences, for a tidy six figures annually.

If November goes well, next year it might be seven figures. But who's counting—you barely spend half the year in the three homes you own as a couple as it is!

Taylor's eyelids flutter open.

"Hi, honey. I love you."

"I love you too, sweetie."

You make passionate love on your king sized bed.

Life really is perfect. So much so that you sometimes wonder how you even got here.

How *did* you get here? It's almost like you just woke up one morning with everything in your life magically slotted into place.

Weird.

But you're not questioning it. Especially not now, when Taylor's starting to feel you up like it's time for round two...

The End. You cheater.

"WOW, THAT, UM, SOUNDS REALLY INTERESTING, BUT UNFORTUNATELY I really need to get back to my desk. Lots of…work to do…" You back away cautiously, as though Debby might pounce.

"But I thought you said—"

"Talk to you later!" You turn and half-run away from the vending machine alcove.

It's only when you've made it nearly back to your desk that you realize you left your Cheez Doodles in the machine.

Jesus fucking CHRIST, you're still hungover, you're starving, you don't have enough cash lying around to replace your Doodle lunch, and apparently you've been sending inappropriate presidential-themed sexts to Debby, of all people. Your life is a mess. You thought rock bottom happened months ago, but no, somehow, right now, you're lower.

You can't help it: you start sobbing, so hard and fast you're half-choking on the tears and mucus.

"Is…is everything alright?"

You turn. Sharon, the head of HR, is standing a few feet away, staring at you. Her face—a leathery web of smoker's lines the color of wood stain—is contorted with a mix of pity and horror.

If you want to tell her you're just having a rough day, go to page 234.
If you want to make up some sort of dead relative to explain your emotional instability, go to page 235.

"FRIEDA...WHILE SHE WAS PLACING THE CRYSTALS, I..." YOU THINK about it. What DID happen, really? A lump of plastic grazed against your naughty bits. Even at the time, it *had* felt distinctly accidental. Plus, you've had worse on the subway. "I just feel... uncomfortable," you finish.

"Of course you do," Debby says, coming over and putting an arm around your naked shoulders. "That means your chakras really needed this." She nods sagely, pushing you back towards the room. "Just give the healing a chance to happen, I promise you won't regret it. SNRCK!"

Sighing, you go in and wriggle your way back on to the table.

"Is everything, hmmmm, alright?" Frieda asks. At least she seems to have stopped crying.

"Yes. Sure. Let's just get this over with," you say, closing your eyes tight.

You could just be imagining it, but the next 30 minutes of crystal healing seem to focus a LOT on the region around your genitalia.

And Frieda's not getting any better at understanding where her fake hand begins and ends.

"Before I step out and let you dress," she says once she's done, "would you be interested in saving 20% by buying a 10-pack of sessions up front? It's a huge savings."

"No," you say. At least you can stand up to this. To the offer of savings. "No thank you."

Go to page 237 to continue.

220

YOU STUMBLE TOWARDS BED, STRIPPING AS YOU GO, WAILING THE entire way. This has quite possibly been the worst day of your life…but on the other hand, you actually can't count how many times you've thought that in the last few years. Or in the last month, really.

Eventually, the soothing rhythm of your continuing sobs lulls you to sleep.

Several hours later you wake up, terrified.

You still haven't started your presentation, the one for the entire marketing and communications team. You're not even really sure what it's supposed to be about.

Tomorrow is probably going to be even. Fucking. Worse.

If you want to try to work out the presentation, tough luck,
it's too late now, The End.
If you want to turn back time and "follow your dreams" instead,
too bad bub, you should have done that 10 years ago, The End.

WITHIN SECONDS OF THE DOOR CLOSING, YOU'VE POURED A PINT glass full of a few ice cubes and a shit-ton of vodka

Tears are still coursing down your face, running into the glass, turning it into a sort of dirty martini of sorrow.

Actually, it tastes really good. There's probably an easier way to get this salty-bitter flavor twist in your vodka drinks, but you don't know what it is.

Still crying, you sit down on the couch, vodka in one hand, remote in the other. You just need to put on something so awful, so mindless and intellectually numbing, that you don't think about your own miserable life.

Thank God you stole your mom's Netflix login last time you visited.

Though halfway through this drink, things aren't seeming as bad. Maybe this will be your funny story that makes you new friends at the bar next week. Or at least you could try calling back from a different number.

You pour yourself another vodka-and-misery. It goes down so, so easy.

Go to page 1 to continue.

"I'm sorry, the truth is…" what is the truth? That you live like a disgusting animal and you didn't want your boss to know? How in God's name can you spin this?

"The truth is, I was embarrassed for you to see the evidence of my…depression?" Oh, that's a good one, mental illness always makes people feel so uncomfortable and it's basically impossible to disprove. "I can manage to keep it together at work, just barely, but once I get home, it's impossible for me to keep up the facade anymore…"

Wait, why are your eyes stinging? Are those real tears?

"I know I've let everything fall apart, and I guess I just…I just didn't want anyone else to see how bad it's gotten."

Oh dear God, you are full on starting to sob. Snotty, choking, possibly-puking-soon sob.

You might be telling the truth. Shit.

"I, uh-uh-uh…you…uh-uh-uh…you know, don't worry about all that, I'll just…" your boss looks around, first at you, then the door, like a caged animal. "Let's just start tomorrow with a clean slate and pretend this never happened, how about?"

"Sh-sh-sure," you weep.

"And, erm, we have great, uh-uh-uh, services for someone in your situation. Perhaps speak with HR about that, they may be able to work out a better…arrangement for you."

"O…k-k-k-kay."

"I'll just be going, then," your boss says, running out the door.

Half an hour later, you've brought it down to just hiccupping occasionally, which the pint glass of vodka in front of you is, counterintuitively, helping to get rid of.

You could go in to HR tomorrow.

But saying, "Hey, my life is a complete wreck and I'm barely even keeping it together," might be too low, even for you.

Who knows about next week, though. Or how you'll feel after you finish this second vodka-and-ice cubes…

Go to page 1 to continue.

"Look," you say, "I didn't want to tell you this, because frankly it's not something I'm very comfortable sharing, but the fact is…the fact is I form…intimate relationships…with pillows?"

You've heard about what they do in Japan. That's definitely a thing.

"Really," your boss says. "Isn't that just, uh-uh-uh, well, self-love?"

"No, it's nothing like that." If this is going to work, you have to commit. You wrinkle up your nose in feigned disgust. "It's like any other meaningful long term relationship. Some people fall in love with the right girl or the right guy, I've fallen in love with my pillow soulmate. He…completes me." Huh. Interesting that you decided your pillow soulmate is actually a guy. How does one even determine pillow gender?

"Well where is he then?" Your boss pushes apart the pile of clothes. "None of this is even a pillow. If you were that averse to my company, you could have just, uh-uh-uh, said something."

"He's in the wash. He wanted to clean up after last night's romantic escapades." You sneer. "He has personal hygiene standards just like anyone else."

Mark the time. A huge chunk of your soul just died.

But it seems to be working. Your boss is looking at you with a combination of puzzlement and fear, but he's edging out the bedroom door.

"You know, I should really be, uh-uh-uh, heading out if I'm going to find a hotel room for tonight. It's not fair to impose on an employee this way."

"I understand," you say as he half-runs towards the door of your apartment. "Sleep well! See you tomorrow at the office!"

Go to page 238 to continue.

"WHAT THE FUCK, DUDE?" YOU DON'T EVEN TRY TO KEEP YOUR voice at a normal volume.

"This isn't what it, uh-uh-uh, looks like."

"Oh, really? Because it looks like you're jerking off to a picture of my ex." You can feel the blood pounding through your ears. Thud. Thud. Thud. Dear God, do not get an aneurysm right now. You cannot die with this being the last conscious thought you have.

"It's just uh-uh-uh, I didn't…" He looks around, as though he's hoping to find an explanation somewhere. "Oh! Since my, uh-uh-uh, wife left me, it's been so hard!" His face briefly lights up, like he's found the toy in the bottom of the cereal box.

"FUCK that. I invited you into my fucking home, which, by the way, was a ridiculous ask—I'm your fucking employee, not your motel—and then you repay me by defiling my things the *minute* I leave you alone."

"It's not, uh-uh-uh…I didn't mean to…"

"Get out."

"I know you're upset, but you wouldn't, uh-uh-uh, tell your coworkers about—"

"GET. OUT."

Sheepishly, your boss scrambles off the bed and pulls up his pants. You try not to look at his still-present erection as he trudges through your apartment and out the door.

So much for brownie points.

If the picture is so tainted you have to throw it out now, go to page 240.
If you just want to gaze at your ex for a while, go to page 241.

"WHAT THE FUCK, DUDE?" YOU CAN'T HELP BUT RAISE YOUR VOICE. But already the wheels in your head are turning.

"This isn't what it, uh-uh-uh, looks like."

"Oh, really? So you haven't asked an employee to put you up, claimed the only bedroom in the apartment for yourself, then become sexually inappropriate in that employee's home, against that employee's will?"

"Hey, what's this 'employee' talk, uh-uh-uh?" Even in the dimness of the room you can see your boss's face going fish-belly pale. "We're pals, aren't we?"

"Are we?" You lean against the doorjamb, staring at your boss in silence until he titters nervously. "Pals return favors, right?"

"Well…I, uh-uh-uh, I suppose so."

You have him right where you want him now. Who thought catching someone defiling your memory of your ex could have such an upside?

"Since we're such pals, I thought you might be able to adjust my sick time a little. I've just been having *such* bad luck this year."

"But that's, uh-uh-uh, I'd be going against—"

"And to thank you for helping me out, friend, I'd be happy not to mention anything about this little scene, or your problems with your wife, around the office."

He looks at you. You try not to stare at his still obviously erect penis.

"I suppose I could, uh-uh-uh, help out a friend that way," he says.

"Excellent, I'll just head back to the couch, then."

"*If…*"

You look at him, suddenly nervous. There weren't supposed to be any 'ifs.'

"*If* I'm able to stay here for a few more weeks. Just until I, uh-uh-uh, get back on my feet. You'd do that for a *friend*, wouldn't you?"

Would you? Go to page 243.
No, you wouldn't. Go to page 242.

"So, I'm not sure if you have any plans this weekend."
Wait, what are you going to do, ask her out? Her mother just fucking DIED.

"Pardon me?" Laura says in her stupidly attractive voice.

You've completely lost your nerve. Apparently there's a reason no one's ever heard of a grief fuck.

"Ha! Oh nothing. I was going to tell you about how I'm going to the…um, IMAX…this weekend," you lie. Is there even an IMAX in town?

"That sounds like fun," she says, obviously confused.

"Yeah, I frequently go to the…IMAX."

"Right. Well, have fun then! Don't sit too close to the screen!"

You give a polite chuckle and hang up the phone in a panic.

Jesus. Who fakes IMAX plans? And why does she have to sound so fucking sexy?

If you want to try to salvage this situation, go to page 244.
If you want to go mope about it in the bathroom, go to page 253.

"So, um, I'm not sure if you have any plans this weekend...but maybe...we could chat...over some coffee?"

You begin to tap your foot nervously on the floor. What on earth did you just do?

The line goes dead silent. There's no response from Laura.

The two seconds that have passed seem like an eternity.

"Sure, that sounds nice. There's a new coffee place in the mall I've been dying to check out." she says.

Who thought asking out a person could be so easy! It's not even so bad that she's a mall-coffee drinker—you have flaws, too, you know that. You should definitely try this approach more often, maybe even on people you've actually met in person.

"Terrific! I'll call later in the week to confirm."

You hang up the phone and do a single fist-pump. You feel fantastic; nothing can bring you down from this high! You start humming that awesome Queen song to yourself. You ARE the champion!

Just as the euphoric feeling is peaking, your cell goes off.

Shit.

It's your doctor.

You knew you couldn't have anything good. Now he's going to tell you that you have mega-cancer or AIDS of the appendix or something.

Great...

It's time to pick up the phone and face the music. Go to page 245.

Y<small>OU TURN AROUND AND PUNCH YOURSELF IN THE FACE</small>. H<small>ARD</small>.

Your vision explodes in what literally look like hundreds of stars. Head-splitting, ice-pick-edged, brain-excavating stars. It would seem cliché if it weren't so accurate.

You turn back to your boss, blood streaming down your face and over your chin.

"I'm blee-dig," you mumble. "I dode thig now is a good tibe for me to take thad call."

He frowns deeply—is there a little fear in the look he's giving you?—and cups a hand around the phone's mouthpiece.

"I'm so sorry, Laura, a…uh-uh-uh, *situation* has arisen here at work, but we can talk about this more later. Say over dinner? Okay. Sure, yes. Speak then." He hangs up the phone and turns towards you, still frowning and refusing to make eye contact.

"Did you, uh-uh-uh," he pulls at his collar awkwardly. "Did you just punch yourself in the face?"

"No, I…" somehow you thought that if you turned your back towards him, he wouldn't realize what you'd done. That's seeming very flimsy, now. "I just stah-ded blee-dig."

"I, erm. I *saw* you punch yourself in the face. Just now."

"Oh, yes, well…"

"How about we go into my, uh-uh-uh, office," he says, shaking his head and striding away.

Go to page 246 to continue.

IT'S ALL TOO MUCH; BETSY'S DEATH—WHICH YOU TOTALLY CAUSED—
your boss being mad at you right now, the hangover.

You can't help yourself. You burst into tears. Loud, wet,
ugly tears.

God, not *again*.

Your boss frowns deeply—is there a little disgust in the
look he's giving you?—and cups a hand around the phone's
mouthpiece.

"I'm so sorry, Laura, a...uh-uh-uh, *situation* has arisen here
at work, but we can talk about this more later. Say over dinner?
Okay. Sure, yes. Speak then." He hangs up the phone and turns
towards you, still frowning and refusing to make eye contact.

You continue bawling.

"Just tell me one thing," he says, "did you sleep with her?"

Sleep with her? With Debby? Wait, why would you
automatically assume that he's talking about Debby—who sleeps
with Debby?

"I'm not sure who you're—"

"Oh for goodness' sake, you know who I mean. BETSY. Did
you sleep with her too?"

Oh my god, *Betsy*? TOO?

If you want to deny sleeping with Betsy, go to page 248.
If you want to try to bro down with your boss and claim
you slept with her, too, go to page 250.

"I COULDN'T HELP BUT NOTICE THE WAY YOU GLIDED THROUGH the room."

"Excuse me?" Alex looks at you, obviously confused.

"Your gait. It's magnificent," you say, with only the slightest of slurs.

"Oh. Um, thank you, I guess." She laughs awkwardly. "No one's ever told me that."

Success! Your plan is totally working. Time to ratchet up your game to the next level.

"These beers are the worst. Am I right?" She smiles wanly. "Why don't we find something a little less terrible?"

"Do they have anything better?" she asks.

"Well I know *I* always keep a few reserve premium cans back at my place." You raise an eyebrow seductively.

"Um, that's okay," she says. "I'm used to drinking the cheap stuff anyhow."

Alex likes the cheap stuff as well! God, she's *actually* perfect for you!

"Well, there's nothing stopping us from slipping a few of these cheapos into our pockets and taking them back to my place." You wink, opening your mouth to get more leverage on it.

"I don't know, it might blow my cover as an international office-supply thief," Alex says, smirking and turning away to another colleague, Gina.

"Then allow me to do all of the dirty work!" You put a hand on her shoulder to get her attention back. Surely you're more interesting than Gina, the receptionist. Plus, Gina's so mean. She's hated you forever just because you *once* said you understood why her ex might have strayed.

The polite smile on Alex's face quickly disappears.

"Look, I'm trying not to make a thing out of this, but you're crossing the line."

"What? Look, there's no reason to be uptight here."

"I'm sorry, but I didn't come to happy hour to be ogled by you," she snaps back.

"Ogled? If anything, you're ogling me," you sputter. Even to you it sounds ridiculous.

"Leave me alone, you creep."

No! The gait compliment was specifically designed to shield you from this.

"You've got this all wrong, Alex."

Alex turns and starts to head off in the direction of an HR representative hovering around the Oreos.

Shit. This can't be good.

If you want to apologize to Alex, go to page 251.
If you want to try to work this out with the HR rep, go to page 252.

232

"SURE..." YOU SAY, HESITANTLY.

As vague and potentially fraught with humiliation as whatever Debby's suggesting sounds, it has to beat watching season two of *Perfect Strangers* alone with a dinner of reheated pizza scraps. Plus, you can always cancel on her later.

"Great, I'll ready the Oval Office, *Mr. President*," Debby says with a wink. "Unless you feel like being Eleanor again, you minx. SNRCK!"

"No, no." Dear God, what are you getting yourself into? "The President is fine."

"I'll expect the motorcade to arrive no later than 21-hundred hours. SNRCK!"

Even though this is easily the weirdest conversation you've had this week, you find yourself enjoying it. Even wanting to... impress Debby for some reason. Huh.

"Sure. We can, um, pretend your underwear is Iraq, so that I can invade it?"

Debby looks a bit taken back. Shit. You clearly botched that attempt.

"Anyway, I'll be sure to text you if I'm running late."

Debby gives you a forgiving smile.

"Sounds good, Mr. President."

As she's waddling past you, she whispers into your ear, "I can't wait for you to apply your oratorical prowess...to my *pussy*."

Jesus. Why does that sentence turn you on so much?

If you want to try to take your mind off all this sexual innuendo with your unfinished presentation, go to page 254.

If you want to stop by the bathroom and give the presidential genitalia a pre-Debby test run, go to page 253.

"Oh, um, that's very...tempting, really, but I have...plans."

"Can't you get out of them?" Debby leans in close, hooking a puffy finger under the rumpled collar of your shirt. "After all, someone as powerful as you should be able to move around an evening's schedule. Even in a wheelchair. SNRCK!"

Oh god, you have to get out of this vending machine alcove before you actually implode from shame. Or get too aroused to turn her down.

"I really can't, unfortunately," you say, backing towards the entryway. "But another time."

"I'll hold you to that," Debby calls after you. "It's my turn to be Eleanor!"

Oh god oh god oh god.

You have to know what those texts said, but you can't face them without several fortifying beverages.

You dash back to your desk. It's 2 PM now. You set your monitor to go dark after three hours and fifteen minutes of inactivity. You'll leave your email up on your phone; if anything massive happens, you'll just be down the block at the BeerXPress.

Go to page 285 to continue.

234

"OH, SORRY ABOUT...ABOUT THIS," YOU SAY, GESTURING TO YOUR leaking face and heaving shoulders. "Don't mind me, I'm just... I'm just having a really rou-rou-*rough daaaaaaaaayyyy*."

Even forcing out just those few words is too much for your fragile psyche. You start sobbing harder. God, just don't puke. This is bad enough, you can't be the person who's pathetic enough to cry-puke in the middle of the hallway.

Sharon walks over and lays a tentative hand on your shoulder. It has all the warmth of a reptilian claw.

"There, there. Just...let it out, I guess." Something about her sandpaper drawl soothes you. Or maybe it's just the human contact, even if it is pretty lizard-like.

Finally, you seem to have gotten most of it out of your system. At least, you're not crying any more.

"I'm sorry about that," you say to Sharon, who's taken the opportunity to step away from you. "Just one of those days, you know?"

"No, I don't. I do know, however, that I'll be recommending you begin some basic therapy immediately. Come to my office and we'll set up an appointment with the staff counselor."

Go to page 255 to continue.

"OH, SORRY ABOUT…ABOUT THIS," YOU SAY, GESTURING TO YOUR leaking face and heaving shoulders. What excuse can you possibly have for your middle-of-the-office mental breakdown?

A dead relative would make sense. A grandma, maybe? But no, you tried that one a few weeks ago, and besides, this level of sobbing is way beyond grandma. You're actually having trouble breathing you're crying so hard now.

"It's just…I recently learned that…my…sister died?" Oh god, that's possibly the most disgusting lie you've ever told. Has it really gotten bad enough for you that the only lie big enough to explain your misery is a dead first-string relative? The thought— combined with your choky, gasping breathing and the mucus fountain running down your nose and throat—makes your stomach pitch.

"If you'll excuse me, I think I'm going to be— BLAAAAAAAGGGGHHHHHHHH." You vomit all over the rug at your feet. And Sharon's feet. She steps back in much more elegant disgust than you'd have expected from someone so smoke-tanned. But even through the tears and the pain you see something else on her face. Pity. And…is that fear?

"Who told you to come in so soon after the loss?" She croaks. "You're obviously unstable. Give me a name."

"No one…" you swallow, wiping at your mouth. At least the vomiting seems to have somewhat short-circuited the tears. Apparently your body is only capable of dealing with one system overload at a time. "No one told me to come in. I just didn't think I had another option."

"Grief-is-a-serious-health-concern-and-we-would-never-endanger-the-health-of-an-employee," Sharon rattles off automatically. God, how many times has she had to deliver this speech?

"It's okay, I'll get through it. It was just the shock of losing my…" Talking about the fake death again makes your stomach churn ominously. You just shake your head instead. "I can clean this up."

"No, we'll call the custodian. You need to get straight to the counselor."

"Well, I doubt anyone would have an appointment on such short—"

"No, the in-house counselor," Sharon's voice softens a notch, from chainsaw-on-rock to sandpaper-on-gravel. "Let me take you there."

Really? Your office has a full-time therapist on staff? You're relieved to be getting away from work for a bit, but something about that is supremely unnerving…

Do you want to try to get it together on your way to the counselor?
Go to page 257.
…or is it finally your chance to let out all this endless, boundless pain?
Go to page 259.

YOU TRUDGE BACK TO THE OFFICE AND ZOMBIE THROUGH THE REST of the day, but you can't get the thought out of your head:

You're starting to really wish you'd taken Frieda up on that offer of another ten sessions.

If you had, you'd at least have a chance at some sort of stiff, plasticky semi-intimacy, at least occasionally. And besides, knowing what you do about the maybe-prosthetic hand, it would be basically consensual-ish. Who knows, maybe someday it would be your hilarious "how we met" story.

Oh Jesus, that's pathetic even for you. You need to drop your mental circuitry in a massive bucket of alcohol and hope it short circuits.

Go to page 1 to continue.

THE NEXT DAY AT WORK THINGS SEEM…DIFFERENT. EVERYONE IS looking at you out of the corners of their eyes, and they're dashing off to obviously fake activities much more quickly than you're used to. Most days you get at least thirty seconds of mindless chatter, but today it's more like a clipped hello and an urgent trot in the opposite direction.

He couldn't have told, could he?

You head conspicuously past your boss's office, making a point of calling out "Morning!" on your way past.

Technically, even as late as you are, it is still morning.

But instead of chewing you out, he nods, a strained smile on his face, and then turns back to his computer, frowning deeply.

You've only just made it to your desk when Debby comes over, looking like a particularly sly piece of beige clay.

"Is it true," she says, smirking deeply. "Have I finally found a fellow *dakimakura* practitioner? SNRCKKK!" She collapses into her hands. It looks sort of like a Japanese schoolgirl giggle performed by a velour-clad Michelin Man.

"I'm not sure what you mean," you say. What is she talking about? That didn't even sound like English…

"Oh come on, you didn't think something that juicy wouldn't get around, did you?"

You lean away from your cube until you can see your boss's office. He's staring your way, frowning disgustedly, but as soon as he sees you looking his eyes widen in something like fear and he ducks behind his monitor.

Awesome.

"Yeah, I suppose not. What can I say, I just had to be honest about my…pillow love. It's who I am. A person who has intimate long term relationships…with pillows."

"Well you're not alone," Debby says, squeezing your shoulder. "On the plus side, they won't fire you now! HR told me that when my own…*proclivities* came to light."

"What? Why?"

"They're afraid of a discrimination suit. Which they should

be, Aki-hoto-san would bring suit in my name even if I didn't. He told me so once, just after we made love. He's so protective of me." Debby stares off into space, dreamily. Ew.

Still, it's useful information. The next day, you bring in a framed photo of a pillow that you found in a department store circular.

No one will eat with you at lunch anymore, of course, and your crush, Alex, skitters away whenever she sees you, as though you might be contagious. But you basically can't get fired now.

Meh. Worth it.

The End.

NOW YOU ACTUALLY DO HAVE TO WASH YOUR SHEETS. YOU ONLY PAID the maid service to clean the living room and bathroom, after all.

You throw them in the machine and return to the bedroom. There's the picture, staring at you from the nightstand, right where he left it.

God, how can you possibly look at your ex the same way after that? You grab the picture between two fingers and drop it in the trashcan, then wash your hands until they're bright red. Then you wash the nightstand with bleach. At least there's one upside to all this: clean sheets and one item of bedroom furniture that no longer has a film on it.

You pour yourself a stiff drink and put on the television.

You can't stop thinking about your ex, now. That pleasant smile. That inoffensive nose. That barrier between you and your own existential, unending loneliness.

God, why'd you ever let that one get away?

You pour yourself a second drink, then a third, but still, you can't get your ex out of your mind. A particularly affecting resolution to the *Perfect Strangers* episode you're watching coincides with a new wave of memories, and you start to cry soundlessly.

You stumble to the trashcan and fish out the picture. You were being too hasty, nothing can taint your memories. Maybe you should call, or text?

Or maybe you should just pour yourself another drink and stare at the picture longingly until you pass out from exhaustion…

The End.

NOW YOU ACTUALLY DO HAVE TO WASH YOUR SHEETS.

You throw them in the machine and return to the bedroom. There's the picture, staring at you from the nightstand, right where he left it.

God, you'd forgotten how sexy your ex was, with those inoffensive looks and that pretty-good body and a personality that you didn't mind. And your ex was always so willing to stand between you and total, utter loneliness.

You pour yourself a drink and return to the bedroom. The longer you look at the picture, the hornier you get. Of course your boss couldn't resist the temptation, who could?

Still crying, sipping occasionally from your drink, you start to masturbate. Maybe, just for a second at the end, you won't feel so deeply unhappy?

The End.

A FEW MORE WEEKS? HE'S ONLY BEEN HERE A FEW HOURS AND already this is the worst night of your week, which is saying more than you'd like to admit.

"That's too much to ask," you say. "You've already outstayed your welcome as far as I'm concerned."

"Fine," your boss says frostily, attempting to hike his pants back into place. "Then I suppose I'll be on my way."

"And I'll be up five sick days?"

"For this? Uh-uh-uh, I don't think so. The best I can do is 'forget' to note your sick time during the last pay period. Which is what, two days?"

Fuck, he knows how much sick time you've been taking? Just in the last two weeks?

Your stomach gurgles with anxiety. This is not going like you expected.

"Yes, I was feeling under the weather last week, and…"

"Let's not, uh-uh-uh, bullshit each other, hmmm?" He stands, fastening his pants. "I'll see you tomorrow. On time, I trust."

"Yes, sir." Fuck, how did he turn this around on you?

The next day, your boss is hanging around your desk when you show up.

"Try to be on time tomorrow, okay?"

"Okay," you say meekly, even though you were barely half an hour late. He continues to hang around you all day. It makes you so nervous that around 2:45 you actually begin to do some work.

You could tell someone in HR what happened, of course. But now you're worried about just how much your boss might know. As it is, at least you're still getting a paycheck. And you have two hangovers' worth of time back, which isn't so bad, right?

Right?

The End.

A FEW MORE WEEKS? HE'S ONLY BEEN HERE A FEW HOURS AND already this is the worst night of your week, which is saying more than you'd like to admit.

Still, the prospect of a clean slate of personal days is too tempting to pass up. Besides, if he's living here, he'll have to warm up to you enough to cut you some slack, right? Or at least feel too guilty to call you out?

"Of course. For a friend I'd be happy to extend a little more hospitality. Though of course you'll have to chip in with the groceries and the housecleaning."

"Of course," he says, grinning in a satisfied way. Too satisfied; aren't you the one winning? "I can even, uh-uh-uh, cover the cable while I'm here. It's the least I can do."

"Alright," you say. "And if this is going to be long term, I'll need my bedroom back. After you wash the sheets."

"Yes, yes, of course."

You retreat to the living room, unsure what just happened.

It becomes clearer the next day. Yes, your sick-day pool is replenished by noon, but by then you've already been in the office a torturous *three hours*. It's essentially impossible to be late when your houseguest works in the same office as you do.

Worse, "cover the cable bill" apparently means your boss feels like he's allowed to pick what you watch every night, which means you're having to suffer through some bug-eating competition that ends in a surgical wedding makeover. God. How can someone watch something so insipid?

And you can't even look for new jobs when you get home, because he's always right there, stutter-laughing in your face, splattering cacciatore all over your couch.

Actually, he *does* make a good cacciatore.

The End.

EVEN THOUGH YOU HAVE A MOUNTAIN OF WORK THAT YOU NEED TO get through, you can't stop daydreaming about Laura. You have to find a way to see her.

You've got it—you can gather up some of Betsy's belongings to bring to Laura, as mementos. That's a reason to see her that's TOTALLY legitimate. You'll even get to know where she lives that way!

You imagine it on the way to her house, box in hand. The two of you will start over somewhere far, far away. Maybe you'll raise llamas. Organic llamas! You'll run school tours, and turn the wool into felted hats, and trade them at the local farmer's market for the freshest eggs…

Barely half an hour later you've made your way across town to the address your cross-search of Laura's various social media profiles turned up. Of course she'll be happy to see you. She has to be, right?

If you want to knock on the door, go to page 261.
If you're having second thoughts, go to page 262.

You can feel a vein throbbing in your neck, your heart's beating so fast. Beads of sweat start pooling around your forehead and your hands are clammy. You pick up the phone.

"Hello?" you say.

The doctor introduces himself, then lowers his voice a bit. "What we're dealing with here with is known as *lipoma*."

You're so terrified you'd rather be dead.

"Um, ok…"

"It's a benign tumor made up of fatty tissue."

All that you hear is the word 'tumor.' You swallow hard as tears begin to well up in your eyes.

"Fuck…"

"Don't worry, it's nothing to be concerned about. Lipoma isn't cancerous and it's rarely harmful," he says. "If it's really bothering you, I can send you over to a dermatologist."

A dermatologist? It can't be that serious then. After all, you saw one of those a few months ago for your back-ne.

You exhale loudly.

"No, that's not necessary. Thank you for letting me know."

You hang up the phone, profoundly relieved, just as a co-worker sidles up behind you.

Oh, it's just Debby, probably looking for someone to talk presidential history with. She's about as awkward as they come, but you never seem to mind talking to her, even with the occasional spittle showers. Possibly because she's one of the few people at the office who can actually remember your name, and still doesn't seem to hate you.

"That sounded serious, SNRCK!" she says. "Everything alright?"

If you want to tell Debby the truth, go to page 264.
If you want to play the "cancer-sounding" sympathy card, go to page 263.

"SO YOU JUST…PUNCHED YOURSELF IN THE FACE," YOUR BOSS SAYS again, fiddling with the things on his desk. It wouldn't sound so strange if he didn't keep *repeating* it. "What made you, uh-uh-uh, decide that was the best course of action just now?"

"I…I don't know." Why *would* you punch yourself in the face? Jesus, is it really so bad around here that you now find it preferable to assault yourself than to deal with—be honest—fairly mundane, ordinary tasks?

Your boss looks at you expectantly.

"I guess I've just…I've been under a lot of pressure lately? I sort of feel anxious all the time…" You've never put it into words, but that's true. The gnawing sense of cosmic failure has been basically constant for the last few years now.

"Do you feel anxious right now? Uh-uh-uh." Your boss tries to smile, but it comes off more like he's trying to hold back a fart.

"Extremely." You have nothing to lose anymore, you may as well be honest.

"Hmmm. Have you ever spoken to anyone about this anxiety? And the compulsive tendencies?"

Who said anything about compulsive tendencies?

"Erm, no, but I assure you that—"

"Because our company takes mental health very seriously. We are in compliance with all regulations regarding disability leave since the incident with…uh-uh-uh, you don't need to know about that, the important thing is we're here to support you on the road to wellness."

"Support me…how?"

"Well, considering the severity of the issue, my recommendation would be a paid leave while you recover in a, uh-uh-uh, *specialized* facility. One prepared to deal with patients with your needs."

"Do you mean a psych ward?"

"No, no." He shakes his head emphatically. "Well kind of. But higher-end. There's a private facility we use in cases like this. Top of the line. And of course your leave will be paid."

Paid leave to play board games and watch old DVDs with a bunch of crazies? It sounds like heaven.

"How long did you imagine I'd stay there?" you say. Please at least two weeks, please at least two weeks, you just need a vacation...

"I would think given the circumstances...60 days? Just to start, of course, it's possible your doctors might think it wisest to extend a little beyond that." He nods reassuringly towards you.

Two months vacation? PAID vacation?

"Well, if you think that's best, I probably could use the help," you say, trying to sound contrite.

"Good. Fantastic. Uh-u-uh, I'll just call them now," your boss says, obviously relieved.

It's better than you could have hoped for. And you'll definitely be able to pick up a few tricks from the lifers in there if you need to find ways to extend your stay.

Who are you kidding, *when* you need to find ways.

The End, you lucky schmuck.

"No," you say, frowning deeply, "I have definitively never, ever, slept with Betsy."

"Oh," your boss looks confused, then slightly afraid. "Good, because that would, uh-uh-uh, be against company policy regarding—"

"Why would you think I'd slept with her?" There's an opening here. Possibly a big one.

"No reason, no reason. Your reaction was just so emotional and heartfelt. I suppose grief made me jump to the wrong—"

"Why would you say 'too'?"

For once—probably for the last time—you have the upper hand in this relationship. You are *not* letting this pass you by.

He gulps.

"Did I…uh-uh-uh, I don't think I said—"

"You definitely did. I assume you were speaking about yourself?"

"I, well…uh-uh-uh, listen, you have to understand, it was years ago, when I was new and Betsy was this stunning older woman. She used to wear these—"

"Sir, I do not need more information," you say, shrinking back slightly.

"Oh, yes, uh-uh-uh, of course." He shakes his head rapidly. "Yes, well, I'd appreciate it if you wouldn't say anything about our conversation today to anyone else. They might not…uh-uh-uh, understand the way grief makes you say things that aren't… well, appropriate."

"I understand," you say. "But I wouldn't want to be in breach of company policy. I may have to think this over…"

"Would a vacation day help you do that?" he says, leaning in conspiratorially.

You say nothing. Will he go for it? Are you pushing it?

"Or maybe two additional days? With that time surely you'd be able to better resolve whether discretion is the smartest option in this case."

"That sounds like a good idea. Two days would definitely

help me work out my concerns."

"Excellent. I'll just, uh-uh-uh, report that to accounting now."

Man, you wish weird old secretaries could die *every* day.

The End.

250

WHAT AN INCREDIBLY STRANGE QUESTION. MAYBE HE'S TRYING TO get you to agree with him for some sort of perverted, "we both hit that" camaraderie?

"Yes. I did," you say. Of course this is when your tears dry up. "That is exactly what happened."

Your boss has a strange look on his face, something you've never seen there before. He seems to be about to say something…

THWACK.

Oh god, your face is exploding. Your entire face is exploding in shards of pure pain.

You squint up between your fingers from the carpet, where you've fallen in a fetal position. Your boss is standing over you, menacingly, shaking out his right hand.

"What the FUCK?" you shriek. Your hands are getting wet with—you pull them away and blink at them—oh yeah, definitely blood.

"I…you told me…" your boss is looking around confused. You dimly sense people entering the room. "She was an ANGEL, okay? Without her, I would never have made it through the first five years. She…uh-uh-uh," he seems to be becoming aware of the gathering crowd.

"I was just saying what I thought you wanted to hear!" you yell, playing it up a bit now. "For Christ's sake, I didn't think you were being serious—I thought it was a JOKE!"

"Oh, I…" his eyes are taking on a feral, trapped-animal look.

It's time to milk what little advantage you have.

"That was straight-up ASSAULT. I did nothing wrong, besides misunderstanding you." The wheels are starting to turn in your head a bit more. "Also, that means you actually DID sleep with her, so…"

He extends a hand towards you, fake-coughing violently to cover your words and widening his eyes meaningfully.

"Let's discuss this further in my office," he says.

If you want to try to get some money out of this whole debacle, page 266.
If you want to play it cool and see hear your boss out, first, go to page 268.

YOU CAN'T AFFORD ANOTHER WRITE-UP FROM HR. YOU DASH frantically after Alex.

"Please, just listen to me for a second."

Alex turns around, lips pursed, silent.

"I'm sorry if I was coming on too strong. I haven't been myself lately," you say. "It's just that...my grandma died recently?" Man, you really hope coworkers don't start cross-checking the number and variety of dead relatives you're claiming.

But for now, it's working. Alex's angry expression disappears.

"She was getting up there, but still, no one saw it coming," you say.

"I'm sorry to hear that. Was it old age?" Alex asks, starting to look almost sympathetic.

"No..." you say. It will sound more realistic if it's something weirder, right? "It was...neglect. From her care workers."

Shit. That was a bit darker than you meant it to be. Where'd that come from?

"Jesus..." Alex mutters.

"Anyway, my emotional barometer has been out of whack ever since."

"If I'd known, I wouldn't have been so short with you," Alex says compassionately. "You should know that I'm also dealing with the loss of a grandparent."

She takes a step closer to you, her arm outstretched. Your heart starts to race.

"I'm sorry for your loss, Alex." She grabs your hand. Holy fuck, it's really happening.

"It's okay. I mean, I still talk to her all the time."

You nod, trying to keep your face somber. Apparently that's how people with *actual* dead relatives sort through things.

"She's a lot nicer to me now that she's gone."

Wait, what?

"She says dying really put things in perspective for her."

If this conversation is getting way too weird for you, go to page 270.
If you're willing to ride this out in the hopes of a hookup, go to page 271.

You drunkenly approach the HR person as soon as Alex walks away from her. She looks tight and disapproving, like she's constantly clenching her asshole.

"How about these Oreos?" you ask chummily.

"I don't think you want to talk to me about that, do you?" she responds curtly. Even her words sound pinched.

You need to buy some time, so you reach around the HR rep for a cookie. You stuff the whole thing in your mouth, trying to think of something to say as you chew.

"Oh, I guess you're referring to that little mix-up with Alex," you finally mumble around a mouthful of cream. "It was just a misunderstanding."

"I'm sure you know how seriously we take sexual harassment around here," she says.

"Sexual har…harassment?" you slur.

"You repeatedly asked Alex back to your house after she continually said 'no,' then proceeded to touch her without her consent."

"Well, when you say it like that…"

"Come with me, we need to deal with this issue immediately."

The HR rep walks you back to her office. She hands you a brochure on "sensitivity training."

You roll your eyes.

"If you refuse to take this twelve-week course, offered immediately after business hours, I'm afraid your employment status will come up for review," she says sternly.

"But who will pick up the kids?"

She fixes you with her steely, unsympathetic gaze. Right, she would know you have no children. Or at least that if you do, you've never applied for an insurance plan that would cover them.

Meekly, you nod. Maybe "sensitivity training" won't be so bad? And after all, it's something to talk about the next time you see Alex, right?

The End.

THERE'S NO WAY YOU'LL BE ABLE TO GET BACK TO WORK WHILE you're this horny. You have to deal with this. Now.

You walk into the bathroom and take a peek under each stall to make sure no one else is around.

Confident that you're alone, you duck into a stall, lock the door tight, and pull your pants down to your ankles. Then you start touching yourself.

Oh man, that *definitely* feels better than inputting numbers into an Excel spreadsheet.

Fap…fap…fap-fap-fap.

You try to keep your mouth closed in order to conceal your moans, but you can't help it. "Ohhhhh…"

Fap-fap-fap-fap-fap.

"Ohhhhhh…"

You're about to co—

Knock! Knock! Knock!

Holy shit, that wasn't the bathroom door, it was the stall door. Your moans must have drowned out the noise of someone walking in. Now there's only an inch-thick plastic door separating you, an obviously masturbating employee, from this non-masturbating employee.

"Occupied!" you scream. "Please just go away. It's occupied!"

Your request is met with silence, but you still see feet beneath the stall door.

"I don't want to go away…" the person on the other side finally says.

You'd recognize that nasally pitch anywhere. It's Morgan! Your divisional manager…and office nemesis!

"Can I…*come* inside the stall?"

If you want to stand your ground and stay locked in your stall, go to page 273.
If you want to let Morgan join the party, go to page 275.

254

THERE'S NOTHING IN THE WORLD LESS SEXUAL THAN A POWERPOINT presentation on ROI analysis. That will help you stop thinking about Debby. Definitely.

You'll just check your personal email quickly before you start. So you don't get distracted later. Because you're *definitely* gonna get some work done on this. For sure.

That's weird. You have a new email from your ex. What could that be about? Maybe you won't have to update your online dating profiles again?

> Jamie wants me to pick up the blender I left at your apt.
> C U tonight?

Right, Jamie. Your ex's new partner. Of course there's still a Jamie.

If you want to agree to meet your ex, go to page 274.
If you want to make up an excuse to avoid seeing your ex, go to page 275.

"So let me get this straight," the counselor—an aggressively bald man in a comfortably schlubby middle age—tents his fingers together. "You're saying you broke down in the middle of the hallway for no reason at all."

"Well, yes. No reason…and every reason. Everything about my life, and my day…I left behind the Cheez Doodles…" You trail off, embarrassed.

"Okay, well, I'm going to have to recommend we begin meeting more regularly."

"But why? I'm stable, management knows that, right?" You start sniffling again. You hate everything about this job, but if they fire you…oh god.

"Yes, yes, of course," he raises a hand as though to ward you off. "But this is exactly my point. I think you're bottling up your emotions, and that it's leading to unhealthy levels of stress."

"But I don't have the money, and after work I'm…busy," the idea that you won't get to leave the building for even a minute longer, let alone a half hour—or more; how long does counseling take?—makes you want to die even more than before.

"Stress-is-a-serious-health-concern-and-we-would-never-endanger-the-health-of-an-employee," the therapist rattles off automatically. Jesus, how often does he have to say that? "Which is why the company is happy to provide mental health care, during working hours, for any employees deemed 'serious.'"

"Wait, 'serious'?"

"It's a technical term. Suffice it to say your sessions will take place during the day, and they'll cost you nothing. We'll start tomorrow."

Well, that doesn't totally suck.

But it does suck that every session makes it clearer and clearer to you that you're emotionally rotting. You hate this job, you hate your life, you hate your bad decision-making, you hate that you're too much of a coward to change any of it. It's like this fat little man has opened a floodgate of misery and you don't know how to turn it off, even after your bi-weekly sessions end.

Which means that, the minute *today's* ends, you'll be heading out the door and straight to the BeerXPress. Maybe all the misery will wash away on a current of beer?

Go to page 1 to continue.

"So you just…stubbed your toe." The therapist, a portly middle-aged man whose head hair seems to have all migrated to his upper lip, squints at you appraisingly.

"Yup, that's me. Just suuuuper clumsy." You clamp your mouth shut tight. If you don't, he'll see you grimace.

"From the little that Sharon's conveyed to me, your outburst seems like a pretty extreme reaction to stumbling."

"Yes, well, I sprained that toe last month, so it was very tender." You frown, hearing how idiotic you sound.

"I'd still recommend you try out a few group therapy sessions."

"But why? I'm stable—management knows that, right?" You feel nervous sweat start to sting at your armpits. You rock back and forth slightly in the chair.

"Yes, yes, of course," he raises a hand as though to ward you off. "But this is exactly my point. I think you're bottling up your emotions, and that it's leading to unhealthy levels of stress."

"But I don't have the time to—"

"Stress-is-a-serious-health-concern-and-we-would-never-endanger-the-health-of-an-employee," the therapist rattles off automatically. Jesus, are they all in on it? "Which is why the company is happy to sponsor a weekly group session during working hours for any employees deemed 'serious.'"

"Serious?"

"I mean qualifying. Either way, you go or I'll mark you down as 'resistant to self-improvement.'"

Clearly you'll go.

• • •

"And, uh, I guess that's why I have a really hard time believing my dad ever loved me," you finish.

Your coworkers stare at you, horrified. Oh, right, like they don't all have a few "accidentally abandoned at the Canadian border" stories of their own.

In fact, their stories are brutal. Broken marriages, autistic kids, permanent colostomy bags—it's like a constant stream of downers.

It's nice to get out of a couple hours of work, but it makes you want to drink the second you leave the room every Thursday afternoon. Like, even more than usual.

It's 4:15 now, if you ducked out a little early to unwind at the BeerXPress, no one would notice, would they?

Go to page 1 to continue.

"So let me get this straight." The counselor—an aggressively bald man in a comfortably schlubby middle age—tents his fingers together. "You're saying you broke down in the middle of the hallway for no reason at all."

"Well yes. No reason…and every reason. Everything about my life, and my day…I left behind the Cheez Doodles…" You trail off, embarrassed.

"And your first thought was to explain your outburst by inventing a dead sister?"

"Well, to be fair, I don't have any sisters, anyway."

"So what made you choose that explanation?" The counselor frowns so deeply it looks like his caterpillar eyebrows are dive-bombing his third chin.

"I needed to think of something big enough that it would explain why I was so…distraught," you mumble. "I would have looked like a crazy person otherwise."

He looks at you, eyes narrowed, slug-thick lips pursed.

"You say 'look like.' Do you *feel* like a crazy person?"

"I don't know. I mean, it can't be *normal* to wake up every day and have the first conscious thought that goes through your mind be, 'It would be better if I'd just died last night,' can it?" You laugh weakly. Ooof. Where'd that come from? Do you really think that *every* morning?

"Alright, I'm going to recommend we take dramatic action, because from what I can tell in even just this past ten minutes, you're at a serious crisis point."

"Crisis point? I'm mostly holding it together, honestly, I…"

"I don't want you to become a risk to yourself or to others. That's why I'm recommending you for inpatient treatment."

"Wait, like…at a mental hospital?"

"Yes."

"But I can't afford that. And my job. I can't lose this…I haven't gotten an interview in months…I can't," suddenly you're crying again. You swallow against a new wave of panic-vomit.

"Don't worry," the counselor says soothingly. "This will be

covered by your insurance. And you'll have disability leave to cover bills in your absence. You'll just rest up for three months, and then, when you're feeling more like yourself, you can return to work."

Wait, he's not firing you?

What could you say that might get him to recommend six months?

The End.

YOU KNOCK ON LAURA'S DOOR.

The sound brings you back to your senses.

Jesus Christ, what are you doing here? There's no way this will go well. What did you possibly think would happen? There's probably still a few seconds to run away or jump into the bushes…

Shit. Too late. Laura's opened the door…and she's even hotter than her voice.

"Hello?" she says. She has her phone up against her ear.

"Oh, um, hi. We spoke earlier today on the phone. About your mother," you say.

She definitely looks a little creeped out.

"One second, Beth," she says into the receiver. "Oh, um, okay…"

"Yeah, I boxed up some of her things and thought I should probably bring them over to you. You know, so that you have a few keepsakes. From her…office…"

"Thanks. That's very considerate of you."

What the fuck is wrong with you? You can feel the dream of llama farming slipping away. But maybe if you just talk to her a little longer you can still fix this…

"Look, do you mind if I come in for a second?"

"Actually, now's not the best time. I'm making a few *arrangements*. Is there anything pressing?"

"Um, no. It's fine. Good then. Glad to have helped."

She nods, frowning slightly, and closes the door on your face.

You start walking towards the street, still holding the box. You're definitely still gonna be eating shitty, poor-person store-eggs now.

Go to page 262 to continue.

262

YOU LEAVE THE BOX ON HER DOORSTEP AND WALK ACROSS THE street, where you sit down on the curb.

From where you're sitting, you can still see Laura through the windows talking on the phone.

She's lovely. And you can never have her.

You pull out your flask—thank God you thought to bring it—and take a massive swig. It's been a hard day. Not unlike most others.

You continue to admire Laura from afar. If you squint hard enough, you can imagine her silhouette naked.

She's perfect.

You take another swig.

Her hair probably feels like angel wings and smells like unicorn tears. She IS an angel. She should be YOUR angel.

You take an even bigger swig.

You want her. You need her. You need to be inside her, living in her skin like a perfect, Laura-shaped sleeping bag.

You down the rest of the booze.

Empty flask still in your hand, you continue to stare at her through the window.

You can't go yet. You'll miss the sight of her too much. You can't even blink.

The End.

IN AN EFFORT TO APPEAR STOIC IN THE FACE OF FAKE ADVERSITY, YOU stand up and walk toward the window, staring off into the distance.

"The prognosis isn't pretty…" you say. "I'm dealing with a…" You pause for dramatic effect. "Well…a tumor."

Debby clasps her hands together and places them over her mouth with a snort of shock.

"Don't worry," you say, lowering your voice. "In times like these it's important to feed our hopes so that our fears starve." For a line that was pulled directly out of your ass, that's not too bad. Of course, it's all too easy for you to say, seeing as how you're facing down a weird, non-threatening fat lump.

"You're so, SNRCKKK!, brave."

You need something to give this moment more weight. More gravitas.

"When my favorite president, Franklin Delano Roosevelt, took office, the economy was in tatters. But did he run away from a challenge?"

"He did NOT!" Debby insta-responds. Wow, she seems much more enthusiastic about that reference than you expected, even with her obvious fixation on presidential history.

"And, um," her enthusiasm has thrown you a bit, "neither will I!"

Debby takes a step closer to you, leaning awkwardly to one side in order to whisper in your ear.

"So about those texts from last night…"

Texts? What texts? That doesn't ring any bells.

"Yes, I remember," you lie.

"Good. Then why don't you, SNRCK, *wheel* over to my place tonight and we can have one of those little…'fireside chats' you told me you wanted."

For some reason, the idea—whatever it is, 'cause you're still extremely foggy on what Debby's referring to—makes your blood start to flow southward.

If you want to take Debby up on what seems to be a sexual offer, go to page 291.

If the whole thing sounds terrifying, go to page 276.

"OH, IT WAS JUST MY DOCTOR WITH SOME TEST RESULTS." YOU pause for emphasis. "It turns out…it was nothing to worry about. False alarm."

"Well, that's good to hear, SNRCKK!" Debby smiles.

Shouldn't she be at least a *little* nervous?

Maybe you're downplaying this "cancer scare" a bit too much. People need to appreciate the minutes—hours, even—of hell you just went through. After all, you *almost* had cancer. And technically speaking, you do have a tumor.

"Well, it's not exactly *nothing*," you say, lowering your voice. "I have…a lipoma."

"Oh, that? That's nothing to worry about! SNRCKKK! Didn't Johnson have that? One trip to a dermatologist and you should be fine."

Debby rolls away from the conversation. Well *that* was unsatisfying.

But if she won't feel sorry for you, then someone else around the office surely will. Especially if you're more vague with the details.

You get up and take a walk around the cubicles.

"I've got some bad news," you tell a coworker whose name you can't seem to remember.

"I've heard. We're gonna miss Betsy so much around here," she says.

Fuck, you'd forgotten about Betsy. You nod sympathetically and escape to the next cube as soon as seems decent.

"This isn't easy for me to tell you…" you say to the next person you recognize.

"I know—Betsy was like a mother to all of us."

Of course, your cancer scare has to happen on the *one* day a receptionist dies. Now no one is even letting you *tell* your harrowing story of near-near-death?

The rest of the day goes by without you being able to elicit a single drop of sympathy, and the glow of your conversation with Laura is starting to fade—the weekend is still so far away, after all. Frustrated, you pull a flask from your desk drawer and take a quick swig behind the ficus tree.

The warmth spreads outwards through your chest almost immediately. It's almost like feeling *not* lonely for a second.

Who knows, maybe someone at the bar will listen to you tonight.

Go to page 1 to continue.

"AND THAT WAS IT. AFTER SEVERAL YEARS OF TORRID PASSION IN THE copy room, and conference room B, and occasionally the break room table, she decided to rededicate herself to her marriage and I…uh-uh-uh…I lost the most passionate woman I've ever known, forever." Your boss shakes his head wistfully, staring off into the corner of his office. "Man, the things that woman could do with a rolodex…"

"That's lovely, sir, but it doesn't repair my broken nose." It's definitely not broken, but it seems like the smart move to open strong. "In fact, given the insurance copays at this office, I don't know if I'll be able to do that at all."

"Oh, about that, I'm, uh-uh-uh…you know it was all a misunderstanding."

"Yes, well, it's a misunderstanding that's causing me a lot of suffering, both physical and emotional. I appreciate that you had history with Betsy, but I think the best thing for me would be to address this with HR, and see whether it's best dealt with internally, or whether I should file a report with small claims court, or the police, or…"

"Nononono," your boss waves his hands furiously in front of his face, "that won't be necessary. Listen, we can take care of this, can't we? Uh-uh-uh. I know you've been due for a raise for awhile, would my putting that through help you find the funds to deal with this fully?"

"Well…" You do some quick mental math. How much do you make in a week? "If you backdated it to when I first applied for it…10 months ago?" You've never formally applied for anything. "That might cover it."

"Sure. Of course, that makes sense, to make it retroactive. Yes, uh-uh-uh, I can do that."

"I may need a day or two of personal time to recover."

"Yes, of course. Take a few days. And HR can…"

"HR doesn't need to hear about my clumsiness, I suppose. I wouldn't want them to get the wrong idea."

"Excellent. Uh-uh-uh. Well then, I suppose I'll get that paperwork started."

Man, you should get punched more often.

The End.

"And that was it. After several years of torrid passion in the copy room, and conference room B, and occasionally the break room table, she decided to rededicate herself to her marriage and I…uh-uh-uh…I lost the most passionate woman I've ever known, forever." Your boss shakes his head wistfully, staring off into the corner of his office. "I asked my wife once to try that one thing she did, with the binder dividers, but I don't know. I guess my wife's just too vanilla."

You cough as broken-nosedly as you can in order to get his attention. He shifts uncomfortably in his seat.

"Of course that's no excuse for my actions now. I just, uh-uh-uh, I thought some context might…but of course I shouldn't have jumped to such an unfounded conclusion."

"Do you have sub tissues?" you say thickly. "I cad seeb to stop the bleedig."

"Oh, yes, sure, yes." Your boss pushes a box across the desk to you. "You just take the box."

"Thags."

He coughs awkwardly.

"I thought it might, uh-uh-uh, clear up any lingering… confusion about what happened just now if you had next week off to recuperate. Paid of course."

You stare at him, expressionless. See how far he'll go.

"And I know you've been having a tough year…*health*-wise, so I thought we could just wipe the slate clean on your vacation and sick time, too. In case you had something planned for later in the year."

"Thag you," you say. "Thad's very gederous."

"I'll just take care of that myself, without involving HR. They don't need to know about any of this; it just complicates things, don't you think?"

You could hold out for more, but you're not going to get a better deal. Plus, what will HR do? Maybe fire him? That's not gonna buy you another 15 hangovers and all of next week to sew your Magikarp costume for ComicCon.

"I agree cubpledely," you say, rising to shake his hand. "I'b so glad we could worg this oud like adulds."

Your boss nods furiously, grinning like an idiot.

Who would have thought Betsy's death would have such an upside for you?

The End.

"Wait, so you're saying you talk to your dead grandma?"

"Well, through a medium of course."

You frown.

"It's called a séance. You know, last time we accidentally channeled the spirit of Melanie Griffith," Alex says, raising her eyebrows in excitement.

You're almost certain that Melanie Griffith is still alive and well, but it doesn't seem worth trying to explain to Alex.

"Wow, that's really…wow. If you'll excuse me, I have to run to the bathroom. But let's talk more about this later, 'kay?" You run away before she can answer.

Why are all good-looking people certifiably crazy? You can't bear the thought of further dismantling your myth of Alex, so you just walk past the bathroom and out of the office.

On the plus side, if you head straight home now, you'll have enough time to cook that family-sized lasagna from the freezer and watch the entirety of *Perfect Strangers* season two.

You're halfway down the block—are they turning that artisanal bakery into another CoffeeXpress?—when you hear someone shout.

"HEADS UP!"

You turn around, trying to see who's shouting.

THUD.

Suddenly, you're lying face first on the street. All you can see is concrete, and everything hurts.

A piece of scaffolding lies on top of you. You can feel blood trickling out of your ear.

Season two of *Perfect Strangers* will have to wait.

Go to page 278 to continue.

"WAIT, SO YOU'RE SAYING YOU TALK TO YOUR DEAD GRANDMA?"

"Well, through a medium of course."

You frown.

"It's called a séance. You know, last time we accidentally channeled the spirit of Antonio Banderas," Alex says, raising her eyebrows in excitement.

You're almost certain that Antonio Banderas is still alive and well, but it doesn't seem worth explaining that to Alex.

"Um, wow, that's so…cool! Tell me more."

Tell me more? Where the hell did that come from? Oh right, your genitals are calling the shots from here on out.

"Why don't we get out of here and head back to my place…" she says, nodding towards the door.

Your heart starts to race. A lot. Heart, please forget all those empanada breakfasts and do NOT have an attack right now.

"…so that we can have our own séance," she adds.

Man. That is not how you'd hoped that sentence would end.

Still, your only plans for the night were that family-sized lasagna from your freezer and the second season of *Perfect Strangers*. And something could still happen with Alex, right?

Go to page 278 to continue.

272

"WHY SHOULD I LET YOU IN?" ON THE ONE HAND, YOU DESPISE Morgan, but you *are* still extremely horny. Why not combine that with some light blackmail?

"I just want to help you out. I swear I'm a good...*kisser*." Those words have never sounded less sexy. You feel blood rushing away from your genitals as fast as it can.

It makes it easier to focus on the blackmailing.

"But then I'll be engaging in 'an inappropriate sexual relationship with a superior.' That would violate our code of conduct."

"I can make sure it's rewarding. Now...and on your paycheck."

You open the door, and Morgan gasps in delight at the sight of you, pantsless. You both squeeze into the stall, Morgan kneeling in order to finish the job.

Just think of your work-crush, Alex. Imagine Alex's beautiful smile. Her luxurious hair. The fact that you could afford to take her out to dinner if this gets you a big enough raise.

"Ohhhhhhh." You can't help but moan noisily as you come.

Morgan stands up, grinning devilishly and gazing at you strangely. Is that...love? You'd say it was, though you don't really have any experience seeing it on another human face.

"Thank you," Morgan whispers, grabbing some toilet paper to clean up, never breaking that gaze. "That was...everything."

Go to page 280 to continue.

"Please, just go away," you say. "This is making me extremely uncomfortable."

Morgan sniffs derisively. But doesn't retreat.

"If you don't leave, I'm going to have to speak to HR about this," you say, your voice wavering.

"By all means. You can have the meeting right after I have mine. Where I report to them that I discovered a fellow-employee masturbating, loudly, in the bathroom during working hours."

That shuts you up.

"I'm sure we can both agree to pretend this never happened," you say, finally. You've never been less horny. Sorrowfully, you pull up your pants.

"I'm sure we can," Morgan says, voice extra-nasal, then marches out of the bathroom.

At first, it seems like things are the same as ever—which is to say terrible, but a terrible you know.

You've forgotten that Morgan is at least two steps above you in the office chain of command.

Soon, the requests for meaningless data analysis start flooding your inbox. The chiding messages about the lackluster nature of your PowerPoints, with every manager CC'd. The emails to your boss "casually" mentioning that Morgan "looked for you to answer a question around 9:15, but couldn't find you anywhere," and so had to assume you weren't in yet.

God, if this keeps up, you're going to actually have to start *trying* at work.

The thought makes you shudder. In fact, with each passing day, it makes you shudder more and more than the thought of what Morgan asked you to do in that bathroom.

But it's too late for that, now. You made your bed. Your cold, hard, early-rising, office-sexless bed.

The End.

THE THOUGHT OF YOUR EX, HAPPY WITH JAMIE, MAKES YOUR BLOOD boil. Still, it can be fun to be mad.

You type:

k

You hit send.

A one-letter response. If that's not laid back enough about "Jamie" and the unexpected visit, you don't know what would be.

Seeming nonchalant about the visit shows your maturity. But you don't want to settle for being just mature, you want to WIN this breakup.

You need your ex to see you with someone new.

If you want to rent a hooker for the evening, go to page 281.
If you want to ask Debby to play your girlfriend for the night, go to page 283.

THE THOUGHT OF YOUR EX, HAPPY WITH JAMIE, MAKES YOUR BLOOD boil. Still, it can be fun to be mad.

You type:

> Unfortunately, I won't be around. I'm super busy these days.
> Maybe we can set something up next week.

You hit send.

You *should* be busy with all of the work you need to do. But realistically, that's not going to happen tonight.

In fact, you're the exact opposite of busy. You're not seeing anyone, you don't have any close friends, you often spend hours staring at the TV before you realize it's not on, and you should probably stop listing the ways you're not busy before you depress the shit out of yourself.

Still, you need to plan *something* that gets you out of the house tonight, on the off chance your ex decides to stop by.

Go to page 285 to continue.

276

"THAT SOUNDS TEMPTING, DEBBY…"

Her eyes widen with excitement.

"…but tonight won't work. I've got prescriptions to fill, family members to alert…"

Her face drops in disappointment, but only slightly.

"I understand, but know that the offer, SNRCKK…still *sits*," she says, waddling out of the room.

You'd be lying if you said you weren't more than a bit intrigued. And aroused. Though you're still not sure why, exactly.

After a few hours fucking around on the internet, you notice the time—shit, you're five minutes late for the weekly office-wide meeting.

You stand up and reach your arms to the sky, thrusting your pelvis forward in order to stretch out your lower back.

FFFFTTTT!

Oops. That one caught you by surprise. Good thing all your coworkers have already headed to the meeting; it's always awkward to overhear someone else farting. Actually, it's probably best to get it fully out of your system before you head into an enclosed space with other human beings.

You grit your teeth and really start to push down.

PHRRRRRP!!! PHRRRRRP!!!

You're almost fart free. Just a little bit more to go…

Oh shit, STOP! That's not a fart…it's a *shart*.

Go to page 286 to continue.

YOU SLOWLY BEGIN TO OPEN YOUR EYES. YOUR SURROUNDINGS ARE unfamiliar, but you're in too much pain to care.

A mustachioed man in a cheap polyester suit stands over your body. He proceeds to take the bloodied gauze out of your ears.

"Ralph Winters, personal injury lawyer."

You try to respond, but you can't seem to open your mouth.

"Relax, relax. Your jaw has been wired shut," he explains. "You've had a terrible accident."

You make a low moaning sound in response.

"Mmmm…"

"Let me tell you the score: CoffeeXPress was in clear dereliction of their responsibility to the public," he says. "And I'm prepared to sue those bastards for all sorts of damages…on your behalf, of course."

"Mmmmm…"

"Don't worry, I work on a contingency-fee basis," he says, looking down at his watch again. "I don't make money until you do. I'll explain more, but first I have to run outside to feed the parking meter."

The lawyer rushes out of the hospital room, leaving behind the scent of cheap cologne.

What all actually happened to you? You'd examine your body more thoroughly if it weren't for the neck brace. And the series of wires holding your limbs in place.

Oddly enough, though, you don't really care about the extent of your injuries. It's just possible this means you won't have to work for the next while…or maybe ever? Surely you'll be able to coast on your settlement for at least a few years. That Ralph Winters looked like a real professional. And the CoffeeXPress is definitely loaded.

You've won the lottery…and all it cost you was a likely lifetime of dialysis.

The End.

"GUILLERMO SHOULD BE HERE MOMENTARILY," ALEX SAYS AS SHE takes off her jacket and shuts the door to her apartment.

"Guillermo?" you ask.

"Guillermo is my medium," she explains. "We met at The Taco Zone."

The Taco Zone? Who meets a medium at a Taco Zone? But before you have time to process Alex's confusing pronouncements, in steps a Mexican goth kid decked out in thick eyeliner and white face powder.

Wait, why are you assuming he's Mexican? He could be Mexican-American. Or one of those other Latin countries—are there many El Salvadorians in this part of town? You try to look at him as non-racist-ly as you can.

Guillermo nods to you. Except it's not really a nod, it's more like he closes his eyes and raises his chin in your general direction.

"Hola," you say. Fuck, immediately with the "hola." Even if he *is* El Salvadorian, that doesn't mean he speaks Spanish. You racist.

Alex acknowledges Guillermo then sits down cross-legged on the rug. She lights a few candles on a nearby coffee table. Dammit, there's probably no way for you to extricate yourself from this now.

"Let us all hold manos," Guillermo whispers.

Oh no, is this thing going to be in Spanish? You definitely don't know any Spanish. You'd say something, but he's already grabbed your hand and started to rock back and forth with his eyes closed. Alex seems to be following suit.

"Spiritos! Ghostitos!" Guillermo cries. *Is* that Spanish? It must be. Maybe Mexicans have a lot of words for "ghost" just like eskimos have all those words for "snow." They must be a more spiritual culture.

Either way, you can't understand what he's saying. This is like the time you had to sit through the original Zorro movie without subtitles.

"Weo tu welcomito, ghostos," says Guillermo.

Hmmm. You're starting to really doubt that Guillermo is

speaking a real language. Is this even official séance procedure?

"Spirits, we give you gracias and praisito," Alex says.

Is Alex fucking with you? She can't believe this is working, right?

Guillermo pulls out a little set of bells from his black jacket and rings them gently as he starts to hum. Alex starts humming along.

It's becoming harder and harder to imagine wanting to sleep with Alex.

"Que es ton questionay?" Guillermo says, opening his eyes to look at you.

What?

"Quando es ti questionarito?" he asks again, looking at you expectantly. Those weren't the same words, were they?

Alex pulls out a Ouija board and pushes it towards you.

"Make sure to ask your question in Mexican," she whispers. "The afterlife prefers Mexican."

Jesus Christ, now you're stuck here the entire evening and it doesn't look like Alex is even going to offer beer. If you died right now, would there be a way to guarantee they wouldn't try to contact you in "Mexican"?

The End.

YOU'LL SAY ONE THING FOR MORGAN: THAT'S A PERSON WHO KEEPS promises.

Within days of your…"encounter," Morgan has called a meeting with you and your obviously confused boss, announcing your promotion to mid-level management.

It comes with a new title, an office with doors, and a $2,200 annual pay-raise, "with the chance for a 3% bump at your next review."

Your suspicions were right, managers really have almost nothing concrete to do. It means you're less terrified about coming in to work—what do you have to fear from a tedious meeting where you "consider" your newly minted underlings' presentations and select your favorite idea at random, mostly based on who's done the least to annoy you personally?

But the boredom is even more crushing than before.

And worse, you know that when your first review comes up, in just a few weeks, Morgan will be the one assessing your "skill set."

Apparently, Morgan thinks you should be checking in quarterly to see how you're progressing.

At least the pay raise is enough to cover how much more you're spending at the BeerXPress, in a failing effort to drink away your shame…

The End.

THERE MUST BE AN ESCORT SERVICE WITH LAST MINUTE AVAILABILITY.
You call the first one in the search results, but they don't have any
girls. The second wants $1,000 for the night—which you couldn't
pay even if you wanted to, considering all the "emergency"
half-slaw combos you've been indulging in at the SaladXPress
this month.

But this one several listings down, "Cheap 'N Easy Escorts,"
might pan out.

You call and a man that sounds like the "after" picture of
smoker lungs answers.

"Could you maybe send someone over who looks a little
classy, say around 7? I just need her to pose as my girlfriend for
an hour or so."

"Got it. Your ass-play willing girl will be there at 7."

"No, I didn't say ass-play, I said—" but he's already hung up.

• • •

You've done a quick tidy up—your living room is officially takeout
container-free for the first time since October—and have just
opened a bottle of wine when the doorbell rings.

"Hey," your ex says coldly, refusing to look at you. "Do you
have the blender?"

"Of course, but stay for a glass of wine! I have a new
girlfriend, she should be swinging by any minute. I'd love for you
to meet her," you say, trying to keep your voice upbeat.

"Really? You? A *girl*friend?" Your ex raises an eyebrow
skeptically.

You just nod, pouring a glass of wine and pushing it into your
ex's hands.

You guzzle wine nervously on the couch as your ex starts to
tell you about Jamie—Jamie has luscious golden hair and donates
it regularly to cancer kids, Jamie volunteers as a rescue paraglider
in hostage situations, Jamie knows all about cheese pairings. The
longer your ex talks, the more you realize how ill-advised it was

to rent this hooker. It's clear your ex doesn't even care about the presence or absence of a partner in your life. And no matter how "classy" the hookers get at Cheap 'N Easy, there's no way they'll send over anything that compares to Jamie.

You're just about to retreat to the bathroom so you can cancel the reservation when the doorbell rings.

You open the door on a haggard, leathery woman of indeterminate age—she could be sixty-eight or a meth-faced thirty-two—in dark lip liner and ripped fishnets.

She is the most comically stereotypical hooker you've ever seen. Except there's nothing funny about this; at $75 for the hour, she's about $75 more expensive than you can afford.

If you want to try to get rid of this hooker, go to page 289.
If you're strangely aroused by the whole "trailer park Lolita 30 years later" vibe, go to page 287.

DEBBY'S THE PERFECT COVER-GIRLFRIEND. NOT ONLY WILL YOUR ex believe you could be with someone like Debby—snorting, unfashionable, formless Debby—but after today's encounter, you know Debby will act the part. Maybe too well.

You send her a message on the office chat service.

"Hey, any chance you'd be willing to drop by my place tonight? I said my ex could pop by for some things, but I'd love to have someone in my corner."

"Of course! I'll bring snacks!" She puts in a sort of squinting emoticon that looks exactly like a Debby snort.

"Great. Come by any time after 7."

• • •

You've done a quick tidy up—your living room is officially takeout container-free for the first time since October—and have just opened a bottle of wine when the doorbell rings.

"Hey," your ex says coldly, refusing to look at you. "Do you have the blender?"

"Of course, but stay for a glass of wine! I have a new girlfriend, she should be swinging by any minute. I'd love for you to meet her," you say, trying to keep your voice upbeat.

"Really. You. A *girl*friend?" Your ex raises an eyebrow skeptically.

You just nod, pouring a glass of wine and pushing it into your ex's hands.

You guzzle wine nervously on the couch as your ex starts to tell you about Jamie—Jamie has a charming tenor that gets puts to good use in that "Make A Wish" a capella group, Jamie once saved the Prime Minister of Bhutan from choking on a quail's egg, Jamie knows all about cheese pairings.

The longer your ex talks, the more you realize how ill-advised it was to ask Debby over. It's clear your ex doesn't even care about the presence or absence of a partner in your life. And Debby isn't likely to make your ex jealous. Especially not if Jamie really is that good about reinventing leftovers. Who would have thought you could make so many things with just one batch of cacciatore?

You're just about to retreat to the bathroom so you can call Debby off when the doorbell rings.

"Oh, that must be Debby now," you say. You hope the sweat you can feel forming at your hairline isn't visibly running down your face.

You open the door.

"Debby, if you don't want to come in, I understand," you say in an urgent whisper.

"Of COURSE I'll stay over. SNRCK! What, did you think I'd turn up such a delicious invitation?" she purrs. It sounds thick, like it's been filtered through a custard.

Your ex looks up at the two of you as you walk in. And there's plenty to see; Debby's really outdone herself. She's wearing too-tight booty shorts in some sort of poor-man's terrycloth, paired with a plunging teal velour v-neck shirt lined with matching marabou at the cuffs and collar, both of which are pinching out a roll of doughy skin.

Is your ex horrified? Uninterested? Jealous—that could happen, right? That shade of teal really brings out Debby's …beigeness.

No, it's worse. It's pity.

"I'll leave you two alone," your ex says, smiling sadly at you. "Thanks for the blender."

And your ex is gone.

Go to page 291 to continue.

THERE REALLY IS NO PLACE LIKE THE BEERXPRESS. IT'S NOT EXACTLY the Witness Protection Program, but most of the people you know feel the need to go somewhere "fancier" with a "drinks menu" and "napkins."

"One beer, please."

You check the time on your phone. It's still pretty early. You'll have to pace yourself.

The waitress brings you a pint of something yellowish.

Maybe you could pass some time chatting with her. She looks nice enough. And it's not like there's many customers at this time of day.

"Busy day?" you ask.

The waitress shrugs and walks away to grab a few empty glasses from a nearby table.

So much for conversation. You head for a table near the back, far away from the other customers. Which currently consist of three older men, at least two of which you're certain are homeless.

You take a long sip on your drink. Ahhhh. People are wrong, the beer here isn't *that* bad. And it still does the job, right?

This was definitely a great idea.

Go to page 1 to continue.

ARRIVING EVEN LATER TO THE WEEKLY OFFICE MEETING ISN'T AN option. It's far from ideal, but you're going to have to head in as-is and toss away your soiled underwear afterwards.

You walk into the meeting, clenching your butt cheeks so hard that it looks like your legs have been duct-taped together.

"Folks, uh-uh-uh, I hate to have to tell you this," your boss says.

You can see a few of the people nearest you starting to wrinkle their noses.

"But we're going to have to cut short Johnson's presentation."

A few employees cry out in disappointment. Really? For a PowerPoint? Jesus, everyone here is the worst.

The man next to you—you think he's from IT—is staring at you with something approaching horror on his face.

"It can't be helped, unfortunately. The, uh-uh-uh, asbestos removal people have to get in here and do their thing. In fact, you should all go home."

"Wait, we have *asbestos*?" shrieks someone from sales.

"Does asbestos have a particular odor?" the IT guy asks. "Like…a shit odor?"

But his voice is totally drowned out by the panicked frenzy breaking out around the room.

Thank god for asbestos…

If you feel celebratory after dodging that shart-bullet, go to page 292.
If you really need to start buckling down on that presentation, go to page 293.

"I'm Patti," the woman croaks to the two of you. "I'm here
for a…lemme just check the name, one second," from somewhere
between her navel and genitals she produces a phone and,
somewhat surprisingly, a pair of reading glasses that she puts on
to peer at it.

"Well of course I know that, hun," you say, trying to force a
smile. "Since we live together. But it's good of you to introduce
yourself to my *ex* over here."

"Did you just call her…but that woman's obviously a…a…"
your ex's face is turning extremely red.

"Okay, I can't find the name," Patti wheezes. The whole
room is already starting to smell like stale smoke and something
pungently acidic that you can't really put your finger on. "But
either way, you gotta sign this receipt right now, otherwise
I'm leaving."

"Oh my god, I didn't even *ask* if you were seeing anyone."
Your ex looks deeply disgusted. "I can't believe you would stoop so
low. And for what, just to impress me for two minutes?"

"Can we do this later," you mutter to Patti.

"Sign the receipt, please," she barks, thrusting a pen and a
mini-clipboard with a receipt attached at your gut. For a prostitute,
this Patti is extremely organized. Seeing no other option, you sign
and hand it back to her.

"Alright, so now you got an hour. Would you like for me to
do some of those downtown ping-pong ball tricks first," she says,
gesturing at her genitalia, "or do you just want to get right down
to the—"

Your ex lets out something between a snort and a shriek.

"Alright, that's just…alright." Your ex won't look at you. "I'm
gonna go now, please never call again." Your ex almost runs to the
door. "Ever."

Dear god, this could not have gone worse. You feel pathetic.
Like no one has ever loved you. Like no one will ever love you
again. Like you just dropped more money than you budget for the
entire week on a single hour with a walking piece of old leather

288

that didn't even do what you meant it to.

Fuck it, the money's gone; you might as well get what you paid for.

"You can, um…take off your…stuff," you say, pointing to the mostly-mesh outfit Patti's wearing. Desultorily, she pulls off her tatters.

"I don't do anal," she says, releasing her deflated-balloon breasts from whatever had been keeping them from dropping below the cut-off point of her crop-top.

You try to caress her, but you feel nothing. Not just no lust, nothing at all. Like a dried out husk of a person with no meaning, and no purpose, and nobody.

Soon, your weeping is too loud and wet to ignore.

"You know, even if we don't fuck, I still get to keep the money. You know that, right?" Patti is edging away from you, clearly uncomfortable. The thought that you're enough to make a hooker back away only makes you weep harder.

"Just…just go," you choke out between sobs. "Just leave. Everyone should just…leave me."

"I still gotta charge you," she says under her breath.

"Fine, whatever. Just GO," you wail.

"I'll have 'em give you a discount next time," she says, throwing on her netting outfit and running out the door.

If you want to just cry yourself to sleep, go to page 220.
If you need the strongest drink you've ever had in your entire life, go to page 221.

"I'M PATTI," THE WOMAN CROAKS TO THE TWO OF YOU. "I'M HERE for a…lemme just check the name, one second," from somewhere between her navel and genitals she produces a phone and, somewhat surprisingly, a pair of reading glasses that she puts on to peer at it.

"Well of course I know that, hun," you say, trying to force a smile. "Since we live together. But it's good of you to introduce yourself to my *ex* over here."

"Did you just call her…but that woman's obviously a, a…" your ex's face is turning extremely red.

"Okay, I can't find the name," Patti wheezes. The whole room is already starting to smell like stale smoke and something pungently acidic that you can't really put your finger on. "But either way, you gotta sign this receipt right now, otherwise I'm leaving."

"Oh my god, I didn't even *ask* if you were seeing anyone." Your ex looks deeply disgusted. "I can't believe you would stoop so low. And for what, just to impress me for two minutes?"

"Can we do this later?" you mutter to Patti.

"Sign the receipt, please," she barks, thrusting a pen and a mini-clipboard with a receipt attached at your gut.

Your ex lets out something between a snort and a shriek.

"Alright, that's just…alright." Your ex won't look at you. "I'm gonna go now, please never call again." Your ex almost runs to the door. "Ever."

You feel pathetic. Like no one has ever loved you. Like no one will ever love you again. Like you've developed a grandma-hooker fetish.

"Sign here, please," Patti says, pushing her receipt at you again, "or I'm leaving."

Well, that's the first piece of good news all night.

"Perfect. Leave," you say, holding open the door. Patti looks slightly abashed. At least you think that's the expression her face is going for; parsing out the meaning in the lined piece of old leather is like reading Sanskrit.

"But wait a second, you ordered…"

"You must be mistaken. And you've already caused enough trouble, seeing as that was my *girlfriend*," you're allowed to fudge the details for a hooker, "so please, leave."

"Well…I…" Patti's face wrinkles even further. You take it for a frown. "Next time you call, you're getting one of our B-list girls."

Oh dear god, you can't even fathom what that could mean. Probably full-body boils, or maybe prosthetic boobs. The kind that are just hooks.

Either way, you hope to never, EVER find out. You'd resort to Debby before that, any day.

Jesus, what a depressing thought. So much so, it actually makes you start to cry.

Go to page 221 to continue.

THE APARTMENT DOOR HAS BARELY CLOSED BEFORE DEBBY'S PUSHED you into a chair and straddled you.

"Oooh, Mr. President, your legs may not work, but the rest of you is operating at full capacity, SNRCK!" She starts groping your chest, and arms, and crotch. "Tell me about your…*domestic policy plans*. GRRGGGHHHH."

"I've, uh…I've got a New Deal for you…Madame First Lady…in my pants," you stutter.

"Oh, yeah, you know how Ellie likes it," Debby attempts to purr. It sounds like two wet fish flapping together.

"I'm over my polio. Now I'm gonna pole-ee-*you*," you say, slapping Debby's ass. It ripples seismically. "This is the wildest ride you'll ever have in a wheelchair," you add.

"GRRRGHHHH, fuck me harder than you're gonna fuck those filthy Nazis," she grunts.

You do.

"ISOLATIONIST FOREIGN POLICY!" Debby screams as she's climaxing.

It's only after she crawls off of you with a coy SNRCK that the shame really kicks in.

This is what you've been reduced to. Weird presidential role-play with a woman you think you might actually hate.

God, it makes you feel so alone. Especially because she's refusing your sleepover offer. You can't ask a fifth time.

At least you still have most of a bottle of vodka hiding out somewhere around your kitchen. And the President definitely doesn't have to live under rationing.

Go to page 1 to continue.

292

THANKFULLY THE SHART WASN'T AS BAD AS THAT MEETING LED YOU to believe. In your many experiences, they rarely are.

You go into the bathroom and toss your shitty underwear in the trash before cleaning yourself up.

You take a step forward as your genitals push up against your pants. Ah, going commando is just so freeing. This must be what Europeans feel like.

With the workday canceled, you're not 100% certain what to do.

You *could* head home and get an early start on the laundry that has been piling up.

But that's no fun. That's like staying inside and doing homework on a snow day.

Didn't Debby say something about *wheeling* over to her house? What did that even mean?

There's only one way to find out. You dial her number.

"Hello, Debby?"

"Well, hello there, *Madam First Lady*. SNRCK!"

Debby's come-hither voice almost makes you forget it's Debby on the other end of the line.

"Are you ready to join me in a little *fireside chat*?" she asks.

Motivated in equal measure by curiosity and excitement, you dive head first into the role.

"Absolutely. Maybe I can give you a *New Deal*," you say. "And I'm not just talking about the signature legislation," you add, trying to make that somehow sound sexy.

"Let's grab the presidential motorcade and get out of here."

Go to page 291 to continue.

THANKFULLY THE SHART WASN'T AS BAD AS THAT MEETING LED YOU to believe. In your many experiences, they rarely are.

You go into the bathroom and toss your shitty underwear in the trash before cleaning yourself up.

With the workday canceled, you're not sure what to do.

The prospect of whatever Debby was talking about still intrigues you, but it's about time you make the "grown up" choice and get some work done back at your place. After all, tomorrow's going to suck even harder than today if you don't finish that presentation.

On the bus ride home, you see a face you recognize from college. You look out the window, trying to pretend you're just taking in the scenery, but soon you hear footsteps shuffling towards your seat.

"Is that…"

Caught. You turn, miming surprise.

"Devan, long time, no see!" you say. God, it's always so awkward feigning interest in someone you haven't seen in a while.

"How long has it been now?" Devan asks. "Ten years? Twelve?"

The idea that any part of your life happened over ten years ago is more than a little upsetting.

You reminisce for a few minutes, catching up on general things. Apparently Devan's just sold a third screenplay. Jesus. You still haven't even finished that short story you keep meaning to send around.

"Anyway, this is my stop," you say, forcing yourself to smile, despite the taste of bile rising up your throat. "Let's catch up sometime, hmmm?"

Devan grins widely. "How about now? Are you on your way to something important?"

You *did* get to leave work early today. And it's not like your presentation is going to take all afternoon AND all evening. And after learning that Devan—blackout Devan, who was always waking up with unexplained blood on the pillow—has sold *three* screenplays, you could really use a few drinks.

"Sure, why not," you say. Maybe Devan will front the first round with some of that screenplay money.

Go to page 1 to continue.

**Well, you've managed to make a
complete hash of your fictional life.
Are you proud of yourself?
Jesus, we saw what happened
with that Debby situation.**

But for all the endings in this book, this isn't the end for
Choose Your Own Misery. Save up your booze money
and keep your eyes peeled for the next installment in
the Choose Your Own Misery series, coming soon
to wherever books (and maybe booze) are sold.

In the meantime, keep mainlining misery straight
into your eyeballs by following the authors online:

Follow Mike on Twitter **@theonald**
Follow Jilly on Twitter **@jillygagnon**

Get new, horrible adventures and updates sent straight
to your inbox by signing up for the newsletter:
www.chooseyourownmisery.wordpress.com

Like the Facebook page:
www.facebook.com/ChooseYourOwnMisery

And be sure to follow Diversion Books, which apparently
decided that publishing this book was a good idea:

Follow on Twitter **@DiversionBooks**
Like the Facebook page:
www.facebook.com/DiversionBooks
Sign up for the Diversion newsletter:
www.diversionbooks.com/newsletter

Hope to do this all again real soon...